ROMANTIC TIM
USA TODAY BESTSE
CONSTANCE

HEART OF

"O'Banyon excels at bring... beauty of the West and its brave pioneers to life.... *Heart of Texas* gets at the heart of the West and its readers."

HALF MOON RANCH: MOON RACER

"Kudos to Constance O'Banyon!"

RIDE THE WIND

"Ms. O'Banyon's story is well written with well-developed characters."

TYKOTA'S WOMAN

"Constance O'Banyon delivers a gripping and emotionally charged tale of love, honor and betrayal."

TEXAS PROUD

"*Texas Proud* is another good read from Ms. O'Banyon. With its excellent characters and strong plot, readers will find enough action and surprises to fill an evening."

LA FLAMME

"Constance O'Banyon tells a tale replete with action-adventure and glorious romance."

SONG OF THE NIGHTINGALE

"Mesmerizing, engrossing, passionate yet tender and richly romantic."

DESERT SONG

"Constance O'Banyon is dynamic. Wonderful characters. [She is] one of the best writers of romantic adventure."

A WANTED WOMAN

"Wade Renault doesn't shoot people," Mr. Liggett said. "He takes them to whoever hires him."

The others fell silent.

Caroline shivered, and this time her whole body shook. What if he had come for her? Her first instinct was to run and hide, but instead she gripped her handkerchief tightly in her hands, twisting it into a knot.

In that moment, the stranger shoved his hat back, and his gaze collided with hers. She looked into eyes that were more intense than any she had ever seen—and saw death reflected in that harsh gaze.

In that moment she knew in her heart that he had come for her!

The bounty hunter nodded the merest bit in her direction while a cruel smile curved his lips. This was no clumsy intruder like the one who had broken into the house in Savannah trying to find her. This man would know exactly what to do: And if he had come for her, she would never be able to escape those watchful eyes.

Other books by Constance O'Banyon:

HEART OF TEXAS
MOON RACER
THE AGREEMENT (SECRET FIRES)
RIDE THE WIND
SOMETHING BORROWED,
SOMETHING BLUE (Anthology)
TYKOTA'S WOMAN
FIVE GOLD RINGS (Anthology)
SAN ANTONIO ROSE
TEXAS PROUD
CELEBRATIONS (Anthology)

The Moon and the Stars

Constance O'Banyon

LEISURE BOOKS  NEW YORK CITY

For Jim,
for the years,
for the love,
for the children you gave me.

And for the men and women who fight for us—
God bless you.

A LEISURE BOOK®

August 2005

Published by

Dorchester Publishing Co., Inc.
200 Madison Avenue
New York, NY 10016

ISBN 0-8439-5542-2

Printed in the United States of America.

THE MOON AND THE STARS

Prologue

Charleston, South Carolina—1868

Autumn leaves scattered across the lawn, driven by a strong wind from the restless sea. Dark storm clouds gathered in the east, and a chill shook Caroline Duncan as she tried without success to loosen the tiny hooks at the back of her wedding gown.

This should have been the happiest day of her life, but it wasn't. Her father had refused to attend the ceremony because he did not approve of her marrying Michael Duncan. There had been a time when their families had been on friendly terms, but that was before Michael's father had remarried after his first wife's death.

Michael had been in Caroline's life for as long as she could remember. They had grown up together, and before long, childhood games of tag and hide-and-seek had given way to picnics and neighborhood dances. Most people had assumed that the two of them would one day wed, and Caroline could not imagine being married to anyone but Michael. As a young girl, she had always shared her deepest secrets with him, and he had come to her when he was troubled about something.

Michael's life had started to go wrong three years ago when his father brought his new wife, Lilly, and his stepson, Brace, into the house.

To make matters worse, Mr. Duncan had died last December, leaving his entire fortune to Michael. But Michael's legal rights did not keep his stepbrother, Brace, from taking control of the household and becoming master of the vast estate. Michael was unequal to the task of taking his inheritance from Brace's firm grip. Brace had dismissed all the servants who had been there for years, and brought in his own people. Michael had told Caroline that the servants spied on him and reported to Brace.

Caroline had not liked Brace from the first moment she met him. The man was somewhere in his thirties, not tall, certainly not as tall as Michael. Brace had dark hair, with just a touch of gray in his sideburns. He had a beard that he kept neatly trimmed. His eyes were his most disturbing feature—they were dark, almost black, and there was never any warmth in them. She might have considered him handsome with his fine features if she had not known about his character flaws. He was vain and liked to dress well, so he freely spent Michael's money on his wardrobe.

It had not taken her long to see that Brace was jealous of everything that belonged to Michael, and that included her. That was when she first started to fear for her friend.

Caroline had come upstairs to change out of her wedding gown and into something more suitable for traveling. She stood before the mirror, focusing on the tiny seed pearls at the neck of her mother's white wedding dress. As a child she had fantasized about one day wearing this gown and walking down the aisle on her father's arm with all their friends gathered for the occasion. She had never dreamed that she and Michael would have to wed secretly.

The door opened and Lilly, Michael's stepmother, poked her head into the bedroom. "You should hurry, Caroline. My son will be back from town any time. He's been drinking, and you know how he is when he's drunk."

Lilly Duncan was a tiny, birdlike woman with long, dark hair that she chose to wear unbound in a style better suited to a much younger woman. The stark blackness of her hair was a startling contrast to her pale complexion and dark eyes. Caroline pitied Lilly, who was a sad creature, living in the shadows of life. She had been twice widowed, and she was terrified of her own son, Brace.

Dread settled around Caroline when she heard thunder in the east, warning of a gathering thunderstorm. She cringed just thinking about what Brace's reaction would be when he learned that she and Michael were married.

Her new husband had thought that if they went on an extended honeymoon, Brace might accept their marriage by the time they returned.

But Caroline knew better. Brace would never acknowledge their marriage. She thought of the many times he had brushed against her or breathed down her neck while cleverly making his action appear accidental, not the lewd and calculated move it actually was.

She despised him, and he knew it. But it didn't matter to him how she felt; he was determined to have her. And when Brace wanted something, he would stop at nothing to acquire it. He was the only truly evil man she had ever known.

She thought back to the first time he had come upon her when she was out riding alone. Caroline had hardly known him at the time. He had roughly pulled her from her horse and pressed his hot lips on hers before she could even object. She had struggled to get away from him, feeling sick inside, and so terrified she could hardly think. She had finally gotten her arm free and had struck him a stunning blow across the face with her riding crop.

She shuddered, remembering how he had run his blunt fingers over the cut and had disgustingly rubbed his own blood across her cheek. She could still hear him swearing and saying that they were now bound by his blood, and he would someday have her, with or without marriage. His threat still rang in her ears. He had told her that if she married anyone else, she would be a widow shortly after she became a bride.

From that day on, Caroline had carefully avoided being alone with him. Only last week he had appeared at a gala held by one of her friends. Brace didn't usually attend any local events because he was not considered acceptable by most of their neighbors. That night he had gone directly to her and grabbed her arm, taking her into the middle of the other dancers. She had smelled the whisky on his breath when he whispered in her ear that if she allowed Michael to touch her, or if she was thinking of marrying his stepbrother, he would see them both dead.

Brace never made empty threats.

The cruel way he treated Michael had worsened since Michael's father had died. Brace never missed an opportunity to torment his stepbrother. Caroline had helplessly watched Michael slip further into gloom. He was gentle and kind, and no match for Brace's ruthlessness. Michael liked to read poetry and good books. She missed the golden days of childhood when they would spend hours reading to each other.

Three nights ago, Michael had come to her at her father's house and, with tears in his eyes, begged her to marry him. He was sure that together, the two of them could stand up against Brace.

Michael had chosen a day when Brace would be busy in town. They had spoken their vows early in the morning, and planned to depart as soon as possible, yet she was still afraid for Michael. She was also afraid for herself.

"You must leave right away," Lilly told her. "You know how bitter and cruel Brace is when he's been drinking." The woman's eyes took on a faraway look as if she had been jerked into the past. "When he was twelve, he threw my lapdog against the wall and killed it just because he was jealous of the little thing." Her eyes swam with tears. "He will do much worse to you and Michael if he finds you here when he returns."

The sudden sound of a shot echoed through the house, making both women jump. For a moment they looked at each other, fearing their worst nightmare had just come true.

"Was that a shot or a clap of lightning?" Lilly

asked, pressing a trembling hand over her heart.

Caroline lifted the skirt of her gown and ran down the hallway, her heart pounding in fear. She flew downstairs and into the sitting room where Michael was supposed to be waiting for her. With an anguished cry, she went down on her knees and gathered Michael in her arms. He was trying to say something, but no sound came from his lips. The red spot on the front of his white shirt was circling wider.

"Run," he finally said weakly. "Get out of here!"

She gathered him close. "No. I will not leave you!"

He reached up to touch her cheek, and then his eyes seemed to freeze and his hand fell limply to the floor. Her tears fell on his face, and she knew he was dead. She saw the gun lying on the floor, and she wanted to pick it up and use it on Brace.

Lilly appeared beside her, going down on her knees, reaching out to close Michael's eyes, then rocking back and forth.

"What shall we do? Get the doctor?" Caroline asked.

"No one can help Michael now."

"Where is Brace?"

"I found him passed out drunk in the study. But he'll come out of it before long, and he'll come looking for you. You have to get away! Run for your life!"

Caroline bent and placed a kiss on Michael's still-warm mouth, her heart breaking. "I will go to my father, and he will see that Brace is arrested for this deed." Tears were trailing down her cheeks, and she didn't bother to wipe them away. "I want to see him hanged for what he's done."

Lilly grabbed her hand. "You don't understand—he

will kill you and your father both. You must leave town now and go to a place where he can never find you."

Caroline stood up, took a lap robe from a chair and gently covered her new husband with it. Sadness tore at her like ground glass. Brace had said she would be a widow if she became a bride, and he had been right.

Lilly ran to the desk and rifled through a drawer until she found what she wanted. She pressed money in Caroline's hand. "Go now! Take the buggy Brace left out front. I'll meet you at the church cemetery tonight with clothing and more money. You mustn't stay here any longer."

Caroline looked down at her wedding gown, which was covered with Michael's blood. For the moment, terror pushed grief aside, and the need for survival took control of her mind.

She fled out the front door and climbed into the buggy, fearing that at any moment Brace would come after her. Putting the whip to the horses, she allowed them to run full out. Deep sobs tore at her throat. "Michael, oh, Michael, what has he done to you?"

It was almost dark when she reached the church where she had been married just that morning. She was grateful that the storm had passed over Charleston with only a light sprinkle. She was also glad that the churchyard was deserted.

She walked down a well-worn path, trying to hold her mind together and keep it from shattering into a million pieces. Many of the graves she passed were of soldiers who had been killed in the war—most of them young men she had known personally.

She came to her mother's grave and fell on her knees.

"I wish you were here to tell me what to do, Mama."

Later, she would not remember how long she had sat there beside her mother's grave, in the wedding gown splattered with Michael's blood. She could not imagine living in a world without him.

She prayed for his soul and for Brace's death.

As long as Brace was alive, she could never go home.

The one satisfaction she had on this tragic day was the knowledge that Brace would never find the gold bars and the bonds that Michael had hidden in a place his stepbrother would not think to look.

Hearing movement behind her, she jumped to her feet, ready to flee, but it was Lilly who stepped out of the shadows.

"Change quickly, and I'll drive you to the train depot." She handed Caroline a leather bag. "I've put some money in the bottom and some things I thought you'd need."

Caroline tore off her bloodstained gown and slipped into a blue print creation while Lilly hooked the back for her.

"It wouldn't be wise for you to contact your father for a while—it would only endanger his life. You know how Brace is."

"I want him to pay for what he's done to Michael."

"And so do I. But now is not the time."

"What will you do?" Caroline asked, feeling fear for the woman who had put her life in danger by helping her escape.

"Don't worry about me. As far as my son is concerned, I am already dead. He doesn't even consider me at all. You're the one I am worried about."

It was almost midnight when they arrived at the depot. Lilly guided the buggy around to the side of the building where deliveries were made. "No one will see us here. You can slip in through the side door."

Caroline was reluctant to get out of the buggy, but she had no choice. "I will write to you."

"No. Do not. That would not be wise. Don't attempt to communicate with anyone here—not even your father. Brace will have someone watching us all. Do not ever underestimate him—he is very clever."

"I understand."

"Change trains several times so it will throw Brace off your trail. And never forget that he will be looking for you."

Caroline suppressed a sob as Lilly hugged her. "I always liked you, Caroline. I wish that you and Michael could have had a life together. Michael is the son I should have had."

Caroline pressed her cheek to Lilly's. "Take care of yourself. And be careful. Brace might turn on you when he finds out you helped me."

"Go now. Run as far and as fast as you can!"

Chapter One

Savannah, Georgia—1869

Rumbling thunder and violent streaks of lightning woke Caroline Duncan from a deep sleep, but her lashes fluttered and closed as she drifted off again, burying her head deeper into the pillow. Even as a child she had loved the sound of thunderstorms. For some reason they always lulled her spirit, perhaps because she was a planter's daughter.

Danger stalked her, and she had trained herself to be a light sleeper, attuned to every noise in the old house. A moment later, her eyes snapped open when she heard a different sound. The front door creaked on its hinges, and there was an unmistakable noise of someone moving about downstairs.

The house belonged to the Lowell family, who had engaged Caroline as governess for their daughter, Vanessa. The family had gone to their country house for the weekend, so whoever was sneaking around downstairs definitely did not belong there.

After six months of living with the Lowells, Caroline had memorized the different noises the house made. The structure was several generations old, but it had been kept in good repair, although some of the floorboards in the hallway were warped and two of the doors downstairs stuck when someone tried to open them. Whoever had come into the house had the heavy tread of a man. She heard him cross the dining room floor and go into the kitchen.

It was certain that the man was not familiar with the layout of the rooms, because he was bumbling through each one, searching them extensively before going on to the next.

Caroline flipped her long hair out of her face and pressed her hand against her heart. She did not know who the intruder was, but she did know that he had come for her. She had been expecting him, or someone just like him, for some time.

Her fear was every bit as stark and terrifying as it had been that awful day when she had fled from Charleston. After she had arrived in Savannah, it had taken her three weeks to venture far enough from her rented room to find a position. She had been desperately in need of money, and she hadn't eaten in two days.

She had been fortunate. Mrs. Lowell had engaged her as her daughter's governess without a recommendation. Even living in the safety of the Lowell house, every day had been a test of her strength. If she closed her eyes, she could still see the vision of her husband dying in her arms.

She quietly moved off the bed, her slight body trembling in fear. This time she would not be taken by surprise as she had been the day Michael died: She had devised a plan of escape in the event that she had to leave in a hurry.

Without pausing to think, she quickly dressed and slipped into her boots, not worrying about hooks and ties. She threw her dark cape over her shoulders and raised the hood to cover her blond hair. Taking a deep, steadying breath, she reached underneath the bed and grabbed the small traveling bag she had packed with the barest necessities.

Her bedroom had two different ways to exit—one which led to the wide hallway and another that led to the gallery that connected with Vanessa's bedroom. Her plan was a simple one: She would wait until the intruder had searched Vanessa's bedroom. Then she would slip into the room and out into the hallway to make her way downstairs while he searched her bedroom.

The night was as black as pitch except for an occasional jagged streak of lightning that illuminated the room. Caroline knew she had one slight advantage over the intruder, since she could find her way about in the dark and he couldn't.

Slowly she opened the door to the gallery and stepped outside, pressing her back against the brick wall, waiting for the intruder to make his way upstairs. Her chances of escaping weren't very good, but she had to try.

A sudden flash of lightning and a roll of thunder shook the house and rattled the windows. Rain peppered heavily against the shingled roof, running off the eaves and splashing onto the gallery. And then as suddenly as it had started, the rain stopped. She was relieved, because now she would be able to hear the man's movements.

She waited for just the right moment to put her plan in motion.

When Caroline heard the labored footsteps on the stairs, she froze. If her plan was to succeed, she knew her timing had to be perfect.

But what if he came out onto the gallery from Vanessa's room? she thought frantically.

Brace would stop at nothing to get his greedy hands on her. He wanted the gold, and only Caroline knew where it was. But she would die before giving the secret up to him. Of course, that meant that she couldn't touch any of the money either, and that left her with only the meager salary she earned from the Lowells.

Her body shook with fear. He would not let her live—she knew too much about Michael's death. He was clever, and he would never stop hounding her until one or the other of them was dead. The intruder's tread was quieter now as he took more care, but the floorboards still groaned beneath his weight. After he had searched Vanessa's bedroom and gone back into the hall, Caroline quietly slipped into the child's bedroom.

She tiptoed across the floor and stepped into the hallway, when near disaster struck: The heel of her boot caught on the edge of the rug, and she almost lost her balance. Bracing herself against the wall, she managed to remain on her feet.

With her heart pounding in her throat, she slid her body into an alcove, shivering when she heard the intruder walk back in her direction to investigate the noise. She closed her eyes and prayed as he passed so near that she could see the pockmarks on his swarthy face. She dared not even breathe when he stopped right next to her and looked toward the stairs. She could have fainted with relief when he finally retraced his steps in the direction of her bedroom. As he disappeared inside, she quickly started for the stairs, cautiously stepping over the third step from the top, knowing that it would creak if she put any weight on it.

When she reached the bottom step, she paused long enough to listen. The man was no longer being cautious. In his frustration and anger, he was shoving furniture pieces and breaking glass. She wondered what the Lowell family would think when they returned to find her gone and her bedroom in shambles. Unfortunately, she would never be able to tell them what had happened. Brace would certainly question them, and it was best that they knew nothing of where she'd gone.

She had no destination in mind as she hurried toward the door. She only knew she had to get as far away from Savannah as she possibly could.

Her whole body shook as she opened the back door. Caroline stepped into darkness so deep and black that it swallowed her in obscurity.

She glanced up at the light shining from her bedroom window. The man had lit a lamp and was probably going through her personal items, looking for clues to her whereabouts.

Running out the back gate, she hurried down the street, knowing that if she didn't escape, she would probably never see another sunrise.

When the next streak of lightning split the night sky, she studied her surroundings and felt disoriented; nothing looked familiar in the darkness. Wet, cold, and shivering in the raw wind, she lowered her head, completely despondent. It was difficult to think about anything but the man who would soon turn his search for her outside the house. Taking a moment to gather her thoughts and catch her breath, she leaned against a tree trunk and lowered her head onto her arms.

Caroline was near to collapsing, and she wondered if she had the strength to continue her flight. By now the intruder must have realized that she had escaped, and he would widen his search. With the next streak of lightning she located the familiar landscape of a garden square and realized that she was only a short distance from River Street.

She prayed as she ran toward the Savannah River that there would be a passenger ship she could board. She hoped that her pursuer would expect her to go to the train station or even to the stage office and direct his search in that direction.

Caroline fled down the ballast stone street, stopping only once to catch her breath and to rest for a moment beneath an aged oak. When she finally reached the river, there were several ships in port. She quickly disregarded the three cargo ships and made her way toward a sleek but small schooner, *The Spanish Lady*. She had no notion what port the ship was sailing to, but when the crew hoisted anchor, she intended to be on board.

She was exhausted by the time she reached the

slanting gangplank and hoped she would have enough strength to make her way up it. The deck was swaying with the rough waves, and she managed to remain upright only by holding on to the railing. She felt her stomach heave and clamped her hand over her mouth—now would not be a good time to become ill.

She swallowed several times before glancing frantically about, not knowing what to do next. Her gaze finally fell on a man who was giving orders; the others seemed to be deferring to him. He was a fearsome sight with black eyes, a shaggy black beard, and a thundering voice that sent his men scrambling to do his bidding.

He frowned when he saw her approach. "What are you doing on my ship, ma'am? You'd best go ashore. We're just now getting under way."

The wind had kicked up again and tore the hood from her head, blowing a blond strand of hair across her face. She swallowed a lump in her throat and said in a trembling voice, "Sir, I would like to book passage on your ship."

He nodded and jerked his head toward the companionway. "If you got the fare, I got an empty cabin." He must have sensed her urgency because he smiled cunningly. "Your fare will be two hundred dollars since you came on board at the last minute."

She swallowed past her tight throat, hoping the ship wasn't headed for China or Africa or some other distant country. "What is your destination, sir?"

He looked at her as if she had lost her mind, and she was sure she must be behaving like a crazed woman. "Why, home port, ma'am. We sail for Galveston, Texas." He took her money and then turned his attention to the upper rigging, which was whipping and snapping in the wind.

The amount the captain was asking was unfair, but she had no choice but to pay it. Later she would worry about the rest of her life; right now, all she cared about was getting out of Savannah, Georgia. Even now, her enemy could be hot on her heels. It would not take Brace long to discover that she had sailed away, and on which ship she had sailed.

A knot formed in her stomach, and she glanced out into the darkness, wondering if she was being watched at that very minute. Her glance fell on the gangplank, which was being drawn in, and she was overcome with relief. She had won this time. But there would be another encounter—of that she was certain.

She was immediately shown to her cabin by a balding first mate who gruffly told her what time they would be serving food and that if she was late, she would get nothing. When he left and shut the door behind him, she waited until she heard his footsteps fade in the distance before she dropped down on the narrow bunk. Lowering her face in her hands, she felt utter despair.

Brace's hired man had almost caught her tonight.

Why hadn't she changed her name when she'd applied for the position of governess?

Feeling utterly alone, she closed her eyes. Tears clung to her lashes and then seeped from her eyes. Where could she go that Brace would not follow? Where could she hide that he could not find her? One thing was certain: Her enemy had a long reach, and he would never give up searching for her.

* * *

It was a week later when *The Spanish Lady* finally sailed past the Florida Keys. The storm that had dogged them most of the way churned the restless sea, and huge waves slammed against the ship, making it bob and sway like a cork in water.

Caroline lay on her bunk, seasick and moaning. The ship had put into several ports, but she had not gone ashore at any of them. The ship's cook had taken a liking to her and gave her fresh fruit to keep in her cabin; that was all she had eaten. But at the moment, the thought of any kind of food only made her feel worse.

It was full dark and raining when *The Spanish Lady* finally reached Galveston Bay. She stared at the lights in the distance, feeling so weak and ill she didn't know if she could make the trek into town. A cold, wet wind drove her forward and soaked her to the skin.

Stumbling down the gangplank, she was jostled by other passengers who were in a hurry to reach their destination; she envied them because they were probably going home to be welcomed by someone who loved them. There would be no welcome for her, no one she could turn to for help. She had only twenty-two dollars to her name, and that wouldn't take her very far.

Weak and weary, she trudged through the mud, always keeping her eyes on the lights of Galveston in the distance. It was dark and cold, and fear dogged her steps as she kept glancing behind her. Once she heard footsteps, and she shrank into the shadow of a warehouse, only to recognize members of the ship's crew with duffel bags thrown over their shoulders, making their way home.

Caroline knew that she could not remain in this town for very long. If she knew Brace Duncan, he had already sent someone to look into every kind of transportation that had left Savannah the night she had disappeared. His man would search every town where *The Spanish Lady* had docked, and it wouldn't take him long to discover that she had come ashore at Galveston.

The rain intensified, making it difficult for her to see more than a few feet ahead of her. For the last few weeks it had done nothing but rain; she was beginning to wish she lived in a desert. Her cloak was damp and slapped painfully at her ankles as she toiled along.

Her mood lightened a bit when she saw the Overland Stage sign swinging in the wind. She climbed the wooden steps and turned the doorknob, and her heart sank. It was locked; the office was closed for the night.

She slumped down on the wooden bench where a slight overhang offered her some protection against the rain. She was determined to be on the first stage that headed west in the morning, and she would go as far as her money would take her.

Darkness closed in around her, and she dropped her head into her hands, too weary to hold it upright. After a time, she realized it would be foolhardy to sit in the rain calling attention to herself.

Exhausted, she took in her surroundings—there was a small hotel across the street and another down the way. She decided to spend some of her money for a room, a hot cup of tea, and a bath.

A few hours later, when night took a turn toward morning, she awoke and dressed, wading in ankle-deep water to cross the street to the stage office.

A man was just unlocking the door when she rushed up the steps. Following him inside, she waited for him to go behind the counter before she placed her money on the well-worn surface. "Can you tell me how far west this amount of money will take me?"

The agent was a grandfatherly-looking gentleman with long white hair and an equally white mustache. His brown gaze rested speculatively on her for a moment, taking in her pale face and muddy shoes. He saw the widow's broach that fastened her tattered cape, and his gaze softened.

"You are very young to lose your husband and to be traveling alone in this country."

Caroline had bought the broach when she had applied for the position with the Lowells, hoping that people would respect her right to mourn her husband and not pay too much attention to her. As for the stage agent, she didn't want to engage his interest, so she quickly said, "I need a ticket on the next westbound stage."

"Just how far do you want to go?" he asked kindly.

"Just as far as the money will take me."

He was silent for a moment and then nodded, taking only ten dollars of her money and shoving the rest back at her. "This will take you as far as San Sebastian, Texas. The stage will be arriving within the hour, and it'll be pulling out by mid-morning. On this run you will only have to change stages twice. Each time the folks at the way station will give you a full meal."

Her hands were shaking as she scooped up the remaining money and stuffed it into her reticule. "You didn't take enough out for my fare," she stated in a quiet voice, knowing she must swallow her pride and depend on his kindness.

"It's enough."

After hiding and running for so long, she was deeply touched by his act of compassion. "Thank you. You are a true gentleman," was all she could manage to say past the tightness in her throat.

The warmth of his smile matched the warmth in his eyes. "Have you no one to go to for help?"

She drew back, frightened, not wanting him to remember her for any reason. "I'll just go outside and wait until the stage arrives."

"Wait," he called out to her, scribbling something on a piece of paper and sliding it across the counter toward her. "You seem to be in some kind of trouble."

She panicked. "No. I'm not in trouble."

He knew better—he could clearly see that she was terrified. "I have a niece who owns the boardinghouse in San Sebastian; that's why I suggested the town. Go to see Nelly when you get there, and she'll help you."

Caroline glanced down at her muddy boots. "No one can help me." She turned her head toward the sound of the arriving stage. "And please," she said in desperation, "I beg of you, tell no one you saw me."

He nodded. "I keep my own business and ask others to do the same. Don't be afraid that anyone will find you through me."

Caroline looked deep into his honest brown eyes and took the folded paper he held out to her. She had a sense that she could trust him. "I will not forget your kindness."

"Seek out my niece," he said, glancing at the stage driver who had just entered and deposited a leather satchel on the counter. "This here is the stage you'll take to San Sebastian." He glanced at the driver. "It'll be all right with you if she boards now, won't it?"

"Yeah. I don't mind if she does," the man said, paying little attention to her.

Words failed her. The stranger's generosity was still on her mind when the stage pulled out an hour later.

Two other passengers had boarded in Galveston, so she pulled the hood of her cloak low across her forehead and pretended to be asleep.

She knew nothing about San Sebastian, Texas, but that was where she was headed. Each mile the stage traveled was taking her farther and farther away from her enemy—and that was all she cared about at the moment.

It was Caroline Duncan who began the long journey into the unknown. But by the time she arrived at San Sebastian, she would be Caroline Richmond.

Chapter Two

Texas—1871

Caroline Richmond, as she was known to the people of San Sebastian, sat near the window so she could catch the last bit of light from the setting sun. Reaching into her sewing basket, she untangled a strand of green thread and threaded her needle. She still had to hem both sleeves before the gown would be finished.

She paused for a moment and allowed her gaze to linger on the sunset that was so brilliant it made the cloud bank to the east look like it was on fire. She was swamped by feelings of melancholy and homesickness that cut deep into her soul. She had tried not to dwell on the past, but in truth it was always with her, lurking just at the edge of her mind.

She tried to concentrate on the view from the window. This part of Texas was mostly flat, so twilight lingered long past the gentle sunsets that she remembered in Charleston. In South Carolina, twilight fell softly across the land. In Texas, when the sun finally did set, it struck against the land like a hammer on an anvil.

She shook her head to dispel her memories, because she could never go home again. She thought of how her father had never fully recovered from her mother's death. He had become a shadow of the man he'd once been. She feared he might have become worse after she'd disappeared from his life. How could she know, since she had not seen or contacted him in almost three years?

Without a doubt, Brace would have someone watching her father's mail; he would expect her to write. In that way she had outsmarted him.

She was resigned to the fact that San Sebastian would probably be her home for the rest of her life.

If she was going to be honest with herself, she owed her very existence to the kind people of this town. When she had first arrived as a stranger, the local families had taken her into their hearts and homes. But sometimes, like now, when she was alone in the still of the evening, when families were gathered about their table together, she longed for a family of her own. Her heart and mind were still attached to the past, and she could never have children of her own as long as Brace was looking for her.

The Gray family lived behind her, and they had seven energetic children whose laughter often floated in her direction, touching the loneliness deep inside her. Even now she could hear the constant slamming of the door as Wanda Gray called her offspring to supper.

Last night the old nightmare had returned, and she had awakened in a cold sweat. She had been too afraid to go back to sleep and had paced the floor until dawn. It had been a long day, and now she was so weary she could hardly hold her head straight.

She did not want to remember holding Michael in her arms, her gown soaked with his blood. She did not want to remember how it felt when he had taken his last breath and there had been nothing she could do to help him. She missed him, she always would.

She reached into the bottom of her sewing basket, pushing thread aside until she found what she was searching for. She carefully unfolded the clipping from *The Union Daily News* of Union, South Carolina. Her hands trembled so badly she could hardly read the faded, three-year-old article:

> *Michael David Duncan, prominent resident of Charleston, took his own life on his wedding day. His grieving brother, Brace, and his stepmother, Lilly Duncan, gave their account of the tragedy. They said that Michael had been despondent for several months, and he seemed to be worse on his wedding day. The deceased's wife, Caroline Duncan, is unavailable for comment and is in seclusion.*

It grieved her that everyone thought Michael had taken his own life. She had hoped that Brace would be a suspect and go on trial for her husband's murder. But he had been very clever; he'd twisted the tragedy to fit his own purpose. Caroline was disappointed that Lilly had lied for her son—but then, she'd probably had no choice in the matter.

Caroline shuddered at the lies that had been printed and accepted by the people of South Carolina.

It was difficult to shake the horrors she had lived through that awful day. The reality of her situation was grim—even in the daylight hours she had to fight against the fear that was always with her. Whenever she was out about town she was constantly glancing over her shoulder to see if anyone was following her.

She laid her forehead against the smooth windowpane while her gaze moved down the dusty street that led to Fort Lambrick. The town had grown up around the fort and owed its prosperity to the army outpost. When she had first arrived in Texas, everything had seemed so alien to her. The blistering summer heat made saddle leather so hot it was difficult to mount a horse. Then there were the harsh, unpredictable winters when a warm, pleasant day could suddenly be struck by a blue norther, plunging the temperature down forty degrees in a matter of minutes.

But this was her adopted home where she had found shelter and friendship.

Caroline laid her sewing aside and went into the small kitchen. By now it was completely dark, so she felt around for the oil lamp and struck a match, watching a warm glow cascade into the dark corners of the room.

Archimedes, a fat tabby, was curled up in a basket beneath the stove. The cat regarded her with a lazy yawn, then closed his eyes and curled tighter into a ball. She had found Archimedes on her doorstep one night and had brought him in, fed him, and brushed the knots from his damp fur. She had given him a name, and he had taken up residence in her house as if it belonged to him.

She bent down and rubbed his fur and smiled at his loud purr. "We are alike, you and I, Archimedes. Neither one of us had anyone; now we have each other."

The animal turned over on his back so she could rub his stomach. He purred louder when she accommodated him. Then he yawned and closed one eye while watching her with the other.

"You are no company to me at all, you lazy cat. All you want to do is sleep," Caroline gently teased, giving him a final rub.

A kettle of water was simmering on the back of the stove, and it enticed her to have a cup of tea. She had to budget her money, but tea was the one indulgence she allowed herself. In the beginning she had made money by taking in washing and ironing for some of the soldiers at Fort Lambrick. She stared down at her hands, which had been rough and bleeding in those first days.

Nelly Aldrich was her best friend and the owner of the local boardinghouse—she was the niece of the man who had helped Caroline when she had boarded the stage in Galveston. With Nelly's help, she had become a seamstress and was doing quite well at it. She made gowns for some of the ladies in town and most of the officers' wives. Lately, she had earned a little extra money by teaching several soldiers how to read and write. She liked to keep busy, because then she had little time to think about her future or to worry about the past.

Although it was long past supper, she didn't feel much like eating alone. She settled onto a kitchen chair waiting for her tea to steep. Glancing about the kitchen, which was small but cheery, she ran her hand over the red-and-white oilcloth that covered the scarred table and matched the checked curtains she had made for the window. The two sturdy chairs had been given to her by Nelly when she had helped her move into the house.

Nelly had taken Caroline under her wing, giving friendship without asking questions about her past. The two women had a lot in common, since Nelly's husband had been wounded in the war and had later died, leaving her a young widow. But he had provided for Nelly by leaving her the boardinghouse, where Caroline had lived for her first year in San Sebastian. Caroline now lived in a three-room house that she rented from Mr. Liggett, who owned the General Merchandise—a store which boasted that it sold almost everything, and it practically did.

Caroline had just reached down to give Archimedes a crisp piece of bacon that had been left from breakfast when she heard a knock on the door. For a moment her stomach tightened in knots as it always did when someone came unexpectedly to her house. She took a steadying breath when she heard Nelly call out to her.

"Caroline, you home?"

Caroline smiled as she opened the door. "I'm so glad you came by. You are just in time for a cup of tea."

Nelly entered and thrust a covered dish at Caroline. "I baked a cobbler today and made some extra for you."

Nelly was several inches shorter than her friend, and

at twenty-three, two years older than Caroline. She had coffee-brown hair and soft brown eyes. She instinctively liked people, and her goodness had helped Caroline heal in spirit. Her friendship had given Caroline the strength to go on when she had wanted to quit.

She closed the door, and lifted the snow-white napkin so she could smell the delicious dessert. "You remembered that mulberry cobbler is my favorite."

When the two women were seated at the table, their tea before them, Nelly placed her cup down and studied her friend carefully. Caroline was much too thin in her opinion, and Nelly worried that she didn't eat enough to sustain her. She knew that most nights Caroline would be seated in the dim lamplight working on her sewing.

A wisp of Caroline's light blond hair had come loose from the tight knot secured at the back of her neck. Nelly suspected that her friend kept her hair pulled away from her face so she would appear older, but even the severe hairstyle did not hide the fact that Caroline was a beautiful woman with smooth skin and sky-blue eyes.

Nelly didn't know exactly why Caroline had come to Texas. But when she had arrived she carried a letter from her uncle, recommending that Nelly look after the young woman. As a result of their meeting, Nelly had the best friend she had ever known.

Nelly traced her finger over the flower pattern on the teacup and frowned. "The talk around town is Captain Dunning asked you to go to the officers' dance with him next Saturday."

Caroline was clearly annoyed that everyone seemed

to be interested in her life. "Yes, he did ask me." She was ready for one of Nelly's lectures.

Nelly frowned. "I also heard that you refused him."

Caroline took a sip of tea before answering. "I had to. As it is, I will barely have time to finish Betty Bostick's gown before the dance. I have no time for frivolous pleasures."

"Is that what you think the dance is—frivolous?"

"Th . . . there was a time when I liked to dance. But I'm a widow now," she stated forcefully.

"Since I've already poked my nose into your business, I may as well keep going. Don't you think you've hidden behind those widow's weeds long enough? Captain Dunning is a very fine gentleman, and he's shown a partiality for you. Don't you want a normal life, children?" She gestured around her. "Don't you want to get out of this little house that belongs to someone else? What could have happened to you that makes you hide away like this? You hardly ever go anywhere or do anything."

Caroline was getting the full blast of Nelly's lecture this time. "If we are going to talk personally," she retaliated, "you might ask yourself why you haven't accepted Yance Grady's offer of marriage. You know you love the man, and he clearly loves you."

"Well," Nelly said forlornly, thinking about her own situation, "I do care for Yance, but his daughter, Judy, doesn't like me. I'm not sure I can be the mother she needs, with her resenting me like she does."

"She is young. Give her time. She still remembers her mother and she is probably worried that you might want to take her place."

"Do you really think that's why she doesn't like me?"

"I'm sure of it. You could make her change her

mind. You are the kind of person who isn't happy unless you can tell someone how to live their life, so give her the benefit of your wisdom." Caroline smiled innocently when she saw Nelly glare at her. "If you set your sights on straightening out someone else's life besides mine, you might have better results."

"I'm not like that."

"Oh, yes, you are. You seem to know exactly how I should live my life."

"You aren't living—you're merely existing."

"You may be right," Caroline conceded grudgingly. "But this is just the way I like it."

"Answer this one question, if you will: Why won't you go to the dance with that handsome captain? People really are beginning to gossip about you keeping to yourself so much."

Caroline fastened the wayward strand of hair back into her chignon and shook her head. "I can't help what people think, and of course I would like to have children of my own, but it's just not possible. I cannot draw anyone into my life or into my troubles—not even you, Nelly. I'm grateful that you have accepted me without knowing who I really am, or anything about my past. You must understand that it's too dangerous for you to know what happened to me before I came here."

Nelly watched Caroline's face carefully. "That's what you always say when you think I'm getting too close to the truth. But if you ever change your mind and want to talk, I'm a good listener—just know that no one will ever hear your secrets from me." She reached out and placed her hand on Caroline's. "I'm not asking you to tell me what you're running from, or what makes you jump out of your skin every time a stranger comes to town. I'm just asking you to trust me as a friend if you decide you need to tell someone what you are hiding from."

Caroline took a sip of tea, found it cold and pushed it aside. "I will never forget all your kindnesses toward me. I hadn't a friend in the world when I arrived in San Sebastian. When I gave you the note from your Uncle Ralph, you took me in and gave me a place to stay. If you will remember, I told you that day that it could be dangerous for you to befriend me."

"I know you were running from someone and you were afraid for your life. You were sick then, and so skinny that a good ole Texas breeze could have blown you away. I was not about to turn you away, and I'm glad I didn't, because then I wouldn't have known you as a friend."

"I never had a better friend than you've been to me. Still, you need to understand something: The man who is looking for me will never give up until he finds me. He is dangerous, and he puts no value on human life."

Nelly's brow furrowed. "I'm not afraid, and you shouldn't be either. You have friends in this town who will help you."

"No one can help me, not even you. Please listen to me and hear what I'm telling you," she said, leaning forward. "The man who hunts me is evil! He has committed unspeakable crimes." Her voice trembled, and she put her hand to her throat. "You can't imagine the things he's done. I was a witness to his crime, and he can't let me live."

Nelly covered her mouth with her hand. "Why don't we go to Sheriff Palmer and tell him your story? You can't spend the rest of your life jumping at shadows."

Caroline stood up, shaking her head, her eyes bright with fear. "I have already said too much. Please don't tell anyone what I said to you tonight. There is nothing that the sheriff can do about this man. And know this: If I think my enemy is closing in on me, I will leave without telling you, and you will never hear from me again."

"You can't do that!" Nelly's eyes widened with anger. "I would never know what happened to you."

"I have done it before, and I will probably have to do it again. My enemy almost caught me once. I have little doubt he will try a second time."

"I don't understand how you can go through each day being afraid. After all, Caroline, this man is only human, and he can be stopped!"

Tears sparkled in Caroline's eyes. "No, he can't. This thing will not end until one or the other of us is dead. May God forgive me, because every day I pray for his death."

"Then promise me this: If you ever think he's found you, you will talk to me before you do anything hasty."

"I promise you that I will do whatever it takes to keep you from becoming embroiled in my troubles."

Nelly stood and hugged her friend tightly. "I wish there was something I could do to help you."

"You already have."

Nelly was afraid for Caroline. She thought that if her friend only had a man to look after her, she might be safe. "You're so pretty. A woman like you can't live in the past all the time."

"I have no future."

"Don't say that. It's time for you to start living again."

"Perhaps some day I can. But not yet."

"I don't understand you."

Caroline wrinkled her nose. "But I understand you. You are trying to play matchmaker and find a husband for me."

Nelly agreed with a grunt. "Well, maybe so. But—"

Caroline lifted the napkin and took another whiff of the cobbler. "Suppose I cut us both a generous slice?"

The town was quiet and most people had gone to bed hours before, but Caroline sat with her head bent, her needle darting hastily in and out of the green muslin. Wearily she sighed as she pricked her finger.

She was swamped by dread and too afraid to go to sleep. Her dream the night before had dredged up all of her old fears, and her conversation with Nelly hadn't helped, either.

Her vision blurred, and she stopped to rub her eyes for a moment, considering whether she should leave San Sebastian—had she stayed too long? It hurt to think of leaving her friends, and especially Nelly. She had very little money, but she could start over again somewhere else. Perhaps she would go to California next time. Surely she could get lost in a place that far away.

Chapter Three

It was overcast, and a rainy mist hung low in the sky as Caroline fell into step with several other people who were headed toward the church at the edge of town. The sound of the church bells was muffled by a sudden heavy fog that swirled about them, and a strange eeriness permeated the air. It had been threatening rain all morning, and as the first drops fell, the group of people dashed beneath the awning of the General Merchandise store, seeking shelter.

Caroline was the first to hear the sound of the rider, and the first to see the stranger as he emerged from the mist, his black horse hardly breaking its stride in the muddy street. The man was dressed all in black from hat to boots. He sat high in the saddle, his head at a formidable tilt, his wide shoulders ridged with muscle. She could not see his features at all because his hat was pulled low over his forehead, but she did see the squareness of his clean-shaven jaw and knew instinctively that he was dangerous, and he meant trouble for someone.

A deep feeling of foreboding slammed into her like a fist, twisting inside her stomach as she heard the whispers that swept through the group.

"I believe that's Wade Renault," Sally Graves marveled. "He used to be a gun for hire, but I heard he'd retired to his home in Louisiana. What's he doing here?"

"That's him, right enough, and he must have come out of retirement," Mr. Liggett remarked. "I heard tell he's the best there ever was at what he does, and I believe it. I wonder if he's come here gunning for someone."

"But who?" Mrs. Liggett asked, clutching her husband's arm and moving a little closer to him. "Who would be so important to bring a man like him to our town?"

Caroline could feel the stirring of unrest in those around her, and it intensified when the gunslinger turned his head to glance in their direction.

"He could've come here for any one of us. Who among us doesn't have enemies?" remarked Mr. Styles, the foreman of one of the outlying ranches. "From all the saddle bums I've fired over the years, I've got a passel of people who would like to see me dead."

"Wade Renault doesn't shoot people," Mr. Liggett said. "He takes them to whoever hires him."

The others fell silent.

Caroline shivered, and this time her whole body shook. What if he had come for her? Her first instinct was to run and hide, but instead she gripped her handkerchief tightly in her hands, twisting it into a knot.

In that moment, the stranger shoved his hat back, and his gaze collided with hers. She looked into eyes that were more intense than any she had ever seen before—and she saw death reflected in that harsh gaze.

In that moment, she knew in her heart that he had come for her!

The bounty hunter nodded the merest bit in her direction while a cruel smile curved his lips. This was no clumsy intruder like the one who had broken into the house in Savannah trying to find her. This man would know exactly what to do: And if he had come for her, she would never be able to escape those watchful eyes.

"I know who he's come after," Victor Liggett insisted, stepping out into the rain and watching Wade Renault halt his mount in front of Nelly's boardinghouse. "I told Arnold Pickens not to hire that saddle tramp he took on last September. I even told the sheriff I'd seen his picture on a wanted poster down in Abilene last August. The sheriff swore he had nothing on him, but I bet Wade Renault knows all about that wanted poster."

Caroline was so frightened, her heart was beating twice as fast as normal. She wondered if Mr. Liggett might be right; could the bounty hunter have come for someone else? She watched the tall stranger fluidly dismount, his black chaps clinging to his long, lean legs. His spurs jingled as his boots touched the ground.

She stared after him until he disappeared into Nelly's boardinghouse.

Hoping no one would notice, Caroline quickly moved to the side of the building and hurried in the direction of her home. She could not go to church and pretend that nothing had happened. Past experience had taught her to be ready to leave quickly.

When she reached the house, she dashed inside, locking the door behind her. She hurried into her bedroom and retrieved the satchel she had stashed beneath her bed. Not knowing what to do next, she hurried into the kitchen and lifted the lid of the sugar bowl where she kept her extra money. When she counted it out, she realized there would not be enough to take her very far.

She blew a tangled curl out of her face and smoothed it into place. Glancing down at her hands, she saw how badly they were trembling. Once more she grasped her satchel and walked quickly to the back door.

She had to get away as soon as possible!

Archimedes chose that moment to saunter into the room after her, looking as if he hadn't a worry in the world. He twined around her leg, purring and rubbing his body against her.

Stricken, she dropped everything and scooped him into her arms. "How will you survive without someone to look after you?" She laid her face against his soft fur while tears gathered in her eyes. "What am I to do, Archimedes? I can't just leave you here, and I can't take you with me."

She was startled by a knock on the front door. She squeezed the cat so tightly that he twisted and squirmed until he was able to drop to the floor.

Caroline backed toward the door. If she could only make it out the back, she might be able to hide somewhere until the next stage left town.

"Caroline, are you in there?" Nelly called out. "Nancy Liggett thinks you're sick or something because you left so suddenly."

Reluctantly Caroline went to the front room and opened the door, noticing the worried frown on her friend's face.

"I was not feeling very well. I have a terrible headache." Her head truly was pounding, and the pain was excruciating.

"You poor dear, you are pale. Why don't you lie down, and I'll get a wet cloth for your head."

All she wanted was for Nelly to leave so she could plan her next move. "I'll be fine. I just need to rest for a while."

Nelly's gaze fell on the satchel on the kitchen floor, and she quickly looked at Caroline. "You're leaving, aren't you? You were going without telling me."

Caroline closed her eyes. "I told you what I would do if I felt threatened. Please tell no one about this until I am safely away. Then tell them I was called home for a family emergency or something of the sort. I'll leave money with you to give Mrs. Liggett for next month's rent."

Tears gathered in Nelly's eyes, and she shook her head. "Why are you doing this? What's happened?"

"A bounty hunter rode into town this morning. I believe he has come for me. You must have seen him. He went into your place."

"You mean Wade Renault." Nelly looked confused.

"He's not here for you. He was asking me about a man I've never heard of. I told him that if he had questions, he should ask Sheriff Palmer."

Caroline took a steadying breath and let it out slowly. "Can it be true that he is not here for me?"

"He didn't ask anything about you. He'll be staying at my place for at least tonight. I suspect he'll ride on tomorrow if the sheriff can't help him, or if he doesn't find the man he's after."

"I don't know what to do." Caroline paced the length of the room and back again. "I was so sure—"

"Mr. Renault has a reputation for always bringing in the man he's after, but I've never heard of him going after a woman." Nelly paused in thought. "No, that's not quite right. I heard a few years back that he rescued some rancher's daughter from the Apache down near San Hidalgo way. But that's not the same as hunting the girl down, is it?"

Caroline was not ready to relax just yet. "What else do you know about him?"

"They say he's quite a gentleman, and I can tell you he's been nothing but polite to me." Nelly smiled mischievously, hoping to put her friend more at ease. "He has this accent—French, I think it is. Notwithstanding what he does for a living, he is one perfect man. Handsome as all get-out."

Caroline remembered those cold, piercing eyes that made her shiver even now. "What else do they say about him?"

"No one seems to know much. I believe I once heard that he lives in New Orleans. That's all I know." She smiled devilishly, still trying to ease her friend's mind. "He isn't married. I'm not fooling you when I tell you he's the best-looking man I've seen around these parts in a long time."

Doubt and fear nagged at Caroline. "I still feel like I should leave as soon as possible."

"You aren't the only one who was spooked by Renault's arrival. A lot of people in town are afraid of him. As I said, he'll probably be moving on soon, and then we can all get back to normal."

Caroline was lost in thought, trying to absorb the significance of what Nelly was telling her. "I suppose, if he was asking the whereabouts of someone else, he wouldn't be looking for me."

"That's right. If I thought he had come to San Sebastian to find you, I'd do everything to help you get away. And besides, even if he were after you, don't you think it would be smarter to face him here surrounded by friends than off somewhere on your own?"

Caroline walked to the window and stared out, swallowing with difficulty. "I don't know what to do. I would like to wake up just one morning without being afraid."

Realizing for the first time the depth of Caroline's concern, Nelly was swamped with pity for her. Whatever had happened to her in the past must have been very bad, or she wouldn't be so suspicious of strangers. "Don't worry about Renault. If he starts asking questions about you, I'll know it."

Caroline didn't like the thought of leaving San Sebastian or of being alone again. "I suppose I could stay for a while."

"Good. Now about that headache—would you like me to make you a nice hot cup of tea?"

* * *

Wade Renault's room was small, but it had the little niceties that only a woman could add: There was a frilly scarf on a sturdy round table, a colorful hand-quilted cover on the bed, and a comfortable over-stuffed chair by the window.

When the landlady had shown him to a room that faced the front of the building, he had quickly explained that he was a light sleeper and that noise from the street would probably keep him awake.

How easily she had obliged him by moving him across the hallway. Now he had a room that looked directly down on Mrs. Duncan's house, and it would be easy to keep track of her comings and goings without even leaving his room.

He had come into town three nights ago when most of the town had been attending evening church service. Mrs. Duncan had not even locked her front door. He had slipped inside, searched every room carefully, and left with her being none the wiser.

He shoved the lace curtain aside and looked down at the small house. What luck that she had been the first person he had noticed when he rode into town today. He had not mistaken the fear in her eyes. It was as if she had been expecting him.

He had already determined that she had friends in this town, and he didn't want anyone getting in his way when he finally decided to make his move. He would bide his time, lull her into complacency by making her believe he was tracking someone else, and then he would take her.

He glanced at the house that was just behind Mrs. Duncan's. He knew that it was occupied by a rather large family; on the other side of her there was an older couple. He expected no trouble from any of them.

He always liked to learn everything he could about the person he was tracking. From what he had observed thus far about Mrs. Duncan, she was not the sterling churchgoer she would have folks believe. He tried to imagine what was going on inside her house at that very moment.

It had been a long time since he had experienced any kind of emotion, but at the moment he was suffused with anger. When he had first started watching her house, he had noticed several soldiers coming and going at all hours. There could be only one reason a man would visit a woman at night. There was little doubt in his mind as to what kind of woman Mrs. Duncan was.

Wade had lost count of how many people he had tracked over the years. He had always charged top dollar, and people had gladly paid it. He didn't need money, and he wasn't sure why he had accepted this one last challenge.

He could not explain what had induced him to come out of retirement, take up his gun again, and agree to locate this woman. For so long, he had needed something in his life, a cause to believe in—and he believed in bringing in criminals. He did have his scruples and a code of honor that he had never broken: He would not go after anyone if he thought his quarry was innocent. He had never hunted a woman before.

He did not feel good about it even now.

But this time was different from all the others: He

was working for a man who wanted to bring his brother's killer to justice. Angel-face down there was not what she appeared to be, and not what the good people of this town thought she was. According to Brace Duncan, his sister-in-law had married his brother, shot him, and taken the money that belonged to the family.

She had been easy to track. A beautiful woman was always noticed. It had taken him only two months to locate her in San Sebastian.

He was a bit puzzled about one thing, though. Why was she living such a meager existence if she had all that money?

He removed the small tintype he carried in his breast pocket and stared at it for a long time. Not that he needed any reminder of how she looked; it had become a nightly ritual for him to stare at her likeness and study the beautiful face. The sweetness of her smile apparently hid the passions of a cold-blooded killer. He traced the long, slender neck, and wondered what color her eyes would be. There was a longing deep inside him to hear the sound of her voice.

"Dammit," he ground out. He did not like the way he was thinking. But if he was going to be honest with himself, he would never have made the trip to Charleston to meet with Brace Duncan if the man had not sent him the tintype in the mail. Something had compelled him to learn more about the woman in the picture, and so far, he was disgusted by what he had witnessed, with the soldiers trailing in and out of her house.

He saw movement out of the corner of his eye, and he stepped back behind the curtain. His jaw hardened when he watched a man in uniform approach Mrs. Duncan's house; the soldier entered at her invitation. Maybe the angel-face had a way of getting what she wanted without spending Brace Duncan's money.

Wade remained patiently at his watch. An hour passed, and then two—then dusk fell and the soldier left. A short time later, she invited another man into her home, and this one remained for well over an hour.

He did not even want to think what was happening in that house, but visions of her locked in a steamy embrace with the sweaty soldier haunted him.

His lip curled into a snarl, and anger coiled inside him. It would be a pleasure to take Caroline Duncan back to Charleston, where she would answer for her crimes.

Chapter Four

It had been a week since the bounty hunter had ridden into town. Caroline had been nervous about venturing out of the house for fear of coming face to face with the man. Although Nelly had tried to convince her that he wasn't after her, doubt still plagued her, and fear had crept into her mind once more. At night when she went to bed, she would lie awake for hours and jump at each noise.

It had been cloudy for most of the morning, but the sun had broken through just after noon. Caroline's supply of thread was scant, and she was running low on food.

There was no help for it—she would have to leave the safety of her home and go to Liggett's store.

It was the last Saturday of the month, and the streets were crowded with ranchers who had come into town for their monthly supplies. Caroline's heart lightened as she stopped to speak to several friends. The Reverend and Mrs. Strand wanted to talk about the harvest-day picnic next week. Before she took leave of them, she promised to bake a chocolate cake, and to help dish out food at the event.

She paused before entering the store and cast a furtive glance toward Nelly's boardinghouse as if she expected Mr. Renault to appear at any moment. She pushed the door open wide and was welcomed by the bell tinkling overhead.

Mrs. Liggett, a gossip but a very kind person who could only find good things to say about her neighbors, greeted her warmly. Caroline moved to the back of the store, concentrating on the threads she needed and choosing among the colored spools. She also wanted three yards of white muslin to finish a petticoat for Nelly. She lifted a heavy bolt and started toward the front of the store so Mrs. Liggett could cut it for her.

In her mind, she was going down a list of things she needed to purchase. She needed a sack of potatoes for the stew she was making for Nelly, who would be having lunch with her after church service on Sunday.

Caroline didn't see the man until she rounded a table piled high with bolts of material and slammed into him. The impact took her breath away and sent the spools of thread she had been carrying rolling in every direction, but she did manage to hold on to the bolt of muslin. When she raised her gaze to him, she could not move or speak.

It was Wade Renault.

She was frozen in place as she stared into piercing eyes that seemed to look right into her mind and discover all her secrets. He was a predator, and in that moment she was his prey.

He smiled slightly and reached out to steady her by laying his hand on her shoulder. His gaze slowly moved over her features as he examined each lovely detail.

She cringed away from him, and shoved the muslin onto the table with the other bolts of fabric. "Take your hand off me!"

Seeing that she was terrified, he dropped his hand from her shoulder. "Forgive me, madame," he said with a clipped French accent. "I was thinking of something else and did not see you. I ask for your pardon."

Although Nelly had told her that Mr. Renault had an accent, when she actually heard him speak, it took her by surprise. She bent down to gather up the thread just so she could have something to do with her hands. She had not expected Mr. Renault to bend down at the same time to help her.

He frightened her so badly that she shot to her feet and pressed her hand over her heart. Caroline did not want to be so close to a hired killer, a man who made money from others' misery.

Renault scooped up the thread and held it out to her, but she shook her head and backed away from him.

"I am afraid you will have to untangle it," he remarked with seeming concern. Then his gaze met hers. "You must be Mrs. Richmond."

He could not have said anything that would have frightened her more than using her name. The lie she would have uttered, denying who she was, went dry in her throat.

She ignored the thread he held out to her and bumped into the table piled high with bolts of material, sending several of them scattering and unrolling across the floor.

"Mrs. Richmond," he said, stooping to retrieve the bolts of material. "Let me help you."

She wanted to run from the danger she sensed in him, but she seemed to be rooted to the spot. She was aware of noises around her—the ticking of the wall clock over the counter, Mr. Liggett talking to a customer, even the sound of a wagon passing by out front.

She watched him place the bolts back on the table and methodically align them as they had been before.

"I must go," she said breathlessly.

"Are you all right?" he asked, his gaze never leaving hers.

Without answering, she darted around him and hurried out the door. At first she just walked fast, and then she ran, not stopping until she reached her house. Once inside, she slammed the door behind her and leaned against it, trying to catch her breath.

When she heard someone coming up the porch steps, she clamped her hand over her mouth to keep from screaming in fear. When she heard Mr. Renault's voice, she cringed.

"Madame, Mrs. Richmond, may I speak to you?"

She didn't move or answer and kept her weight pressed against the door, hoping he would just go away.

His voice suddenly became mocking and arrogant. "I know you are in there because I saw you enter."

His high-handed attitude shoved every sane thought out of her mind, and she was left with only anger. How dare he follow her home, and then demand to enter her house? Without hesitation she whisked the door open and glared at him. "You have no right to be here. Why did you follow me?" she demanded.

There was nothing threatening in his pose at the moment. He seemed genuinely puzzled by her attitude. "I ask your pardon, madame, if I have frightened you. I only wanted to return this." He held her reticule out to her. "You dropped it when you left in such a hurry."

Her anger died and embarrassment took its place; the telltale sign of her humiliation showed on her flushed cheeks.

"I . . . didn't realize I had dropped it." Slowly she raised her gaze to his, and she had the feeling that she was drowning in those penetrating eyes. "Thank you, sir."

He handed her the purse. "Madame, I am accustomed to people having an adverse reaction to me. I suppose it's because of my profession."

Nelly had been right, this had to be the most striking man she had ever met. He stood at least six feet two. He was lean, and his shoulders were wide. His hair was so dark that it almost had a blue sheen to it. His eyes, which she had first thought to be brown, were actually an unusual amber color. His face was rugged and handsome, and his demeanor, even while he smiled, was intimidating.

On first seeing him, she had sensed that he was not a man to trifle with, and that impression was even stronger now. She knew in her heart that he was dangerous and unpredictable. If he had come for her, she would not stand a chance of escaping him.

As if he sensed her fear, he retreated down the steps. "Are you all right, madame? You seem upset about something."

She shook her head because she was having difficulty finding her voice. She gripped the door handle and stepped back inside. "Thank you for bringing me my purse. Please go now."

He settled his hat on his head and gave her a nod. "As you wish. If I can be of any assistance to you, my name is Wade Renault, and I'm staying at the boardinghouse for a few days."

Her heart was hammering in her ears as she heard the man's retreating steps. Her short encounter with him had been far more frightening than the incident in Savannah.

The truth hit her hard. She would not run this time because if he was after her, he would catch her in the end. Nelly had been right; it was better to face him here among friends than to be on her own again. He had given her no reason to suspect him—not by word or deed. It was just a feeling she had deep inside.

She opened her purse to see if anything was missing. To her surprise, the thread she had dropped in Liggett's store was there, and it was untangled—she wondered how he had accomplished such a feat in so short a period of time. And had he paid for it? He must have. Otherwise, he could not have just walked out of the store with it.

Caroline had just taken the last stitch on the gown for Captain Flynn's wife. She had promised to deliver it to the fort as soon as it was finished because Tessy Flynn was going to wear it for the ball tonight.

She arranged her straw bonnet on her head and tied the blue velvet ribbons beneath her chin. She carefully picked up the folded gown and draped it over her arm so it would not wrinkle. It was only a mile to the fort, and Caroline enjoyed the walk along the river.

As she stepped outside, the sun was shining brightly even though there was a bank of storm clouds in the west. She would have to hurry if she was going to get the gown to Mrs. Flynn before it started to rain.

As she walked through town, a cowhand tipped his hat to her. She paused long enough to hear Mrs. Simmons inquiring about Mrs. Gray's toothache and to advise the lady to pack it in cinnamon oil.

She was relieved when the gown was safely delivered without mishap. She stayed with Tessy long enough to take a cup of tea before starting back to town.

Heavy raindrops had just begun to fall as she reached Main Street. She ducked beneath the overhang of the *San Sebastian Gazette*, waiting until the shower passed. After a few moments the clouds scattered, and she continued on her way home.

She heard a rider approaching, and she glanced up just as the man dismounted in front of the post office. He had looped his horse's reins around the hitching post and climbed the steps toward her.

It was Wade Renault.

He casually leaned against a post, his entire attention focused on her. She felt the heat of his gaze, and she realized he was willing her to look at him, but she kept her head lowered

"Mrs. Richmond," he said, touching the brim of his hat.

She started to step around him, but he blocked her path. She raised an angry gaze to him. "Move aside."

"I was only going to wish you a good day."

She felt an intensity in him that made her step back. Her heart was hammering in her breast like a wild thing, and she felt as if it might burst out of her body at any moment. She was so frightened she could hardly think straight.

"How do you always manage to find me?" she demanded, finally looking into his eyes.

He smiled slowly. "You are assuming I came in search of you?"

Much to her embarrassment, she felt a flush climb up her face. "You always seem to be where I am."

He tapped a letter against the palm of his hand. "This is the post office, is it not? I am here to mail this letter."

"I . . . yes, I see."

"Good day to you, madame."

She dashed around him with hurried steps. She wanted to run, but she didn't want him to think she was afraid of him. No matter what he said or did, she knew in her heart that he had come to San Sebastian to look for her.

Wade stood by the window, glancing down at Mrs. Duncan's house. She had been terrified of him again, and that bothered him, although he could not have said why. He seated himself in the overstuffed chair and propped his long legs on a cowhide ottoman.

He reached into his pocket and withdrew the small tintype and traced the lines of her lips. He had seen those lips tremble in fear today. He had stared into her eyes—he now knew they were a deep blue. The picture did not show the suppleness of her full mouth. For nearly three months he had wondered how her voice would sound. Now he knew. This afternoon, like the day in Liggett's store, her voice had trembled in fear, but the trembling did not hide the melodic tone or the fact that she spoke each word distinctly with a delightful Southern accent.

Brace Duncan had told him about his sister-in-law's past, and it did not fit with what he had seen of her today. She was the only child of a prominent Charleston family. Her mother had died years ago, and he knew that her father's health was failing because he had visited Mr. Richmond before coming to San Sebastian. He had introduced himself as one of Michael Duncan's friends. The father had been more than willing to talk about his daughter, and he did not even realize that Wade had been directing questions at him.

Mr. Richmond had been out of his mind with worry for his daughter's safety. He had not seen her since before the marriage. The elderly man had been distressed by Michael Duncan's death, and he had felt it was somehow his fault—though he did not share with Wade his reason for feeling that way.

There had been tears in the old man's eyes when he confessed that he feared his daughter might be dead. He had raved on and on about the evil in the Duncan household, and how no decent woman would go near the place.

Wade closed his eyes, trying to remember what else

Mr. Richmond had told him about his daughter. He had said that he had not heard from her in three years, not a letter, nothing. The man had been pitiful when he swore that if she would return, all would be forgiven. Wade had not had the cruelty to ask him the one question that nagged at him. Did the father suspect that his daughter had killed Michael Duncan?

He also wondered how a daughter could so blatantly neglect her sick father. Not one letter in the three years since she had left Charleston. That was cold-hearted.

Wade became fully alert when he heard a squawking sound outside his window. He rolled to his feet, keeping in the shadows and glancing down at a young private who stood on Mrs. Richmond's doorstep, dangling a chicken by the legs. His jaw clenched as he watched Caroline Richmond invite the soldier inside. Was the price of her favors no more than one scrawny chicken? Did she offer her bounty to every man in uniform who made a trail to her door?

Something about the whole thing was not right, but he could not find the flaw. Why would she live such a meager existence when she had all that Duncan money?

He dropped the tintype on the floor and crushed it beneath his boot. Somehow he did not want to believe that Caroline Duncan was a woman of such loose morals. He picked up the bent tintype, and a small ache throbbed inside him because he had crushed it in a moment of anger. He shoved it into his saddlebag. Why should he care if she went to bed with every soldier at the fort?

He did, though. He cared a lot.

Her face had haunted him from the time he had opened the package sent by her brother-in-law. And seeing her in person, even knowing what kind of woman she was, had not changed his longing for her.

His steely gaze pierced the darkness of his room. He had never lost his head over a woman before, and he wasn't about to lose it over this one. He would carefully set his trap for her, and she would eventually walk right into it.

Wade swore under his breath as the soldier emerged from her house. This one had not even lingered for half an hour. Disgust grew in his heart. His landlady, who seemed to be a decent woman, befriended Caroline Richmond. She could not know about her promiscuous habits.

He would feel no guilt for bringing Mrs. Richmond to justice. In fact, it would be a pleasure to see that she got what she deserved.

Chapter Five

Caroline was having more trouble than usual falling asleep. Her thoughts were jumbled with the fear that pressed in on her like a swirling tide of darkness. Taking an exasperated breath, she opened her eyes and sat up, clasping her arms around her folded legs. Had those two meetings with Mr. Renault been accidental, or had he somehow contrived them? Was she being overly distrustful? Probably. But she had reason to be cautious.

Around midnight she was still thinking about the bounty hunter, and what she would do if he came after her. It was hot in her bedroom because it was on the side of the house that caught the setting sun. She pushed her damp hair out of her face.

How could she fall asleep in this heat?

A sudden gust of wind stirred in the leaves of the oak tree outside her bedroom window, and the branches scraped against the roof of the house. Cringing inside, she remembered that night in Savannah when she had been forced to flee for her life.

Mr. Renault had come to town for someone—he certainly wasn't there for sightseeing. But if he was after her, she was sure he would come at her straight on and not sneak into her house in the middle of the night.

Realizing that she was not going to fall asleep at all, she decided to make herself a cup of tea; perhaps that would help settle her mind.

She slid out of bed, pulled on her tattered green robe, and went into the kitchen. Archimedes greeted her with a yawn, and then stretched and hopped out of his basket, rubbing against her leg. She picked him up and held him close, rubbing his fur. It consoled her somewhat to hear his soft purr while he snuggled against her.

Even though it was hot in the house, Caroline was too afraid to open a window at night. She pushed a tumbled curl away from her neck, wishing the weather would turn cool. She moved out of the kitchen and through the front room. Opening the door, she stepped out on the porch and sat down on the top step, hoping to find some relief from the heat.

Ordinarily she would not have come outside in her robe, but it was the middle of the night, and she imagined that everyone would be asleep. She glanced up at the full moon that had just emerged from behind a cloud bank, showering its brilliance into the darkened shadows.

Archimedes seemed willing to lie in her lap as long as she stroked his fur. It was so quiet at this time of night. Somewhere near the Grays' house she heard a dog barking, and an angry rebuke by Mr. Gray.

She was overcome with feelings of moroseness. There was no one she could tell her deepest secrets to, as she had with Michael. There was Nelly, but Caroline would not burden her friend with her problems. There was no one to advise her on what she should do now. If only she could talk to her father, he would know what to tell her.

She had to keep so many emotions locked inside, and sometimes the weight of them was almost more than she could bear.

She didn't know what made her glance up at the boardinghouse, her gaze moving to the middle window. Her breath hung in her throat, and she was barely aware that the cat jumped from her arms and ran around the side of the house. Her attention was focused on the silhouette of a man. There was no doubt in her heart that it was Wade Renault, and no doubt in her mind that he wanted her to know he was there, because he stepped closer to the window.

Nelly had not told her that Mr. Renault's room overlooked her own house, giving him a good position to watch her every move. He would know every time she left the house, and everyone who came to visit her. Now that she thought about it, he had probably seen her leave the house that day she had gone to Liggett's store—he must have timed his departure just right so he could meet her there.

The encounter between them had not been an accident at all.

She rose quickly to her feet, clutching her robe together where it had gapped open in front. Backing up the steps without taking her gaze off him, she felt for the door handle and fumbled with it until it opened. She stumbled inside, slammed the door, and locked it behind her.

She slid down to her knees because her trembling legs would no longer bear her weight. After her heart rate slowed, she dashed about the rooms, making sure all the curtains were pulled together so no one could see inside the house.

After dropping down in the rocking chair and resting her head in her hands, she finally became more rational. But there was no reason to go back to bed, she would never be able to sleep now.

She picked up the petticoat she had been working on earlier and threaded her needle. She might as well do her sewing—perhaps it would take her mind off what had happened. Whether her fear was real or imagined, it remained on the edge of her mind until the first streak of sunlight touched the sky.

After a sleepless night, Caroline wrestled with the notion of staying home and not attending the church picnic. She certainly did not want to take a chance on meeting Mr. Renault again, and he would probably be there.

She spent the morning making the chocolate cake. When she slid it into the oven, she fried the chicken for Private McCaffrey. The homesick young man was only seventeen years old and away from his family for the first time. He had mentioned to Caroline that he did not enjoy Texas-fried chicken—he liked it cooked with spices the way his mother made it back in Alabama.

Caroline had taken Private McCaffrey under her wing, along with his friend, Private Foster. Both of them were so young, and neither one of them had been able to read or write until she started teaching them.

It was actually Mrs. Liggett who had suggested that the young men talk Caroline into teaching them, and she had enjoyed watching them learn. They insisted on paying her two dollars a month, so she used the money to buy books to give back to them. In the last two months several other young recruits had joined the reading group, and she now had twelve students. They were all polite and respectful to her and made her feel as if she had a dozen younger brothers.

It was almost eleven o'clock by the time she had iced the cake, and a very happy Private McCaffrey had arrived at her front door. After heaping praise on her and thanking her at least five times, he walked away, carrying his fried chicken with him. Caroline stood on the porch, smiling as she watched him reach inside the canvas bag, grab a chicken leg, and take a big bite.

Going back into the house, she removed her apron and hung it on a peg. She had decided that she would just take the cake to the picnic and then return home. Nelly wouldn't like it, but she was in no mood to visit with anyone today. Maybe she could come home and nap.

Tying her bonnet beneath her chin, she lifted the cake and went out the front door. Her gaze was drawn to the boardinghouse window, and she was relieved that no one stared back at her.

As she made the short walk across town, she joined several other people headed for the fairgrounds, where the festivities were being held.

When she reached the spring-fed pool, Caroline stopped to watch one of the Grays' children dive into the water, gleefully splashing his siblings. She smiled at their laughter and the loud splash that came when they all jumped in the pool at once.

She was suddenly overcome by a feeling of melancholy. The last time she had gone on a picnic was with her father in Charleston. She missed him, and she knew he missed her, too. If only she could go home.

Nelly reluctantly approached Yance Grady's children as they stood near the pond watching the other children swim. Judy was the eldest, at ten, and she had made no secret of her dislike for Nelly. At the moment, the girl was glaring at her and defiantly gripped her five-year-old brother's hand.

"We don't want to see her or talk to her, do we, Seth?" Judy frowned and stuck out her chin, reminding Nelly of her father. "You're not our mama, and you never will be!"

Nelly bent down so she would be eye level with the girl, whose dark gaze flared with resentment. "I don't want to take your mama's place, Judy. No one ever could. But I'd like to be your friend."

The child stubbornly shook her head. "I don't want you for a friend, either."

Seth reached out and patted Nelly's cheek, then glanced at his sister, not certain what to do. "I like you," he said earnestly, rebelling against his sister. "And our papa does, too." The boy was remembering the times his papa had taken him to the boarding-house, when Mrs. Aldrich had served them food and given them dessert. He liked her cooking. It was better than the food his papa gave them, and he couldn't remember his mama's cooking.

Judy gripped her brother's hand and jerked him back. "No, you don't like her—tell her that you don't want her near us." Her lower lip protruded at Nelly. "It was a good picnic before you came along."

Seth looked uncertain, but the painful grip his sister had on his hand made him decide in her favor. "We don't want you near us, I guess." He hung his head and kicked at a stone. "But Papa wants us to like you."

Nelly stood up as Yance approached, and she tried to smile for his sake. "No matter how you feel about me, Judy, I will always be your friend. And I like you both very much."

Yance lifted his son in his arms. "It looks like everyone here is having a good time, right, Seth?" He glanced at his daughter. "And how about you, Judy—are you having fun?"

The girl's glance fastened on Nelly's face, and she ducked her head, knowing her papa was going to be mad at her for sassing Mrs. Aldrich. He had warned them before they came to be nice to her.

"We were getting along just fine, weren't we, children?" Nelly asked, watching the girl's face redden.

"No, we weren't," Seth said, pointing at his sister. "She was just telling Mrs. Aldrich that—"

Nelly took the boy from his father, not giving him

time to finish what he was saying. "Judy was just remarking on what a good day it is for a picnic."

Judy looked startled. Seth was confused. And Yance looked pleased. "You two run along and play with the Gray kids. Mrs. Gray wants you to eat with them. There's gonna be fireworks tonight if it doesn't rain."

Nelly set Seth on the ground, and Judy looked up at her in uncertainty. "Let's go." She gave Nelly a guarded look before darting away with her brother in tow.

Nelly knew it was going to take a lot to win Yance's daughter over, but she would have no trouble with Seth. They both needed a mother—Yance tried hard to take care of them, but Judy's hair needed a good brushing, and Seth's shirt was wrinkled. She looked at the man she loved. He needed someone, too. It had to be hard for him to come home after working on his ranch all day and be both mother and father to the children.

There was one thing that was certain in Nelly's mind: She would never marry Yance until both his children welcomed her into the family. It just wouldn't work otherwise.

Chapter Six

The day was sultry, and Caroline was glad she had worn the lightweight blue-and-white gingham gown. She placed her chocolate cake on a table with the rest of the desserts and looked around for Nelly. Apparently, she hadn't arrived yet.

"Caroline," Julia Salazar said, uncovering a bowl of corn. "You're just the person I need. The food is ready, and we don't have enough servers. Will you help us? I think you were on the list to serve."

Caroline glanced quickly around and did not see Mr. Renault, so she felt easier in her mind. "I'm your woman," she said, picking up a spoon. She went down the row of food, helping uncover the bowls.

She was surrounded by the familiar faces of people she knew and liked. She got hugs from many of the children and smiling nods from their parents. Over time, she had become a part of this community. She had a life here, but she had a dreadful premonition that it was about to come to an end.

She was assigned to serving the green beans and mashed potatoes, and it kept her busy for a time. When the line thinned, she handed her apron to one of the other ladies and walked up a nearby hill, hoping to catch a cool breeze. A curl sprang from beneath her bonnet, so she crammed it back inside.

From her vantage point she could observe the countryside, which was rife with Spanish oaks and mulberry trees. She watched as families spread their quilts beneath the shade of a pecan grove and listened to the laughter that floated up to her. Somewhere just out of sight, someone was strumming on a guitar and singing a plaintive tune.

A familiar restlessness stirred within Caroline, and she felt a deep familiar longing for a family of her own: But a family was something she could never have, and she would probably end her days alone and afraid.

She removed her bonnet, allowing the slight breeze to play against her cheek. The sun reflected off Las Brisas Creek with its clear water that was fed by the Rio Grande some thirty miles away. The creek was a favorite swimming hole with the people from Fort Lambrick as well as the townspeople. She envied the children their freedom to splash in the cool water on such a hot day.

With her back against a pecan tree, Caroline listened to the wind rustle through the branches. Daisies dotted the area, and she watched them twist and dance in the breeze. She smiled when she saw Nelly, loaded down with food, making her way up the hill toward her with Yance Grady at her side.

The day would come when those two would marry, and they would have a good life together, and a houseful of children. Nelly had already told her that if she married Yance, she would sell the boarding-house and live at his ranch with him. Nelly shared Caroline's love for children, and it would just be a matter of time before Nelly won Yance's son and daughter over to her side.

As Nelly approached, her face was flushed, and Caroline knew it had nothing to do with her climb up the hill, but more likely something Yance had said to her. The man was hopelessly in love.

"How do, Miss Caroline," Yance said, shyly looking down at his boots as if examining them for flaws. "It's always a good day when we can meet like this—don't you think?"

"Yes, I do, Yance," she agreed. "It's always nice to break bread with friends."

"We brought enough food to feed an army," Nelly remarked, going down on her knees and spreading out a pinwheel-patterned quilt while Yance set a picnic basket on the grass.

"Yance," Nelly remarked with her usual straightforwardness, "please go and get us something to drink."

Yance was a bear of a man with skin darkened by long hours in the saddle. He had curly blond hair and a deep baritone voice. His mere size caused intimidation in some folks, but not Caroline. She saw gentleness when she looked into his eyes—the blue of them deepened when he looked at Nelly. It was evident to anyone who cared to look that Yance wanted to marry Nelly.

"Yes, ma'am. I'll be glad to," he answered, giving a salute and a deep laugh. "I always know when the ladies want to talk about woman things and send the men off on chores."

Nelly watched him leave before she spoke her mind. "Knowing you like I do, I figured you wouldn't eat unless I brought you something." She eyed Caroline critically. "Why are you up here all by yourself? You have friends down that hill who like to be with you."

Caroline helped unload the picnic basket. "It's a good place to watch other people with their families."

Nelly's gaze was fraught with sorrow. "It doesn't have to be this way. You should accept some of the invitations you get, and I know you get a lot."

"Don't scold me today. Let's pretend that you aren't running from happiness yourself," she retaliated. "Let's pretend that you have accepted Yance's marriage offer and that you have already set a date for your wedding."

Nelly became pensive. "It wouldn't take me that long," she said, snapping her fingers, "to marry Yance if Judy would accept me. But if I married him with the way she feels about me right now, it would eventually hurt all of them. That's something I'll never do."

Caroline watched Yance walking up the hill toward them, a pitcher of lemonade in one huge hand. "All right, let it pass today. Let's just enjoy the picnic. I am here with my good friends, and I want to have fun."

"Speaking of good friends, unless I miss my guess, that'll be Captain Dunning riding up. He can only be here because he wants to see you."

Caroline had little doubt that her friend had encouraged the captain to attend today. He was interested in her, and she didn't want him to be—it complicated her already complicated life. As he walked up the hill toward her, he removed his hat and gave her a dazzling smile. She liked him. He was from Georgia, and they had a lot in common, but she also had a side to her life that she could never share with him or any man.

"Mrs. Richmond, I was hoping you would be here today." His gaze rested on her for a long moment, then he became aware of the others and his need to acknowledge them as well. He turned to Nelly and nodded. "Ma'am." He shook hands with the rancher. "It's good to see you, Grady."

"We have plenty of food, Captain, so why don't you join us?" Nelly asked, eyeing Caroline carefully. "Sit right down and make yourself comfortable."

The captain ran his hand through his already neat brown hair, and his gray eyes sparkled. "I'd be obliged to, if Mrs. Richmond doesn't object."

Caroline could not send him away, and Nelly knew it. "I would be happy for you to eat with us. As Nelly said, we have plenty of food."

The four of them soon settled onto easy banter, and Caroline began to relax. Captain Dunning had the polished manners of a trained officer. He was knowledgeable and funny. She realized that she was having fun, and that hadn't happened to her in a very long time.

They had just finished the last of Nelly's jelly roll when a shadow fell across Caroline's face, and she glanced up to see Mr. Renault. She tensed and drew back, resisting the urge to scramble to her feet and run down the hill. She rose to her knees and then reconsidered, sitting back down. How could she be in any danger with Yance and Captain Dunning there to protect her?

"I hope I'm not interrupting anything," the bounty hunter said in his aristocratic French tone. His gaze went to Nelly. "The whole town emptied out, and I came to see what the inducement was."

"Mr. Renault," Nelly said politely. "Please, won't you join us?"

"Thank you, madame, but I would not want to intrude." His words were for Nelly but his gaze was on Caroline. When he came toward her, she could see the gold in his eyes turn rock-hard. She was reminded in that moment of how dangerous he was, and her instinct warned her to be vigilant.

She could not let her guard down for a moment.

"Nonsense," Nelly stated, unaware of the tug of war going on between her boarder and Caroline. "You would not be intruding at all." She knew the bounty hunter was the last person Caroline wanted to be introduced to, but good manners dictated that she should make the gesture. First she introduced Yance and Captain Dunning, then turned to Caroline. "I don't believe you have met—"

"Ah, but we have," he remarked, cutting Nelly off in mid-sentence. "We bumped into each other just the other day, didn't we, Mrs. Richmond?"

Caroline met his gaze and found his expression as sharp as the blade of a knife. The heaviness of his presence lay on her like a weight. He was examining her thoroughly, and she understood how a rabbit might feel while being inspected by a hawk.

She was surprised at how steady her voice sounded when she answered him. "Yes. I do recall the incident. I believe we met twice."

"You never told me the two of you met," Nelly said in astonishment. "Well"—she shrugged, and held out a clean plate to the man—"I hope you're hungry, Mr. Renault."

Captain Dunning could see that Caroline was nervous around the bounty hunter, and he could understand why a woman would not want to be near so dangerous a man. He was irritated that Renault had hardly taken his eyes off her—it was as if he were deliberately trying to make her uncomfortable. "Tell me, Mr. Renault, how long do you intend to stay in San Sebastian?"

Wade turned his head in the captain's direction. "Not much longer, I should think."

Captain Dunning was not satisfied with his answer and tried to pin him down. "How long? A day, two?"

Wade smiled at the officer, but his gaze was cutting. "I tell you what I will do; when I am ready to leave, you will be the first one to know."

Nelly gasped at Mr. Renault's rudeness while Yance slid a calming hand over hers and said, "None of us can figure out what you're doing here in the first place. I heard you have a big fancy home somewhere in Louisiana. What can our poor little community offer a man like you?"

Wade reached for a chicken salad sandwich and took a bite, chewed and swallowed while the other four people waited for his answer, none more tensely than Caroline.

Renault took another bite, aware of the strain on those around him. "This is very good, Mrs. Aldrich."

Nelly met his gaze, asking in a straightforward manner. "Why are you in San Sebastian?"

Renault smiled tightly. "Why, madame, I am hunting." His gaze slid to Caroline. "A quarry of the most elusive kind."

Nelly tried to digest his meaning. She was sure his being in town meant trouble for some poor unsuspecting person, but who?

Caroline knew what he meant, and she was certain that *she* was the elusive quarry he spoke of: With that knowledge, calm settled around her. She was just too weary of running and hiding—she would not do it anymore.

"What have you done?" Nelly asked, seeing a bandage on Caroline's hand and trying to channel the conversation in a different direction.

Caroline unwrapped the bandage and held her hand up for inspection. "It isn't worth mentioning. I agreed to fry a chicken for Private McCaffrey. When I was frying it this morning, some of the hot grease popped on me. It isn't bad at all. I had forgotten all about it."

Wade's lids hooded his eyes. That answered the question of the chicken, but it did not change his mind about the woman. It was what she and the private did before she cooked the chicken that he wondered about.

Captain Dunning smiled and asked, "McCaffrey is one of your students, isn't he?"

"He was the first one who came to me and asked if I would help him learn to read. I have several now."

The captain chuckled. "I shouldn't tell you this, but most of those recruits who asked you to teach them to read already know how."

"What!" She stared at him in disbelief. "Why would they do such a thing? It cannot be true."

Nelly rolled her eyes, and Yance gave a deep laugh. "You tell her, Captain. Explain it to her," Nelly said.

Captain Dunning took Caroline's hand and helped her to her feet. "I think I'll just let it go at that." He smiled at her. "The afternoon has cooled off somewhat—would you like to take a stroll along the river?"

She nodded, willing to do anything to get away from Wade Renault. "I would like that very much."

Renault tossed the remainder of his sandwich on the plate and stood, taking a step that brought him close to Caroline. Her lips were trembling, and he found himself becoming preoccupied with their full shape. "It's always a pleasure when I run into you, Mrs. Richmond."

She felt herself unconsciously gravitate toward him as if he had some strange power over her. When she realized what was happening, she jerked back. "Good day to you, Mr. Renault," she said stiffly, placing her bonnet squarely on her head and tying the ribbons. "Nelly, I will see you later. Try to remember what we talked about a few days ago."

Nelly shook her head in puzzlement, and then her eyes brightened with realization. Caroline was talking about leaving San Sebastian.

Caroline felt Wade Renault's eyes on her as she walked away beside Captain Dunning. Under other circumstances she would have enjoyed the walk along the river, where she could watch the children playing in the water. But today all she could think about was the bounty hunter. Brace had hired the man to take her back to South Carolina, of that she was sure.

They paused beneath a mulberry tree, and the captain looked uncertain for a moment before he asked, "Would you mind if I call you Caroline?"

"Of course I wouldn't. Since we have been acquainted for over a year, I believe it's acceptable, Daniel."

He stared at her hand as if measuring its smallness compared to his own. "I have made no secret of my deep feelings for you, Caroline. I have been patient because you lost your husband, and I wanted to give you time to grieve."

She twisted her hand out of his grip. "Don't, Daniel. You are a very fine man, and I respect you too much to let you believe that we can ever be anything but friends."

He took her chin and turned her face up to his. "Are you saying you aren't attracted to me?"

At that moment she wanted nothing more than to tell him everything about her past and lay all her troubles in his capable hands, but she shook her head. "Under other circumstances I could be, in another life, at another time. But please take this as the truth, Daniel: You do not want to love me."

He gently traced her jaw line. "It's too late for your warning. I have already lost my heart."

Tears moistened her eyes. "You must not feel anything for me, Daniel. My heart is not free to love anyone."

"I understand if you still have feelings for your husband." He touched her cheek. "I am prepared to wait a little while longer."

"You need to find someone who can give you the love you need. I cannot be that woman."

"I still have hope."

"Daniel, I don't know if I'll ever be ready to love anyone again."

"You will. Just give it time."

She laid her hand on his. "I enjoyed today."

"So did I." He raised her hand to his lips. "I will hope for many more days like this one." He looked deep into her eyes. "Only perhaps next time we can be alone."

Out of the corner of her eye, she noticed Mr. Renault mounting his horse to ride back to town. She could not go another day until she faced that man and demanded that he tell her the truth.

"I have to go now," she said, tightening the ribbons on her bonnet. "Please tell Nelly that there was something I needed to do."

The captain had seen Renault ride away, and he knew that whatever trouble Caroline had somehow involved that man. It did not seem that Caroline had any warm feelings for the bounty hunter; it even appeared that she was afraid of him. And as for Renault, he had acted overly attentive to Caroline as if he were trying to annoy her, or was there something much more sinister going on between the two of them?

As Caroline made her way across the narrow road toward town, she noticed the gathering storm clouds on the western horizon. What happened today when she finally faced Mr. Renault would determine the rest of her life.

Chapter Seven

Caroline climbed the steps of the boardinghouse with a purposeful gait. After today she was no longer willing to hide from life, and she wasn't going to run anymore.

She was going to face her worse fear.

And that fear was Wade Renault.

It was strangely silent in town since almost everyone had gone to the picnic, but that did not deter her—she would face this man alone. She moved through the dining room, her steps just a whisper on the polished wood floor. When she came to the stairs, she made no effort to disguise her steps. She knew in her heart that the bounty hunter would be waiting for her.

And she was right.

The door to his room was open, and he stood with his back to the window, watching as she stopped in the doorway.

"I have been waiting for you," he said, his gaze cold

and hard, his Creole accent giving the words more emphasis. "You arrived even sooner than I had expected."

"My brother-in-law sent you, didn't he?"

"Mr. Duncan, *oui.*" He came slowly toward her, watching her hands as if he expected her to have a gun. He knew that even the most innocent-looking person could become dangerous when trapped. That was especially true of this woman.

She stood her ground when he reached out and took her purse from her stiff fingers. With indignation she watched him open it and examine the contents before throwing it onto his bed.

"Madame, you will oblige me by raising your gown. From what I know of you, I expect you to have a concealed weapon."

"You know nothing of me if you got your information from Brace. And I will not raise my gown for you or any other man."

"I know you better than you think I do." He nodded at the hem of her gown. "Now raise it."

Caroline was seething with anger, but she raised her gown past her knees. "Maybe you would also like to search my person?" she asked haughtily, not really expecting him to perform such an outrageous deed.

"That, madame, is exactly what I intend to do."

Before she could react, his hands clamped on her shoulders, and then they slid along her bodice and down to her waist. She closed her eyes, her face flushed with embarrassment at the methodical and detached manner with which he examined her. Even Brace at his worst had not made her feel this kind of shame.

"Let me know when you have finished," she said, not bothering to hide her anger.

When he was satisfied that she had no weapon hidden on her person, he stepped away from her, his gaze hard. "Caroline Duncan, we can do this the easy way, and you can come with me willingly, or you can resist, and I will be forced to make you accompany me. One way or the other, you will be with me when I leave this town."

She had been startled when he called her by her married name. "I have not thought of myself as a Duncan in a very long time," she said, her lips trembling. She raised her gaze to him, feeling defeated—she couldn't run, and there was nowhere she could hide from him. She was simply no match for a man such as him.

"Just how do you plan to get me out of town?" Caroline asked scornfully. "I have friends who will search for me—you must know that."

She was right—he couldn't just take her away without any explanation—but he had already planned for that event. He would have to move fast, because he did not want to have to answer any questions that the people of this town would demand to know.

"I took the liberty of choosing a horse and traveling attire for you. You will go with me now to your house and change clothing,"

"And if I refuse?"

He picked up the folded clothes, a pair of boots, and a hat from the foot of his bed, nodding at her purse, which still lay there. "You may now take that with you."

She folded her arms over her chest and planted her feet. "You can't make me go with you."

He scooped up her purse, tossed it to her, and she

caught it. "I have my ways of persuasion. Make no mistake about it, you are leaving here with me today. And I don't much care how."

She vacillated between wanting to fly at him to claw his face and going down on her knees to beg for mercy, but she did neither. She merely stepped out the door, knowing he was following close behind her.

When they reached the dining room, he took her arm. "Don't think you can stall until your friends come to your rescue," he warned, forcing her to take two steps to each of his long strides.

If he could have read her mind, he would have known that she didn't want anyone to intervene on her behalf. Renault would not take kindly to anyone's interference, and she didn't want any of her friends getting hurt on her account.

Thunder rolled in the distance, and dark clouds boiled across the sky. She hurried toward her house, knowing the rain would drive the picnickers home. When she stepped inside her home, he handed her the clothing.

"Put these on and be quick about it."

She looked confused. "But these are men's trousers! Surely you can't expect me to wear these? I would look ridiculous. No," she said, backing away from him. "I will not do it!"

"Why do you pester me like this? You are only making it harder on yourself. Do exactly as I tell you to do. You cannot travel in that gown; therefore, you will wear what I have provided for you," he stated in a matter-of-fact tone.

She knew it would do no good to argue with him,

so she walked into her bedroom, her steps heavy with anger. She would have closed the door, but a booted foot blocked it.

"Leave it open. I will give you the privacy you need," he told her, turning his back but bracing his shoulder against the door jamb. "Don't try anything. You will be unable to outrun me."

She was angry as she undid her ribbons and hooks. She kicked her gown away and started to remove her shift but thought better of it. Looking at the trousers with disgust, she stepped into them and pulled them up. She stuffed her shift tightly inside them, attempting to distribute the material so it wouldn't be lumpy. She discovered that Wade Renault had left nothing to chance; the trousers and shirt fit perfectly. She sat down on the foot of the bed and wiggled her feet into a pair of socks, knowing the boots he had chosen for her would probably be the right size as well. They were.

"I'm ready," she said, looking about the room that had been her sanctuary for so long. Her heart was breaking because of the friends she would be leaving behind.

He turned to look at her, nodded approvingly, and handed her the hat. "You will need this tonight for the rain, and the rest of the time to keep from burning in the sun."

She looked at the Western hat with leather straps to hold it in place. "I can't wear a hat like that."

"It may seem unstylish to you, but it will serve you well before we get to where we are going, madame."

She took it from him and crammed it on her head. "There. Does that satisfy you?"

"Of course. Now," he said with authority, "I want you to write a note. And don't try anything, because I will read it after you have finished."

She had no choice but to do exactly what he told her to do, and anyway, Nelly deserved some explanation from her. She scribbled the letter quickly and held it out to him. "Does that suit your purpose?"

He took a deep breath and read aloud. " 'Nelly, you will remember when I said I might one day have to leave without telling you. Today is that day. Do not worry about me. I am in no danger.' "

He nodded in satisfaction, then took her arm and led her toward the kitchen. "We will leave now. The horses are tied out back."

"You've forgotten nothing, have you?" She opened her purse and took what money she had, held it up for his inspection, and then stuffed it in her shirt pocket.

"Why would I?" he remarked, leading her in the direction of the kitchen.

"Wait!" she cried, jerking her arm away from him. She ran to her sewing basket and dug around until she came to the newspaper clipping with the false account of Michael's death and shoved it into her trouser pocket.

"Are you quite ready now?"

"Not yet." She went into the kitchen, bent down to the basket beneath the stove, and scooped Archimedes into her arms. She rubbed her face against his soft fur, which soon became damp with her tears.

After a moment she looked up at Mr. Renault and saw the strained expression on his face. If she didn't know better, she would have sworn that he was sorry for what he was doing. "I'll need to feed him before we leave. I'm sure Nelly will take care of him after I have gone. He cannot"—she wet her trembling lips with a flick of her tongue—"he cannot survive on his own."

Wade leaned casually against the door, the hardness in his eyes warning her that he couldn't care less what happened to the cat. "Go ahead. I can wait long enough for you to feed it."

An idea came to her, and she blurted out, "I don't know what my brother-in-law is paying you, but if you will give me time, I can pay you more."

His eyes became hooded. "I don't think so."

"But I can—"

"Madame, my patience is wearing thin—you are pushing me too far. And believe me, you would not like me that way."

She stood for a moment undecided, and then turned her attention to Archimedes. She could feel the bounty hunter's agitation as she poured milk into a saucer and then crumpled several slices of crisp bacon into a bowl.

She rubbed her hand over Archimedes, determined not to cry again. "You must be a good cat." She placed a kiss on his face and stood. "I guess I am ready." It took all her courage to stand before him without trembling. "Well, are we going or not?"

He muttered something under his breath and held the door for her, then followed down the steps.

She saw that his black horse was tied to her wash-tub, along with a white-faced roan. "I have never ridden astride," she said, looking wide-eyed at the heavy Western saddle. "I'm not sure I can."

He untied a yellow slicker from the back of his saddle and tossed it at her. "You will need this before the night is over."

She put it on, deciding he might be right. It was definitely going to rain before too long. But that was the least of her problems.

"Are you a good horsewoman?"

"Of course—side-saddle."

His hands spanned her waist, and he lifted her onto the saddle. "Then you will have no trouble hanging on."

She bit her lip and gathered the reins, wondering if she could outrun him if she urged her horse forward.

Before she realized what was happening, he had clamped a handcuff on one wrist, locking the other end around the knobbed saddle horn. "I chose your mount with care," he said, as if reading her mind. "Believe me when I tell you, this filly will never outdistance my horse."

She pulled and jerked on the handcuffs until he reached over and laid his hand on hers. "Do not do that. You will only hurt yourself."

By the time they rode out of town, the first drops of rain were beginning to fall, and she was glad for the hat, though she would never admit it to him. She turned her face into the rain and allowed herself to cry, knowing he would be unable to see the tears.

She turned once to glance behind her. This would be her last view of San Sebastian. She watched the sign above the boardinghouse sway in the wind. She had never had a sweeter friend than Nelly, and it hurt to think she would not be seeing her again.

"We need to hurry," he told her. "I want to make it to Uvalde before nightfall."

She was wet to the skin. Rain always seemed to follow her when she was in trouble, and this time she was in real trouble.

At first it felt awkward to be wearing trousers and riding astride, but she soon felt comfortable on the horse except for the handcuffs that restricted her one hand.

After they had been riding for over an hour, he halted and motioned for her to do the same. "I will take the cuffs off now if you give me your word you will not try to escape."

She felt as if she were dying from the inside out. She had no hope, no way to escape the fate that awaited her. But she would hang on and fight to the bitter end, because this man could not be cajoled or persuaded to set her free. "I can assure you that if I get the chance, I'll run so far away from you, you'll never find me again."

He was thoughtful for a moment, almost troubled. "Why didn't you try to convince me to trust you? You might have succeeded, and then you could have waited for a chance to escape."

"Because," she said with all the dignity she could muster in such a humiliating situation, "I don't give my word unless I intend to keep it. I will give you my word on this: If I get a chance to escape, I'll take it. So you had better watch me closely."

He nudged his horse forward. "Do not worry. You will never be out of my sight."

Chapter Eight

The rain had finally moved away, allowing weak shards of moonlight to strain through tattered clouds. Renault and Caroline rode along silently, although she had many questions that nagged at her.

She glanced at the man who rode beside her. He certainly wouldn't feel obliged to answer any of her questions, so she might as well save herself the trouble of being rebuffed. Misery engulfed her like a dark shroud. Life was unbearable, and it was only going to get worse.

Time passed, she did not know how much, but she was weary and so sleepy she could hardly stay in the saddle. Since she was unaccustomed to riding astride, she ached in places that had never before bothered her when she had ridden horseback. She shifted her weight, drawing a sharp glance from her companion.

She felt incapable of going another mile, but she stiffened her back and held her head high. She would almost rather fall down dead than to ask that man for mercy. But after a while she slumped in the saddle, and her head kept falling forward. Her hand was cramped because she couldn't move it.

"Please," she said at last, "can't we stop for a little while?" She studied his face and saw no yielding. "Just for a moment?"

He swung out of the saddle, unlocked one end of the cuffs, and unhooked the other from the saddle horn. She felt the power in his hands when he grasped her around the waist and placed her on the ground. "Do what you must, but we will only remain here for a few moments."

The moon was riding high in the sky when they rode into a wide valley. Caroline felt she could not go another mile. Pain shot through her cramped body with each jarring step the horse took. Just when she thought she couldn't stand another minute, she saw the distant lights of Uvalde.

As they approached the town, they passed through a graveyard, and then a wagon yard. Because of the late hour the town was quiet and the streets deserted but for the tinny music that came from one of the saloons.

When they at last halted in front of a hotel, she wasn't sure if she had the strength to dismount by herself, but that decision was taken out of her hands when Wade removed the cuffs and gripped her waist, swinging her to the ground. His nearness made her forget about her physical pain for the moment, as she tried to get as far away from him as she could.

She stumbled and might have fallen but for the firm grip he kept on her arm.

"Just a little farther and you can rest." He turned

her to him, a serious expression on his face. "Do not give me any trouble in this hotel. I will let the clerk think that you are my wife. This I do only to save you embarrassment. Do you understand?"

She jerked away from him, knowing if she didn't escape from him now, she might not get another chance. If she could just make it around the corner of the building, she might lose herself in the darkness.

She came to an abrupt halt when his hand clamped down on her shoulder and she realized that her struggle was ineffective against Wade Renault's superior strength. Out of sheer exhaustion, her body finally became limp, and she dropped her head against his shoulder. She could feel the stir of his breath on her cheek, and her chest rose and fell with effort.

"Do not try that again."

It took a moment for her heartbeat to calm to a steady beat. Since she couldn't speak, she nodded as she moved away from him. As she approached the door of the hotel, he was right behind her, blocking any escape attempt she might have made.

"That was foolish," he told her.

"I had to try."

He opened the door for her and she went inside, so tired her legs felt like weights. A sleepy clerk handed them a key and pointed to the stairs, yawning. With a steadying hand on Caroline's arm, Wade Renault directed her up the stairs and into a dark room.

She stood swaying wearily while he lit a lamp; then she dropped down on the edge of the bed, wanting nothing more than to lay her head on the pillow.

He helped her out of the slicker and draped it on the bed post while water pooled at her feet.

"Your trousers and shirt still got wet. I will leave you so you can get out of them before you catch a chill. But," he warned, "I will be just outside the door listening, so do not try anything."

She turned her back to him, angered by his tyrannical tone. "I won't undress, and you can't make me," she stated forcefully, turning to see that he had already left, and her words had fallen on an empty room.

She was cold and miserable, she admitted to herself. She undressed, glad that she had worn the petticoat. Even though it was damp, she would use it as a nightgown. She practically dove beneath the covers to get warm. Caroline was not about to call Wade. He could just stay out in the hallway all night, for all she cared. It occurred to her that she would be at his mercy here in this room alone with him. She could not see him molesting a woman: The image just did not fit with the behavior of the bounty hunter. In any case, Caroline was just too sleepy to worry about him.

As her body sank into the lumpy mattress, her eyes closed. She did not hear Wade reenter the room and drape her damp clothes on the chair so they could dry.

She was unaware of the moment he blew out the lamp and moved a chair in front of the door. He unbuckled his gun belt and let it slide to the floor. He sat down in the chair and rested the gun on his lap.

He was a light sleeper, and he knew every time she moved. He heard her sigh in her sleep, and he watched the moon play across her beautiful face. How innocent she looked in sleep. He wondered why she had killed her husband when he would probably have given her the world for one of those smiles that had so captured Captain Dunning at the picnic.

Wade's head drifted backward to rest against the cushioned chair, and he closed his eyes. She might look like an angel, but there were horns on that pretty head. The old story of roses having thorns would fit her just right.

Caroline was sleeping soundly when a hand lightly touched her shoulder. "Wake up, Mrs. Duncan."

In confusion, she blinked her eyes, disoriented for a moment, and then her eyes widened on Mr. Renault. Everything came rushing back to her at once, and she sat up so quickly the covers fell to her waist.

"What do you want?"

His gaze slid down her shoulders to her breasts, which pushed through the thin chemise. His heart slammed into his gut, and he quickly turned his back to her. His voice was low when he said, "Madame, I will be waiting for you outside the door. You need to get dressed. I left breakfast for you on the dresser. Eat quickly. I want to leave Uvalde before sunrise."

Caroline was shaking with horror. She had forgotten she had removed her clothing because it was wet. She clutched the cover up to her chin. Had he thought she was trying to entice him with her body? She was so horrified he might think that had been her plan, she didn't have to be told twice to get dressed. This man had already seen more of her than she cared to share with him.

Later, a single lamp lit the dimness of the lobby as he led her out of the hotel. No one was about.

"Do not speak if we should meet anyone," he warned, sliding his fingers through hers so it would appear that they were a married couple. Suddenly he stopped, glancing at her hand and frowning. He raised her hand toward the lamp and examined it carefully. "The cuffs have bruised your wrist. Why did you not say something?"

"You put cuffs on people all the time. You must have noticed what they do to your prisoners," she said angrily, jerking her hand from his grip.

He reached for her hand again and led her closer to the lamplight, touching the red, raw streak. "Your skin is so soft. I never thought the cuffs would hurt you." He looked into her eyes, and she could have sworn she saw contrition in his gaze. "I know you are sore from riding. I have liniment that you can rub on your body tonight when we stop. It would not hurt to rub some on your wrist as well." His tone was deeper, his accent more pronounced than before. "When we get away from town, I will pad your wrist so the cuff will not cut into it."

"Why should you care?" she asked stingingly.

His brow arched, and he gave her a hard look. "I always like to bring my prisoners in without bruises."

His words hit her full force. She was his prisoner.

The blood-red sunrise found them riding in open country. Caroline remembered her old nurse once telling her that a red sky in the morning was an ill omen that something bad was about to happen. She had never been superstitious before now, but something bad had already happened to her. She wondered what Brace had told Mr. Renault about her, and how much money he had paid him to bring her back to Charleston.

She had not yet lost hope—there was still a long

way to go, and she might get a chance to escape before they reached Charleston. She wanted to go home, but on her own terms, and not cuffed by this man.

Her little filly had spirit and, at Caroline's urging, shied sideways and tossed her head in protest. Wade reined in his mount and waited for her to bring the horse under control.

"I feel the need to remind you, madame, that you cannot outrun my horse, so save yourself the trouble."

She gave him a scathing glare and pulled against the handcuffs. "If I were a man—"

"If you were a man," he cut in, "it would be a pity."

She lapsed into silence as his laughter drifted back to her, and she mumbled under her breath, biting back an angry retort.

The day had been sweltering, and Caroline pulled her hat low over her forehead, knowing she would be sunburned if not for the hat he insisted she wear. That angered her—in fact, everything about him angered her. Wade Renault never missed the slightest detail. He had seemed genuinely bothered by the bruise on her wrist, and that confused her. If he was as heartless as he appeared to be, why should he care?

They had been riding all day, stopping only when necessary. Dusk fell just as they crossed the Frio River, and she was glad it was cooler. As they rode along the riverbank, Caroline could see nothing but dense thickets, and she wondered how they would ever maneuver through the thorn bushes.

She fell behind Mr. Renault, and he guided them to a well-worn path that had been hidden by undergrowth.

The sun was making its last splash across the western horizon, and it was not yet full dark when they rode out of a craggy limestone canyon that stretched out to a grassy plateau. Renault held up his hand for her to halt.

"We will camp here for the night," he said, dismounting.

Caroline waited while he unlocked the handcuff from the saddle horn and clasped it around her other hand. She gritted her teeth as he lifted her from the saddle and set her on her feet.

The first step she took was jarring. She could hardly walk without pain shooting through her thighs and legs. But she would sooner die than let him know how sore she was.

"Where are you taking me?" she demanded, dropping to her knees, completely exhausted.

"I thought you knew," he said, leading the horses forward. "To Charleston, of course."

"I mean, are we going to travel all the way on horseback?"

He studied her for a moment before he answered. "Of course not. I will make other arrangements once we get to San Antonio."

She stood, slowly suppressing a groan of pain. She moved to the edge of a hillside, staring at the buttercups that were intermingled with sage bushes and cactus. The wilderness seemed so far-reaching it appeared to go on forever, and it felt as if she and Mr. Renault were the only people on earth.

Too weary to stand any longer, she once more dropped to her knees. She could not remember ever being as tired as she was at that moment.

As she sat there dazed, she watched Mr. Renault unsaddle and hobble his horse. She assessed him for the first time as a man and not an adversary. He did not wear the clothing she would have expected a bounty hunter to wear. She watched the way his green shirt molded to his shoulder muscles when he lifted the saddle from her horse and settled it on the ground. He carelessly tossed his hat on the saddle as he bent to hobble her horse. She liked the way his dark hair fell neatly across his broad brow. He wore black trousers and black boots, but not the Western boots that everyone in Texas seemed to prefer—his were English riding boots—and of course there was the gun belt slung low over his hips.

His golden eyes were dangerous for any woman who became trapped by their intensity. She leaned back on her elbows, trying to imagine what his life might be like. But she had no notion of what a bounty hunter did when he wasn't out hunting someone.

She studied his profile and was once again struck by how handsome he was, though not in the traditional sense. His features were too ruggedly chiseled for classic male beauty. He turned to her and found her assessing him, and there was a questioning expression on his face. A woman would feel safe under his protection. Not her, of course, he would probably be the death of her. For all she knew, he might have a wife; no one knew much about his life, and he was not forthcoming with details.

He walked toward her with long strides, his voice deepening several tones when he said, "If I take the cuffs off, you must give your word that you will make no attempt to escape."

She could not think straight, so she merely nodded her head.

"And," he stipulated, as he bent down and unlocked the cuffs, "I will leave them off tonight if you will promise not to try anything."

She glared at him. "I promise not to run away right now—I'm too tired to get very far anyway. But I already told you that I will most certainly escape if I get the chance."

He seemed not to hear her, but instead stared at the angry redness where the cuffs had cut into her skin—the one wrist was raw and nearly bleeding. "Why did you not tell me that the padding had fallen off?" He raised his gaze to hers.

"Why should I? You have no pity for anyone or anything, and I would never lower myself to beg mercy from you," she stated mutinously.

He clamped his jaw tight and left her for a moment. When he returned, he handed her a bottle of liniment. "As I told you before, you will want to rub this on your body wherever you ache—it will help with the soreness. You should put some on your wrist as well." He paused as if he did not know what else to say to her. "I am not in the habit of mistreating women."

"You just singled me out for that honor?"

She glared at him as he walked away, and he turned back to her in time to see her fury. He actually smiled, which only made her angrier.

"I will make camp just over there," he told her, nodding to a glade of trees. "Come on over when you are ready. I am sure you must be hungry."

She watched him until he disappeared from sight, trying to decide if he was the cold-blooded killer she imagined him to be, or if he had a soft side and really cared that her wrist was hurt.

The pain in her backside reminded her that she would have to take her trousers down to apply the liniment. After the deed was awkwardly accomplished, she followed the smell of bacon frying. She was hungry and willing to endure Wade Renault's company as long as he gave her something to eat.

After she had eaten her fill of bacon and beans, she watched him douse the campfire. Her gaze followed him when he spread a blanket beneath the tree. "Don't think I'm going to lie beside you," she said, coming to her knees and then standing up and holding her body stiff.

"Madame, we are in perfect agreement on that," he remarked as he unfurled a second blanket several paces from his, and smoothed it. "It has always been my habit to sleep alone."

She stared into the darkness and flinched when she heard an owl hoot in a nearby tree. "Are there very many wild animals out here?" she asked in a shaky voice.

"Of course. This is their habitat." He unbuckled his gun belt and placed it beside his blanket. Then his hands went to the leg buckles on his chaps, and he slowly began to unbuckle them one by one. Erotic thoughts coursed through her mind. She became fascinated, wondering what pleasure those hands could stir alive in a woman if he so chose.

She felt her face flush. There should be nothing intimate about the way a man removed his chaps, but he performed the deed in a manner that sent her heart slamming into her throat. He was the most masculine man she had ever known. It sounded trite, but he was like a work of art.

Angry with herself, she looked away when he eased himself down on his blanket and stretched out his long frame.

She heard him cock his rifle, and knew he had placed it close at hand. "You should not concern yourself about wild animals—I always hit what I shoot at." He spoke without conceit, merely stating a fact.

She reluctantly settled on the other blanket. "I just bet you do."

"If you are not sleepy, why do you not tell me about yourself, Madame Caroline Richmond Duncan?"

"Lovely weather we're having," she said, unwilling to share any part of her personal life with him.

"I know what you are doing, madame." Amusement laced his voice. "You do not want to talk to me, so you resort to speaking about the weather."

She liked the sound of his clipped accent and found herself wanting to know more about him. "It isn't that I have nothing to say," she said, swinging her head in his direction and offering him her most haughty glance. "It's more that I was taught if I was ever in the company of a person that I didn't particularly want to converse with, I should mention the weather."

There was an amused twinkle in his eyes. "Anyone will concede that you are a properly brought up Southern lady."

"There are clouds in the distance," she said in an uninterested way. "I hope it won't rain again."

"So it is to be the weather."

She noticed the irritation in his tone and smiled to herself; it was the first time she'd penetrated that thick skin of his, and it felt good. "But then again," she continued, "I could be wrong about the rain. The storm may very well pass us by altogether."

He laid his head on folded arms. "You just do not know when to stop, do you?"

"You do not want to talk to me?"

"Good night, Mrs. Duncan."

She wanted to throw something at him. "I certainly don't wish you a good night."

"I hope you have one," he said half to himself. "Otherwise I do not expect to get any sleep myself."

She said nothing, but her gaze swept him from head to foot. She had never known a man like him, but then, she had never before met a bounty hunter. He appeared to have fallen asleep; she could see the steady rise and fall of his chest.

Caroline suddenly had the most outrageous fantasy: What would it feel like to lay her head against his chest and allow him to hold her? She wanted him to be her protector, not her captor. She was afraid of him, and yet there was a part of her that wanted to pour her heart out to him.

Why was that?

After a while, her eyes grew heavy and the ground grew harder. She had already moved her blanket once because a root was jabbing her in the back. Now she was even more uncomfortable, and she tossed and turned, trying to find a position in which she could fall asleep.

She heard him mutter a soft oath and watched as he

rolled to his feet. "Madame, will you settle down! You will not be fit to travel in the morning if you do not get some sleep."

"I never slept on the ground before," she answered tartly. "You may be a brute and accustomed to such sleeping conditions, but I am not."

He stalked down the hill and soon returned with an armload of grass, which he spread on the ground, then made a second trip and repeated the deed. "Move your blanket onto this padding and maybe then we can both get some sleep."

She ached all over, and now she was exhausted. Nothing in her life had prepared her to deal with a man like him. She moved her blanket as he had instructed, and he bent down beside her to help smooth it out.

Just as he was about to move away, she heard the cry of a wolf and then several other answering howls. She dove at him, pressing her body tightly against his.

"Will they come into camp?" she asked, looking up at him with fright in her eyes.

He eased her away from him and stepped several paces backward as if he needed to put some distance between the two of them. "There is nothing for you to be concerned about."

"Those creatures sound very near," she said, scooping up her blanket and moving closer to his. "Are you sure they won't come near us?"

"I told you not to worry." He sounded frustrated. "Now, dammit, go to sleep. The wolves will not harm you, and neither will I."

She turned her face into the blanket. He said he

would not harm her, but he already had. In making her a prisoner, he had degraded her, but the worst was yet to come. If she didn't find a way to escape, she would soon be under Brace's control. She could not let that happen. Brace would kill her without feeling any remorse.

Her eyes fluttered shut, and she sighed. She would just sleep for a little while. Maybe an hour or so. . . .

Chapter Nine

The sun had just touched the eastern horizon and tinted the sky a deep pink. The nocturnal creatures of the wilderness had already sought their safe dens and burrows, whereas the daytime creatures were embarking on their never-ending quests for food. Caroline awoke slowly and stretched her arms over her head.

With a soft groan she made it to a sitting position. There was not a place on her body that didn't ache. Gripping the rough tree trunk, she used it for leverage to move herself into a standing position.

She glanced around camp and found that Mr. Renault was nowhere in sight. She heard the neighing of horses and assumed that he must be tending to them. She was amazed that he had built a campfire and even cooked breakfast without waking her. The smell of fresh bacon made her stomach rumble.

When he led the horses toward her, she groaned, dreading the thought of getting back onto a saddle.

She shook her head. "I can't get back on that horse today. Must I?"

He stared at her grimly, slapping a pair of leather gloves against his thigh. "I should have taken into account the fact that you are a woman and made arrangements for us to travel by stagecoach to San Antonio. Of course, you probably would have caused me trouble if I had done that."

Her eyes widened. "I am astonished. Are you admitting that you made a mistake?"

He tried to suppress the smile that played on his lips, but he was not entirely successful. She was such an enchanting woman, with a sense of humor and obvious intelligence. "Does it please you to know that I miscalculated?"

"Well, yes, it does," she admitted. "You always seem to have everything planned out in advance. I'm surprised you made just this one little mistake."

He walked toward her, and she took several steps backward. She wondered why he always seemed to stalk, instead of walking like everyone else. There was an air of arrogance and self-assurance about him that had intimidated her from their first meeting. And it still did.

"Did you apply the liniment like I told you to?"

"Of course I did. But it's not a miracle cure-all, if that's what you think," she remarked bleakly. "I am very sore."

He glanced down at his boot as he considered his options. "I will allow you to rest today if you will agree to apply the liniment several times. Even with this delay, we should make it to San Antonio in three days' time."

"And if I don't want to get back on that horse?" She was testing him, which was a dangerous thing to do, and she knew it. "What will you do then?"

He gazed down at her, his lips set in a tight line. "I do not much care in what condition you arrive, as long as you can stay in that saddle." His gaze drilled into her. "Or I could throw you across the saddle, although I have heard that is not a very comfortable way to travel."

"You are inhuman."

"I have been told that. It is good you believe it."

"You are . . . you are—"

"Madame, I know exactly what you are thinking. You do not have to voice your every grievance. Just be quiet!"

And she was quiet, but only for a moment. "If you are married, I wonder how your wife puts up with your dreadful attitude toward women," she said ungraciously.

He caught and held her gaze. "If I ever do marry, I will make sure my wife does not want to shoot me like you shot your husband."

She was aghast. "You think—" She shook her head. "I did not shoot my husband. How dare you say such a thing to me! You are a fool!" she stated with fury building inside her. "A complete fool."

His eyes swirled like molten lava. "No one before now has ever called me a fool."

"Well, you are one!" She walked toward him, anger making her forget about the pain in her muscles, as well as the need to be cautious around him. "Brace told you that *I* shot my husband, and you believed him?"

He watched her closely, the first feelings of doubt surfacing. "He said something like that."

"Nothing is beyond that man. He is totally without honor." She looked at Wade in confusion. "But you must have already guessed that about Brace, haven't you? I never considered that he would make such an outrageous charge against me. I don't know why I didn't expect him to do something like that, but I didn't."

"What did you expect?"

She was trying to gather her thoughts. What did Brace hope to accomplish by making such an outrageous fabrication? "You wouldn't understand even if I told you."

He looped his horse's reins around his hand. "I understand this, Mrs. Duncan. In all my years of tracking criminals, I have yet to meet one who did not swear he was innocent."

She took a step that brought her right in front of him. "I see how it is with you, so I'll save my breath and let you think what you will. You have already made up your mind about me, anyway."

He led the horses away, leaving her to stare after him. She was as confused as she was angry. She would probably shoot him if she had a gun.

When he was out of sight, she began to pace back and forth. Brace was an evil man; she had always known that—but to blame Michael's death on her was beyond understanding. When she stopped to think about it, she could see how his mind would work. If he could make people believe that she had shot Michael, it would solve both his problems. If she was convicted of murder, he imagined that the Duncan estate would go to him. She stopped a moment and leaned back against the tree trunk. But he had told the authorities right after it happened that Michael had shot himself. He was building a bed of lies. The truth was not in that man.

Nonetheless, she was in real trouble.

Her knees suddenly went weak, and she slumped to the ground. This was one of the bleakest days of her life. She dug her fingernails into the bark of the tree while her whole world tilted and blackness crushed in on her.

She fought against a fear that was so dark it felt as if she were smothering in it. She wiped her tears on the back of her hand, angry because Brace's evil had taken her by surprise once again.

Besides herself, there was only one other person who knew the truth about Michael's death. Lilly had helped her escape from Brace the day of Michael's death, but would she help her if it meant accusing her own son of murder? Caroline was not sure.

She knew that she had to get back to Charleston as quickly as possible, and she had to face Brace one last time before she could go on with her life.

She wasn't feeling well. She was achy, but maybe it was just being saddle sore. She touched her forehead, and thought she might have a fever, but it could be the heat.

She could not get sick now.

She had to keep going, no matter what. Brace was not going to get away with accusing her of shooting Michael.

* * *

They had been riding hard for two days. Mr. Renault expected to reach San Antonio by the next day. When they stopped for the night, he made camp beside the San Antonio River.

Caroline picked up the tin plates and cups and walked down to the river, thinking she wasn't nearly as sore as she had been the first two days of their journey. She carefully made her way down the slope and bent to wash the dishes in the clear water.

She could feel Mr. Renault's eyes on her, but then, he was always watching her to make sure she didn't try to escape. She stood for a moment looking longingly at the cool water.

With determined steps she returned to camp, dried the plates, and slid them in the canvas bag as Wade always did. "I am going to take a bath."

He was polishing his rifle and looked at her over the barrel. "Can you swim?"

"Of course I can. And anyway, the river doesn't look more than four or five feet deep."

He closed one eye and looked through the barrel, and then inspected the stock. "The swiftness of that river can sometimes take you by surprise. Even though it is not wide, it flows all the way to the Gulf."

She drew in a breath. "I am not going to swim away, if that's what you think."

He glanced up at her with a sardonic twist to his lips. "I know that. Because I can swim faster than you." He smiled slightly, catching her off guard. "I could go with you to make sure you do not try to escape."

She turned her back to him. "Up until now, you have been a gentleman, but I trust you a little less than a rattlesnake." Her cheeks flamed, and the thought of him being nearby while she bathed sent her heart pounding. She wondered why she should have such erotic fantasies about him.

He reached for his saddlebag, opened the flap, and tossed her a bar of soap. "I was not suggesting I watch you, Mrs. Duncan."

"Well, I . . . well—"

"Take heed of how swift the current is. I do not relish going in fully dressed to rescue you."

Without a word she picked up her blanket and stalked off down the shadowy riverbank. She had worn the same clothes for days, and she intended to wash them in the river and wrap herself in the blanket, even if she had to show some of her skin. She could not abide going without a bath for another day.

As she walked along, she undid her hair and allowed it to flow down her back. When she rounded a bend, she found a secluded spot that suited her purpose. She was surprised to find that she trusted him not to follow her. But he would be listening, and she knew his hearing was very good.

Caroline was pushing her trousers down her hips when she hesitated. He had displayed a code of honor where she was concerned, but just the same, she waded into the water fully clothed and then undressed, taking off everything but her shift. Then she washed her trousers and shirt.

Soapy foam flowed through her fingers as she lathered her hair. It felt glorious to be clean. She did not hear the heavy tread of the man who had squatted down on the bank watching her in the moonlight. Soap was stinging her eyes, so she dunked her head under the water. She was startled when she heard a deep voice.

"Well, now, I never did see a prettier sight in my life," the stranger said, watching her closely. "No, ma'am. I never did."

Caroline crossed her arms across her breasts, as fear rose up inside her. The man was heavyset and at least six feet tall. He appeared to be in his thirties, and he wore a gun in his holster.

"Go away," she said, moving toward the middle of the river.

"I think I'll just come in there with you." He removed one of his boots and tossed it behind him. "I been needing a bath, and nothing could be sweeter than having a good-looking woman to wash my back."

She took another step back. She had two dangers to contend with, the man and the swift current. She chose to take another step backward and felt the underwater flow pulling at her. She planted her feet wide, trying to keep her balance, not knowing how long she could keep the swift water from carrying her downstream.

"If you don't leave now, I will call my friend."

He grinned at her and removed his other boot, then tossed it up the bank beside its mate. "If you call out, I'll pick your friend off before he can help you. I don't wear this here gun for show." He stood up and whipped the gun out of the holster, aiming it at her. "If I was you, I'd just keep quiet."

"I don't want any trouble. Just please go away," she said, taking another step back and feeling the dangerously surging current.

"Nope, can't do that. You can like it or lump it—you already tickled my fancy."

Wade seemed to appear out of nowhere. Caroline saw him, but the stranger had not detected his presence. Wade quietly stepped just behind the man and said, "You had better tickle your fancy somewhere else." He pulled the hammer back on his gun and placed the barrel against the man's temple. "Lower your gun or you are a dead man."

"I'll shoot her," the man countered.

"If you try, you will be dead before you cock the hammer of your gun," Wade stated in a deadly calm voice.

"I like to know the name of the man who draws down on me," the man said. "My name's George Samples."

"I am Wade Renault."

"Aw, hell. I should'a known it was you with the French accent," Samples said, dropping his gun as if it had burned him. He thrust his hands over his head. "I ain't gonna mess with you, Renault. I know your reputation—you'd as soon shoot me as not." He wiggled his fingers to show that his hands were still in the air. "I might be dumb, but I ain't stupid."

Wade reached down and picked up the man's gun, then threw it into the river.

"Renault, that was my pa's gun. Couldn't you just take the bullets out and give it back to me?"

"The gun stays where it is." Wade's tone was deadly, establishing the fact that he would suffer no argument from the man. "You tied your horse in the clump of bushes to my left. Mount up and ride away—right now. If I do not hear your horse clearing that hill before I can count to twenty, you will be a dead man." He started to count. "*Un*, *deux*, *trois*."

"But my pa's gun—"

"Think of it this way—you get to keep your life, so consider yourself fortunate." Wade realized he had been counting in French and changed to English. "Four, five, six."

"Hey, lady, I'm sorry. I didn't mean any harm. I was just funning."

"Seven, eight, nine—"

"I'm going—I'm going!" George Samples grabbed up his boots and sprinted through the bushes, unmindful of the thorns that stabbed his bare feet. He jumped on his horse and rode away as fast as he could. He was thinking that no one in Uvalde would believe him when he told them Wade Renault had pulled a gun on him and he was still alive to tell about it—if he made that hill before the bounty hunter finished counting to twenty.

Wade turned his attention to Caroline. "You can come out now. It is safe. Monsieur Samples will not be returning."

She faced another danger—her feet were beginning to slip from under her. "I can't."

"Caroline, do not make me come in after you."

"I can't move. The current—" She was suddenly swept under as if some force had dragged her down. She fought against the surge of the water and tried to reach the surface, but the current was too strong for her. She twisted, turned, and kicked her feet, but nothing helped. Just when her lungs were starving for air and the fight went out of her, strong arms lifted her up, and she was carried to the surface and away from the dangerous flow.

She coughed and sputtered, expelling river water. She was so weak she had to lean her head against his shoulder and allow him to swim toward the bank.

The moon cast its golden light across the water, and the ebony skies were alive with thousands of stars. It seemed to Wade as he glanced down at Caroline that the stars were reflected in her eyes.

Caroline felt at a disadvantage, since she was scantily clad in a transparent shift, and he was fully dressed. She turned her face against his rough shirt, fighting against the hot feelings that ran through her when his eyes swept over her body.

His mouth was near her ear. "You did not heed my warning: I told you the river was swift." He was aware of each breath she took, of each movement she made, and it stirred the fire higher and hotter within him. Reluctantly he lowered her to her feet in knee-deep water.

"I was afraid." She stumbled and almost fell, so he lifted her in his arms and carried her onto the bank.

"You should have known I would not let him hurt you."

She cuddled close to him, closing her eyes. "I knew you would take care of that man. What I was afraid of was that I was going to drown."

His grip tightened on her, and her arms slid around his neck.

"I was not going to let that happen either," he stated with force.

"No, I don't suppose you would. Brace wants me delivered to him alive. He probably wouldn't pay you if I were dead." She pushed against him. "Would he?"

She felt his deep intake of breath as he lowered her to her feet.

"You might want to retrieve your trousers and shirt before they drift downstream," he told her, his French accent deepening—a habit she had noticed from time to time.

She moved away from him, and when she looked back, he was walking toward camp. She had been in his arms wearing very little, and he had not even noticed. He had been fully dressed, and she had certainly been aware of him. She bent to pick up her trousers and shirt and wrung as much water out of them as she could. Then she gathered the blanket about her and stared at the river. She would probably be dead now, or worse, if it hadn't been for Wade.

She frowned. But if it were not for him, she would never have found herself in a dangerous situation where she could either be ravaged by a strange man or swept down the river to the Gulf of Mexico.

She stood on the riverbank for a long time, staring at nothing in particular. She had seen the predator in Wade tonight. That stranger had been terrified of Wade, and with good reason. Wade would have shot the man if he hadn't dropped his gun. She knew it, and the man had known it.

Something had happened to her when he had taken her in his arms and carried her out of the water. Her heart was still hammering inside her from the experience. When she had felt his hands on her, she had wanted him to touch every inch of her body.

She had wanted him to kiss her and never stop.

Caroline was certain that she must be losing her mind.

Chapter Ten

Wade's Colt was wet because he'd had to go in the river fully clothed. He removed the bullets and ran a rag through each chamber. He inspected it and dried it again. It had always been his habit to keep his guns in perfect condition; they could be the difference between life and death for him.

His hearing was very acute, and he picked up the sound of Caroline returning to camp. He heard every move she made and attributed the heaviness of her tread to anger.

He did not want to think of her as a woman, but when he had carried her scantily clad body out of the river, and she had nestled in his arms, he had wanted to press his mouth against those trembling lips. When he'd reached shallow water, he had had to force himself to set her on her feet.

He wanted to possess her mind and her body. He wanted her to belong to him in every way a woman can belong to a man. His body swelled and throbbed just thinking about her. Angrily, he spun the chamber of his gun. He was thinking nonsense. Michael Duncan had probably had those same feelings, and look where they got him.

He had to remind himself that she was a woman who had killed her husband. But he remembered the stranger aiming his gun at Caroline, and then the river almost sweeping her away. The woman was nothing but trouble for any man.

He blew his breath through the Colt chamber and spun it around again. Then he thought about how he could always tell what Caroline was thinking by the way she smiled. If she was amused, her blue eyes sparkled. And when she was angry, they were like gathering storm clouds. He was entranced by the delicate gestures she made with her hands when she was attempting to make a point about something. He could not imagine those hands pulling a trigger to kill a man.

He had watched her sleep last night, wondering how her hair would look if it fell freely down her back. He ached to touch her, not to just make love to her, although there was that too—he wanted to hold her body against his, to feel the softness of her skin, to feel the fullness of her lips against his.

He wanted her to want him as much as he wanted her.

He took a deep breath. Caroline Duncan was the last female he could ever get tangled up with. He was taking her to Charleston to face her accusers, no matter what.

He slid bullets in the six chambers of the Colt and then with more force than was required, he shoved the gun into his holster.

He was trying to remember the faces of some of the women who had warmed his bed over the years, and there had been plenty of them. But at the moment he could not remember a one—none of them had left a lasting impression. No woman had ever touched that certain part of him that had come alive with Caroline. In the past, when a woman pleased him, he would stay with her a day, maybe two, but no longer than that. He had not been with a woman in over five months. He had not wanted another woman since the package with Caroline's picture had come to him in the mail.

He leaned back against his saddle. Caroline was different from any other woman he had known. He flattered himself that he was a good judge of character, and unless she was the best actress he had ever met, he could not see her taking anyone's life.

She was within sight now, and her footsteps sounded lighter, perhaps she had lost some of her anger. He closed his eyes, pretending to be resting. She was trying to move quietly so she would not disturb him, but he heard her when she draped her clothing over the branches of a tree.

When she sat down to remove her boots and pour the sand out of them, he opened his eyes to watch her. He wondered what she thought about as she stared across the river. She was barefoot and clutched the blanket about her as if it were a lifeline. He already knew how soft she felt, and his imagination had stripped off her undergarment. Her wet hair fell down her back, and he wanted nothing as badly as he wanted to kiss each golden strand.

He rolled to his feet. His problem was probably nothing more than being in the wilderness alone with a woman he could not touch.

She turned her head and gave him a small smile. That was almost his undoing. He wanted to take her in his arms and kiss her until his hunger for her was satisfied.

Instead, he pulled his rifle out of the holster. "Do not be startled if you hear gunfire. I will try to bring back fresh meat for dinner." He slung the rifle over his shoulder and turned back to her. "Do not go near the horses. I will have them in my sight."

She glared at him but said nothing.

When Wade returned to camp an hour later, his heart rate had settled back to normal. Caroline was wearing her trousers, and her hair was twisted into a tight bun at the back of her neck.

She knelt beside the campfire and nodded. "It's a good thing I opened a can of beans since you returned empty-handed."

He looked beyond her into the darkness. "My mind was not on hunting tonight."

"I know. I have been thinking about that man, too. Do you think he will come back?"

"No. He will run that horse until he gets to the nearest town."

She gave a short laugh, and said in a teasing tone, "He was rather afraid of you. You are such a big, bad man."

He laughed. "And you are not as good a swimmer as you led me to believe."

She spooned beans onto his plate and handed it to him. "Who does the cooking for you when you are at home?" she asked, sitting cross-legged and holding her plate on her lap.

He took a bite and nodded in approval. "Mary cooks for me."

Disappointment hit her like a fist. He had said he wasn't married, but she hadn't thought he would be living with a woman. She could not have said why she should care who he lived with, but she did.

"Mary Murphy is as Irish as they come and an excellent cook. She is fifty years old, runs my house, and tries to run my life." He did not usually share facts about his private life with anyone. He wondered why he had told Caroline Duncan about his housekeeper.

"Does she know that you go hunting for innocent people so you can collect the reward?"

His reply was noncommittal, "Some might believe that, but Mary would not."

Caroline suddenly cried out in alarm and knocked her plate onto the ground when something fell off the tree and plopped onto her sleeve. She was frozen with fear as the little green creature regarded her with round curious eyes.

"Help me," she pleaded. "Please get it off me!"

Wade lunged toward her and gently gathered the creature in his hand. "This will not hurt you." He placed the creature unharmed on the ground, and they both watched it scamper into the brushes.

"What was it?"

"It is merely a harmless lizard." His mouth clamped

shut, and she had the feeling it was to keep from laughing at her.

He saw her visibly shiver. "I can't abide anything reptilian."

He moved closer so he could sit beside her. "You should know after today that I will not let anything happen to you."

Lowering her head, she said softly, "It's just that I am not accustomed to all of this."

She seemed so vulnerable, he felt a sudden rush of protectiveness toward her. "Why don't you get some sleep? You hardly slept at all last night." He eased back away from her and stood up. "I will douse the campfire."

Her gaze was glued to the spot where the creature had disappeared. "How are you going to arrange to turn me over to Brace?" She wasn't sure if it was real or if she had imagined it, but she thought she saw him flinch. "You do have a plan, don't you?"

"Do you want me to make you another plate?" He bent to pick up the one she had dropped. "You hardly ate anything."

"I'm not hungry."

After he put out the fire and cleaned the campsite, he spread out her blanket for her. "You should lie down."

"I'm not sleepy."

"Try not to think about your brother-in-law tonight."

"That's all I do think about."

He had a sudden suspicion. "You do not have a fondness for him, do you?"

She gave him a disgusted glare. "He is the last man in the world I could feel anything for except revulsion. As you already know, he will stop at nothing to get his hands on me."

He wanted to know more about her, and she seemed willing to talk tonight. He was curious about many aspects of her life. Mostly he wondered what had driven her to kill her husband. He was beginning to wonder if Brace Duncan had not been honest with him about Caroline.

"Why do you think he wants you back? Is it so he can turn you over to the law?"

She leaned her head back against the tree. "You wouldn't believe me if I told you."

"Try me."

"Brace was actually my husband's stepbrother, not his real brother. His mother, Lilly, married Michael's father, so you see, the two of them were not related by blood."

"But they did have the same last name."

She nodded. "My husband's father never actually adopted his stepson. Brace took his last name anyway." She paused, not knowing how much to tell Wade, or how much he would believe. "Brace thought he would inherit a portion of the Duncan estate when Mr. Duncan died. But everything went to my husband."

"And your husband's possessions should, by law, now belong to you."

"Yes."

"Tell me what he was like, this man you married." He didn't know why he had asked such a question, but he wanted to know about the man she must have loved at one time.

"Michael was gentle and kind, and certainly no match for Brace's scheming treachery."

"You mean he was weak," Wade taunted, hoping he could goad her into telling him what he needed to know. "A coward," he said with a contemptuous curl to his lip.

"No! Do not ever say such a thing to me about Michael." Her tone was sharp, her manner indignant, and her eyes sparked like a hammer on an anvil as she defended her dead husband. "How dare you suggest such an outrageous notion? I grew up with Michael, and I should know what kind of man he was. I have never met another man with his compassionate nature." She paused and said in a painful whisper. "Until his spirit was crushed."

A funny feeling crept up the back of Wade's neck, the kind of feeling he always got when he was about to learn something important. "Who crushed his spirit?"

She turned her anger on him. "Why should I tell you? You couldn't possibly understand a man like Michael, because you judge everyone by your own standards. He would never have treated a woman the way you have treated me. So don't tell me he was weak, but rather concentrate on your own imperfections. Brace is the kind of man who is not happy unless he is causing someone pain. He delighted in killing and torturing his own mother's pet lapdog. He set fire to the stable, killing twelve horses, because he was jealous that a stallion he coveted belonged to Michael!"

She jumped to her feet and turned away from him. "Leave me alone!"

He followed her and stood just behind her. "I believe you are about to tell me that Brace Duncan killed your husband."

She defiantly turned her head and met his gaze. "You can draw your own conclusions. I will tell you nothing more. But you have been made a fool of by Brace. The mighty Wade Renault—the mere name made that man today quake with fear and throw down his gun. You have been outsmarted by Brace Duncan!"

She stalked over to her saddle and picked up the yellow slicker. "Did you go to the authorities in Charleston and ask them how my husband died?"

He had that feeling at the back of his neck again. "When a family member tells me how a crime was committed, I usually take his word for it."

She unfolded the clipping and stared at it for a moment. "Brace has told different versions of what happened that night, but he has yet to tell the truth." She handed him the newspaper article. "This is only one version—he told you another."

He quickly read the old article and glanced up at her. "Brace told me this himself. He said that he had tried to protect you in the beginning. According to him, his conscience has been bothering him. He worried that his brother could not be buried in consecrated ground because everyone believed the lie that he took his own life. Perhaps you can tell me the truth."

She sat down and lowered her head. "It has been a very long day."

He was not ready to give up his questioning. He had to know her side of the story. "What happened that day, Caroline?"

She shook her head in disgust. "I don't feel that it's my duty to enlighten you. You are Brace's hired gun."

He would act as if he believed the death was a suicide and see if she took the bait. "Perhaps the newspaper article is the true version of what happened. Perhaps your husband did take his own life."

"No, he didn't. Michael would never do such a thing."

"How did Michael feel about Brace?"

She laced her fingers together and stared at her hands. "You are the supposed marvel—find out for yourself, or better still, ask Brace if you are gullible enough to believe anything he says."

"Tell me just this one thing," he roughly demanded. "Do you have your husband's money hidden away somewhere?"

She held out her arms. "Search me."

"Then does Brace have the money?"

She shook her head. "No. And he never will find it."

"Is the money important to him? Surely he inherited a portion of the estate from his stepfather."

"Mr. Duncan left him nothing. He did leave Brace's mother a small sum, and the right to live on the estate during her lifetime. With good reason, Mr. Duncan didn't like his stepson very much."

Wade could smell the clean scent of soap in her hair, and it was distracting him. "And just why was that?"

"He saw through Brace, and you didn't."

"You expect me to believe you?"

"No. I don't. You kidnapped me, and then accused me of killing my husband. You are the last man I would expect to believe me. But just suppose for a moment, this one time, you are wrong. Why would I kill someone I wanted to help?"

He frowned, looking into her eyes as if he could find the truth reflected there. "Are you trying to tell me that you married Michael Duncan because you wanted to help him?"

Wade had come too close to the truth, and she blurted out, "I don't want to discuss my husband with you. I'm very tired."

"Yes, I see that you are." Again the gentleness had crept into his voice. "You must rest."

She raised tear-damp eyes to him. "I was in over my head with the cruelty I had witnessed in my husband's house. I could not fight the evil, and in the end, may God forgive me, instead of staying and demanding justice, I ran for my life. And now I am going back to face the man who destroyed everything."

Wade reached out and gripped her arm. "And I can see that you are more afraid of Brace Duncan than you are of me." His grip tightened. "I wonder why that is."

They stared at each other for a long moment. She noticed that he looked exhausted, and realized he probably hadn't had much sleep either. Good! "Neither you nor Brace has given me any reason to trust you."

A long moment passed before he nodded. "I was merely curious."

"Don't ask me any more questions, because I won't tell you anything else. Let Brace be the source of your information."

Briefly his eyes closed, and his hand dropped away from her arm. He stalked off into the dark. He had a lot of heavy thinking to do.

Caroline watched him disappear into the night.

Every move he made was slow, thoughtful, and calculated. He never did anything without first thinking it through. She wondered if he would make love with the same intensity he applied to his occupation. Shivers of delight ran up her spine, and she felt a tightening inside just imagining what he would be like if he made love to her. Slow, measured, attentive.

Was she crazy?

She would rather have a rattlesnake coiled up beside her than have him touch her!

She squeezed her eyes shut, trying to be honest with herself. Every day she spent with him made the ache inside her grow worse. If he touched her at the moment, she would probably melt into his arms.

She was disgusted with herself. She had to get a grip on her feelings. She took several deep breaths and opened her eyes, staring at the star-sprinkled night, reminding herself that he would as soon shoot her as make love to her.

At least he had a clear head, even if she didn't. He certainly never thought of her as a woman. Wade Renault was the prefect, cold-blooded bounty hunter, and he only saw her as his prisoner.

Chapter Eleven

Caroline had awakened that morning feeling as if her head were going to explode. After a cup of coffee, she felt somewhat better, but she dreaded the thought of getting back in that saddle—mostly she dreaded the handcuffs.

They were riding at a fast pace now, stopping only once to rest and water the horses at a small stream. It seemed to Caroline that Wade was strangely quiet, as if he had a lot on his mind.

It was an hour later when they descended a steep hill to rougher terrain dotted with oak trees and cactus. She felt a yank on the handcuffs every time her horse took a step.

Suddenly her stalwart little filly stumbled down a hill and almost unseated Caroline before she could bring the animal under control.

"This horse needs to rest," she said, slumping over the saddle, her heart beating fast. "And so do I."

Wade swung out of the saddle and with long strides

came to her. He bent his head to unlock the cuffs, then lifted her into his arms. "*Ma chère*, are you hurt?"

In a surprising move, he laid his cheek against hers, and her breath became trapped inside her chest. "While you may be superhuman, I am not, and neither is this horse." She was surprised she could speak at all with him holding her so close.

"You are such a small woman, and this has been too much for you." His eyes were full of guilt because he had pushed her so hard. "You can rest for a while."

Her head fell back on his shoulder, and she had the feeling that she would like to stay there forever. She felt his warm breath stir a lock of hair at her cheek, and she turned her face to press it against his neck. "I was not hurt, but I was afraid the horse was going to fall."

With steady steps he carried her to an oak tree and placed her down in the shade. He knelt beside her and tilted her face up to him. "You would tell me if you had been injured, would you not? I know how stubborn you are."

"I was just scared." She looked into his eyes and saw genuine concern reflected there. "It is difficult to handle the animal with my hand cuffed."

"I do not want to put the cuff on you, but you have assured me that you will escape if presented with the chance."

"It was a promise, and I always keep my word. Anyone who knows me can tell you that."

He gazed into her blue eyes as if hoping they would give up their secrets. "I believe you." He rose to his full height, his demeanor suddenly cold and distant.

"I may yet elude you, Mr. Renault. It is best that you keep the cuffs on me."

His jaw tightened. "I must see if your horse was hurt in the mishap. If all goes well, we will reach San Antonio by early afternoon."

The scenery suddenly changed when they rode out of the rolling hills onto a well-traveled road. They galloped past several men on horseback and ate the dust from a freight wagon before they overtook it and left it behind. A Butterfield stagecoach lumbered past, going in the opposite direction. At one point they were forced to mingle with cattle being driven across the road by several determined cowhands.

Wade noticed that Caroline had bent over her saddle in an attempt to hide the handcuffs when a column of soldiers rode toward them. He also noticed that every man in the outfit stared at her with interest. Did she realize that she drew the attentions of men like a magnet? It had been his experience that beautiful women knew exactly how to use their looks to get what they wanted from a man. He did not mind getting caught in a lady's well-laid trap; in fact, most of the time he welcomed it, as long as they understood that he would never be bound to them in any way.

He had never had trouble measuring a man by his appearance and attitude, or most women, but Caroline Duncan was another story. He glanced at her now, and his heart caught in his chest. He was becoming aware of her in every way. He wanted to take the handcuffs off her and throw them as far as he could. He had to think of something besides her face, which was smudged with dust, making her so damned adorable. He wondered what she had been like as a child. He wanted to know how much she had loved her husband.

Disgusted with himself, he nudged his horse forward, and she did the same to stay abreast of him. No matter how he tried to channel his thoughts into a different direction, they always came back to her. He had called her by an endearment when he had thought she was injured by the horse. He had never used those words with anyone else. He had wrestled with himself to keep from kissing that tempting mouth that could slide down into a pout or curve upward in a dazzling smile.

He tightened his grip on the reins, reminding himself that she might be a mistress of deception. No matter how innocent she appeared, he was not altogether convinced that she had not killed her husband.

The roadway was now crowded with ranch wagons and buggies. When Wade glanced at Caroline, he became aware of her growing embarrassment because of the handcuffs, and the attention they were drawing from the people on the road.

He motioned for her to halt, and he removed the handcuffs. "Speak to no one. I will do all the talking. You will do just as I tell you, or I will put the handcuffs back on you. Do you understand?"

She nodded, rubbing her wrist. "I understand."

They halted once more, and Wade allowed Caroline to rest for an hour before leading her mount forward. She wearily climbed onto the saddle, wondering if they would ever reach their destination.

The closer they got to San Antonio, the more interested she became in her surroundings. She glimpsed a tall church steeple in the distance, and there was another church with a bell tower just to her right. San Antonio seemed to be a thriving town, with throngs of people from every walk of life mingling and conducting their business.

They rode past the main plaza, where a man dressed in Spanish style was haggling with another man who appeared, from the cut of his clothing and his manner of speech, to be of German descent.

As they grew closer to the center of town, the streets became more congested. Cowhands rode their horses beside well-dressed ladies in fancy carriages. When they rode past a saloon, Wade moved his horse closer to Caroline in a protective manner. She had expected him to stop at one of the hotels, but they passed them by, riding through a section of town with small houses and hovels.

Eventually they crossed a narrow wooden bridge and rode down a boulevard lined with mansions. She was taken by surprise when Wade halted before a pink stucco, two-story residence.

"Caroline, we will be staying here for a day, perhaps two." He lifted her from her horse and set her on her feet. "This is the home of friends of mine, Nate and Dolly Housing. You will like Dolly—everyone does. She will see to your needs while we are here."

He glanced at the front door. "I would ask that"—he paused as if trying to find the right words. "I will not tell her that you are in my custody, so she will not know unless you tell her yourself."

"What about her husband? Will you tell him about me?"

"Nate is a very discreet man, and you can trust him to tell no one, not even his wife, about your situation."

She flung her head back and glared at him. "I'm sure that is true, but what will he think about me? Will he think that I am your light-of-love, or your soiled dove?"

He flinched, and his golden eyes took on a deeper hue.

"He will not ask questions that will embarrass you. And Dolly will assume that I would not bring someone of questionable reputation into her house."

She walked away from him, then paced back toward him. "You think I murdered my husband, and you don't think that would give me a questionable reputation?"

"You are presentable."

She was so angry it took her a moment to find her voice. "It never occurred to you that I might be more comfortable in one of those hotels we passed? There I would have been anonymous. You don't understand how humiliating this will be for me."

"*Non*. I confess I did not think about that."

She was too weary to argue with him. The sun felt like fire on her cheeks, and her head ached dreadfully. "Do you think they will have a place where I can rest for a while?"

He guided her forward. "Let us get you in out of this heat."

Caroline's foot had just touched the top step when the door was pulled open, and the most charming creature she had ever seen came rushing out, catching Wade in a tight hug. Caroline guessed the woman to be somewhere in her fifties. Her red hair was streaked with gray, and it feathered softly against her plump cheeks. There was hardly a spot on her face that wasn't freckled. She was not very tall, so when she spoke in a boisterous voice, it took Caroline by surprise.

"Wade, we were so happy when we got your telegram last week. You're a welcome sight: It's been too long since you came to see us."

"It has been much too long." He turned his attention to Caroline. "Dolly, may I present Mrs. Caroline Duncan. I am accompanying her to Charleston, which is her home."

Dolly turned a bright smile on Caroline and took her hand, pumping it in a vigorous handshake. "Well, honey, you can just consider our home yours as long as you're here." Dolly led her guest inside, talking to them all the while. "You're just as welcome as you can be." She stepped back and assessed Caroline's trousers. "Well, we will have to do something about those."

Caroline had never gotten such an enthusiastic welcome from anyone. She glanced about the comfortable room, talking in the lace curtains at the wide windows, and the couch and three chairs upholstered in green tapestry. She knew the rug she stood upon was woven of silk. Although her hostess's pale blue gown was made of the finest muslin, it seemed to Caroline that the woman would be more at home on a ranch than in these opulent surroundings.

Wade had been right about Dolly's personality: No one could help responding to her kindness. "Thank you, Mrs. Housing."

"No, no, no. I'll call you Caroline, and you'll call

me Dolly. We don't hold with stiff customs around here." She looked Caroline over from head to foot. "My, but you are a tiny little thing." She hardly paused for breath. "And you must be tired, coming all the way from San Sebastian on horseback. Why don't I get you to bed and have Trudy take you up something to eat?"

"Thank you," Caroline said in relief. "That would be very nice."

After Caroline had slipped out of her clothing and into the nightgown Dolly had provided for her, she sank into the soft feather mattress and fell asleep almost instantly.

She was asleep when the maid, Trudy, brought a tray of food to the room, then tiptoed out without waking her. Caroline slept through the afternoon, waking sometime during the night, trying to catch her breath.

Frightened, she got out of bed and walked around the room until she could finally take a cleansing breath.

She lay down across the bed and did not wake until sunlight filtered through the window and fell upon her pillow.

She sat up and looked about. Yesterday she had been too exhausted to notice her surroundings. The bedroom was tastefully decorated in soothing colors of cream and maroon. Her head still ached a bit, but she thought the headache might go away after she ate something.

She suddenly became distressed when she slid off

the bed and looked for her clothing. It was gone. Her head was pounding painfully, and she could hardly think.

Her gaze fell on several boxes stacked on a cream-colored lounge chair. She started to lift the lid of the top box when someone knocked on the door.

Dolly whisked into the room. "Good. I see you are awake. You slept the afternoon away yesterday."

Caroline had taken an instant liking to the chubby little woman. "I am sorry, but your bed was so comfortable."

Dolly plopped down on a chair, shoving a tangled curl out of her face. "We didn't want to disturb you, because you were just plumb worn out."

While Dolly chatted on, a sudden idea hit Caroline: Perhaps Wade had taken her clothing because he was afraid she would run away in the night. "Dolly, do you know what happened to my clothes?"

"Sure I do. I threw them away. I got a telegram from Wade before you got here, asking me to get you some new duds." She laughed and slapped her knee, rattling on, hardly giving Caroline a chance to reply. "That man told me your exact size on everything." She frowned. " 'Course, since the time was so short, I had to get store-bought things, so they might not be the best fit. I can't think why you'd go gadding about the country dressed like a man when you are so pretty."

Caroline knew that Dolly's comments were meant kindly—she was a woman who spoke her mind, and Caroline liked that about her.

There was another knock on the door, and Dolly

went to admit the maid. "This is Trudy," she said, nodding at the girl, who carried a tray of food. "If you need anything, just ask her."

Caroline nodded at the tall, willowy girl with a shy smile. "Thank you, Trudy."

"You should eat a nice breakfast," Dolly told her. "Especially since you missed supper last night."

Dolly was so energetic, she was like a whirlwind sucking up all the air in the room. She instructed Trudy to put the tray on the small table near the window, then walked her to the door, instructing her to bring up the tub and bathwater in an hour.

"Dolly," Caroline asked, "where is Mr. Renault?"

"Why, he's gone with Nate to make sure the private railroad car is ready for your trip home."

"Your husband has a private railroad car?"

"No, indeed, not Nate. The private car belongs to Wade. You didn't know that's how you'll be traveling, did you?"

Caroline dropped her head. "No, I didn't."

"Men! They think they can take care of everything and not bother 'the little woman' with details." She motioned for Caroline to sit at the table. "My Nate is the same way. Thinks he's doing me a favor by keeping everything from me."

Caroline agreed with a nod. She wasn't always clear on what Dolly was talking about. "I don't really know that much about Mr. Renault."

Dolly looked puzzled for a moment, and then her face eased into a grin. "I can tell you a few things about him where you are concerned. He's never brought a woman to our house before. He's always been a loner, never allowing anyone to get very close to him except a few friends and business associates. Of course, there's Jonathan, but I'd bet the boy doesn't know Wade much better than we do."

"Wade has never mentioned anyone named Jonathan to me."

"Now, there you go—that just proves what I was talking about. Jonathan is a boy Wade found one night in a rainstorm. The kid was living on the streets of New Orleans and didn't have a home. I guess the boy's situation reminded Wade of his own childhood."

"His childhood?"

"I probably shouldn't have said anything about that."

Caroline was trying to imagine Wade as the benefactor of a waif—she just could not see him in that way. "How long have you been acquainted with Mr. Renault?"

Dolly motioned for Caroline to eat. "Let me see now. Wade and my Nate go back a long way. He's been awful good to both of us through the years." She swept her hand outward. "We wouldn't have any of this if it wasn't for his generosity."

"I see." She didn't see at all, but it didn't matter. She touched the delicate handle of the china teapot and traced a swirling vine pattern with her finger. "Mr. Renault seems very fond of you."

"Wade takes an interest in all the people he cares about." Dolly watched Caroline's face as she said, "He let me know that you were particularly fond of tea, so Nate got you some down at the general store last week."

Caroline frowned. How could Wade have known about her passion for tea?

"Well," the older woman stated, "I'm going to leave

you alone so you can eat and take a bath. Come on down when you're ready."

Caroline sat silently for a long time after Dolly had gone. Wade was a complex man, and it seemed there were many sides to his personality that she didn't understand. It didn't make sense to her that he made his living as a bounty hunter if he had enough money to own a private railroad car. Did a bounty hunter make that much money? She wondered how much money Brace had offered him, and how Brace thought he would get the money to pay Wade. She had no doubt that Brace was taking all the profits from Michael's estate, but that would never be enough for him—he would want it all.

She pressed her hand against her temples, wishing her head would stop hurting. At last, hunger induced her to eat an egg and a biscuit dripping with butter and jam. She was pouring her second cup of tea when Trudy returned with a bathtub.

After fussing around to make sure the bathwater was the right temperature, Trudy left.

Caroline placed her empty cup in the saucer and stripped off her nightgown, tossing it on the bed. She sank into the water and closed her eyes, enjoying the luxury of hot water, something she had not been able to do for a very long time. Her bathtub in San Sebastian had been nothing more than a small washtub, and she hadn't even been able to unfold her legs in it.

Caroline smiled delightedly when she saw that Trudy had left lilac bath salts and soap that smelled of vanilla. But after she lathered her hair, it felt as if a heavy weight were pressing on her chest. She gasped and lay back until the feeling passed. It wasn't until the water had cooled that Caroline climbed out and wrapped herself in a thick towel.

She cautiously opened the first box and lifted out a yellow silk taffeta gown with several rows of seed pearls around the edge of each sleeve, and back-pleats that swept to the floor. There were undergarments, stockings, and a pair of yellow doeskin slippers.

While she was sliding her foot into one of the slippers, she felt flushed and hot. Her head felt as if someone were hitting her with a hammer. She had not been feeling well for several days. She feared she was coming down with something. She could not be sick! There were things she had to do.

When she was dressed, she stood before the full-length mirror and studied her image. The garments might be store-bought, but they were very fine. Everything fit perfectly, even the corset and shoes. No one could guess her size from head to toe without some kind of help. Even Wade was not that good.

She frowned at her reflection. She would demand to know how Wade had come by that bit of information, and how he knew so much about her. He could not have guessed her sizes or her preference for tea over coffee.

Chapter Twelve

Caroline thought Wade must have heard her on the stairs, because he was waiting at the bottom for her. His gaze swept over her, and he nodded. "Everything is a good fit, is it not? I hope you are pleased."

She didn't answer for a moment, because she was staring at him. He looked so different wearing a dark blue suit and a stiff white shirt. "The gowns I have at home also fit me well." She held out the skirt of her dress. "I would not have needed these things if you had allowed me to bring my own clothing."

He ignored her irritation, his eyelids falling to half-mast. "Do you have everything you need? If not, just tell me and I will see that you get it."

"It would seem you have forgotten nothing. Dolly did exactly as you instructed her. This is certainly better than the wardrobe *you* forced me to wear when you took me away from San Sebastian. Tell me—just how do you know my exact sizes, and how did you know that I have a preference for tea?"

He led her away from the stairs and paused. She saw that he was undecided for a moment, but nothing caught him off guard for very long, she thought, so she pressed her point. "If you don't tell me, I will only use my imagination. And you may be aware of how far a woman's thoughts can take her—especially this woman. You were sneaking through my house, weren't you?"

He saw no reason to deny it. "I visited San Sebastian a week before you saw me ride into town," he admitted. He did not tell her that he had watched her from afar for several days, or that he had carried her likeness next to his heart.

"I should have guessed you would never leave anything to chance. But it's strange that no one mentioned seeing you in San Sebastian before that morning in the rain. How did you manage that?"

He shrugged. "It is very simple. I did not intend that anyone should see me until I was ready. I was ready the day you saw me ride into town."

She stared into eyes that seemed to dance with amusement. "Just how did you accomplish all that?"

"There were several times I slipped into town at night while most people were sleeping. Another time I was there when you were in church."

She poked her finger against his chest. "And what did you do with your time there? Spy on me?"

He caught her hand and held it firmly. "I have always been truthful with you, and I will not lie to you now. As you suspected, I went into your house." His arrogant gaze as much as told her that he was making no apology for what he had done. "There were things I needed to know about you."

She wriggled her hand free of his. "I can hardly believe you were so bold as to trespass on my privacy." She covered her eyes for a moment and shook her head. "You were in my house, going through my belongings?"

"It pains me to admit it, but *oui*." He pinned her with a direct look and smiled slightly. "Archimedes was my partner in crime. He stayed with me while I learned your trouser and boot measurements."

"You went through my clothing?"

He glanced away. "If I do not ask your pardon for anything else, I do ask you to forgive my going through your personal belongings. It was necessary."

What shocked her most was that he would dare to ask her pardon for such a deed. "I will never pardon you. Never! You broke into my house, spied on me, and made me wear those horrible trousers. But worst of all was when you accused me of shooting my husband. I will never forgive you for all the things you have done and said to me."

He seemed undaunted. "I thought you might see things that way." His words were laced with heavy irony. "Before I met you, I had never known a woman to try my patience as much as you have, Caroline. If you had been a man, I would have come for you without all the extra fuss. You have been nothing but trouble."

She took a breath before answering him furiously. "Good! I am glad. I may be your prisoner, but you will never conquer me."

He was standing near a table where a world globe was displayed. With a hefty spin he sent it twirling, but his eyes were on Caroline and not the world as it spun on its axis—he had become fascinated as she paced in front of him. Every move she made, every gesture of her hand, enchanted him. Did she know how adorable she looked in that yellow gown?

"One conquers in a war. I am not one of your soldiers who fall all over themselves to get your attention."

"No. You are not."

"And you continue to trouble me, madame."

She drew herself up tall and gathered her wits. "I'm happy if I have inconvenienced you in any way. I want you to think about me, and remember what you did to me long after I am out of your sight."

His eyes narrowed. "I will not soon forget you."

"I'm counting on it."

He glanced away from her. "Looking at the situation from your point of view, I suppose it may seem—"

She pressed her hands over her ears. "I won't listen to anything you have to say in your defense. I hate you!" She watched him flinch at her angry words, and she was glad if she had pierced his thick skin.

"I hope that is not true, Caroline."

She reconsidered, softening her stance a bit. "I don't really hate anyone except Brace. You, I just don't like."

"But you are no longer afraid of me."

"I was at first."

"Yet in San Sebastian you came charging to my room to confront me. I see something of the survivor in you."

"I have had to confront many people in my life."

She rubbed her temples again, wishing her headache would go away. She was not prone to headaches, but this one was persistent. "I should have left town that day."

"I would only have caught up with you."

She nodded. "Yes. You would have."

"Caroline," he said, his tone deepening. "I wish it could have been different. I did not set out to hurt you."

She was staggered by his statement. "And what do you call what you have already done to me? Can you not see that?"

He was thinking how adorable she looked when she was mad. He was thinking the sun that shone through the front window fell on her hair and streaked it with gold. He was thinking she had the bluest eyes he had ever seen. "I believe we should join our hostess."

She hesitated when he extended his arm to her, but when Dolly suddenly entered the room, Caroline decided not to make an issue of it, and quickly placed her hand on his sleeve.

"Why, honey, you are just as pretty as you can be." Dolly walked around Caroline, inspecting her carefully. "It's no wonder Wade has lost his head over you."

"I'm . . . not, he isn't—"

"What Mrs. Duncan is trying to tell you," Wade said, coming to her rescue, "is she does not think of me in that way." He nodded down at her. "I am right about that, am I not?"

"Wade told me you are a widow," Dolly said soothingly. "It's too bad that you lost your husband at such a young age. The passing of time will dull the grief."

Caroline was uncomfortable talking about Michael with Dolly. "I loved my husband very much."

For the first time, Dolly saw the angry flush on Caroline's face, and she realized that she had come in on a confrontation between the two of them. "I'll just wait for you in the sitting room. You can come in when you want to. I told Trudy to bring in the tea when you're ready."

Dolly disappeared through the arched doorway, and Caroline turned her attention back to Wade. "It is unthinkable for me to deceive that kind woman. When do we leave?"

"I have business that will keep me in town today." He reached out and tilted her face so she was forced to look at him. "San Antonio is a rowdy town for a woman alone. You will not want to venture outside the house."

She pulled away from him. "My life has not been my own since the day I met you." She took several quick steps away from him. "Or should I say since the night you went prowling in my house without my knowledge?"

"I will return later this afternoon."

She watched him walk away as an unsettling feeling hit her. She should be furious with him, and she was, but she had been with him for so long, she almost panicked at the thought of his leaving her. Her headache was getting worse, and for a moment she could not take a deep breath. Caroline knew she was ill. But she could not let anything delay her return to Charleston.

After several tries, she was finally able to take a deep

breath. She was slightly lightheaded and held on to the stair railing until the dizziness passed. After she had composed herself, she moved toward the sitting room, thinking a cup of tea might make her feel better.

Dolly was sitting before a large tapestry frame, her needle darting in and out of the canvas with vigor. She looked up, smiled at Caroline, and nodded for her to be seated in the chair by the window. "I'm sorry if I busted in on the private talk you and Wade were having."

"Please do not be concerned. It amounted to nothing."

Dolly frowned as she took a stitch. "I knew when I first saw you and Wade together that he's in love with you."

Caroline was taken aback by Dolly's incorrect assertion. She could not tell Dolly that the intenseness with which Wade watched her had more to do with intimidation than any soft feelings he might have for her. "You are mistaken. I can assure you he does not feel that way about me." She searched for the right words. "Mr. Renault and I have a sort of business arrangement."

Dolly was curious, but she was too polite to press Caroline on the matter. But she did know Wade, and he was smitten with Caroline. "You see, Wade has a way of looking at people as if he were measuring them for a pine box. But when he looks at you, there isn't a doubt in my mind what he's thinking."

Caroline was glad that Trudy chose that moment to enter. There was only one cup on the tray the maid placed on the small round table beside her. "Dolly, will you not have tea?"

"I never developed a taste for it. I'm an old west-Texas gal and the only thing I'd drink hot is strong coffee."

Caroline poured a cup of the steaming brew and added cream. "Will I be meeting your husband?"

"I'm 'fraid not this time. He had to go to South Carolina today. Some kind of business for Wade."

Caroline's spine stiffened. "Charleston?"

"I'm not sure of the name of the town."

Caroline's hand began to tremble, and she was afraid she would drop the delicate cup, so she carefully placed it on the tray. Her throat seemed to close, and she could not catch her breath. Frightened, she leaned back in her chair. After trying several times, she was able to breathe. "I did not know that your husband worked for Mr. Renault."

"Goodness, yes. Nate worked for Anton Renault until he died; now he works for Wade."

Caroline wanted to know more about Wade. Perhaps she could find a weakness in him somewhere. Dolly seemed more than willing to talk about him, so Caroline shamelessly asked, "Is his mother still living?"

Dolly was amazed that Wade hadn't told Caroline about himself. But then, he had always been a very private person. She had no qualms about telling this young woman whatever she needed to know. In the end, Wade and Caroline would wind up married—she was sure of it.

"Wade never knew who his mother or father was. Anton Renault found him sleeping in one of his warehouses down on the docks and took him home with him. He was half starved at the time."

Dolly talked ceaselessly as she stuck her needle through the canvas and leaned back to give Caroline her full attention. "Anton's wife died some years back, childless. So he finally adopted Wade, and the boy became the son Anton had never had." She calculated on her fingers. "At that time Anton figured the boy was around six or seven, we don't really know his true age. The one thing Anton was sure of was that the boy was Creole. He might've come from the streets, but he spoke French like one of those uppity people." She grinned, her eyes dancing with a teasing light. "You know, the same way you speak American, all prim and proper."

"I have been accused of having an accent."

"And so you do. Why, if Wade is of a mind to, he can rattle off that French as well as anyone."

"I have heard him at times."

"Well, Anton didn't like him speaking French. He told the boy if he was going to live in this country, he could just speak the language."

Caroline suddenly saw Wade as a boy, and pity for him washed over her. "Mr. Renault does not know who his parents were?"

"No, he doesn't. But if it bothers him any, he never says so. I doubt the truth of his past will ever be known."

Caroline took another sip of tea, her heart hurting for the boy Wade had been. Having grown up with a mother and father who loved her, she could not imagine what he must have gone through in his lonely childhood. Even if his adopted father loved him, that did not give him a past. Now she could better understand why he was such a loner.

"It is easy to see that he has had a very good education."

"Well, for a time he did attend one of those fancy schools. Then he and Anton had a falling-out—I never knew what it was about, and, of course, Wade would never say. But he took off, heading here to Texas. He stayed with me and Nate for a while." She shook her head. "He actually became a bounty hunter for a time, and he was good at it, from what Nate tells me."

"I have heard about that myself." She wondered what Dolly would do if she told her the truth. She decided against it. She would take care of Wade in her own way.

Dolly's expression was sorrowful. "Then Anton got sick and sent for Wade. He went home, and they settled whatever it was that was wrong between them before Anton died. Wade took up the family business and even made it more of a success than Anton had. But he's a restless soul, always looking for something that is just out of reach. I hope he will find it in you."

Caroline saw no reason to state the obvious, because Dolly was determined that she and Wade belonged together. She certainly could not tell her she was actually his prisoner. "Mr. Renault informed me that we would be leaving tomorrow."

Dolly rubbed her hand over her knee is if it hurt from sitting for so long. "That is what he told me, too."

"Why does he have a private railroad car?"

"It's used mostly for business. Wade has to travel a lot, and sometimes my Nate uses it. I traveled in it a few times myself, and I can tell you it's better than riding in a public railroad car or a stagecoach."

"Yes, I suppose it would be."

Dolly went back to her tapestry, but she continued to talk. "Honey, I can tell you're mad at Wade about something. But be kind to him. He's about the most alone person I know. We only see him as a man, but there's some of the little boy in him, too. It's like he's looking for something to hold on to."

"I have never seen him in that way."

"If I was as pretty and young as you are, and if I didn't love my Nate so much, I'd set my sights on him. Even at my age, when he speaks to me with that exciting French accent, my knees go weak."

Caroline could not help laughing. "I think the woman who decides to take on Mr. Renault will have her hands full."

Dolly winked and chuckled. "You're probably right—but wouldn't it be fun just the same?"

"I don't know what kind of business Mr. Renault owns."

"He's got several large warehouses in New Orleans and Baton Rouge. Then there all those big barges that go up and down the Mississippi to bring back cotton, indigo, tobacco, and sugar cane."

Caroline sat forward so she could catch the breeze that stirred the curtains, but when it touched her face, it was like a blast from an oven. She felt as if a fist were clenching her chest, and she gasped for breath. Something was wrong with her. Dolly was taking out a stitch and did not seem to notice that Caroline was having trouble breathing. She suddenly had the feeling that everything was closing in on her, and there was a ringing in her ears. "Dolly, would you think it rude of me if I went upstairs to rest for a while?"

"Not at all, honey. You just rest all you want to. If you'd like, I'll have your lunch tray brought to your room."

Caroline walked to the door and turned back to her hostess. "Thank you for the tea. It was delicious."

Dolly noticed after Caroline had gone that she had not even finished a full cup of tea. She had a suspicion there was more to the situation between the young woman and Wade than either of them would admit. She could not be wrong about Wade's feelings for Caroline. But why were they traveling together, and why had Wade sent Nate to South Carolina to make inquiries about her?

Chapter Thirteen

Caroline opened the window and stood staring outside for a time before she started to undress. She unhooked her gown and then removed her corset, thinking she might be able to breathe better without it. The world tilted a bit and then righted itself.

She was feeling very ill.

She leaned against the casement, wondering what she should do. If she were in San Sebastian, she would go to Dr. Davis and he would help her. The real problem she faced was keeping her illness from Wade, and that would not be easy because he noticed everything that went on around him. She moved to the bed and eased her body onto it. She ached all over. Then she was struck by a sudden chill, so she pulled the covers over her and finally fell asleep.

She was not aware that the maid came in to bring her lunch tray. She slept through the day, too weary to lift her head. When night fell, she still had not awakened.

Wade himself came into the room to see why she had not come downstairs for dinner. He knocked softly on the door, and when she did not answer, he went inside. He stood over her, watching her for long enough to determine that she was asleep. Guilt was a new emotion for him—he had pushed her too hard. He quietly left and softly closed the bedroom door.

It was sometime during the night when the fever struck. She was hot one minute and shivering the next. She was under the covers and then on top of them, wrestling with her illness all night.

Just before sunup she slid out of bed and got dressed. She had to hold herself together so they could leave today. She brushed the tangles from her hair and secured it to the back of her head in a chignon. Just the chore of dressing and doing her hair exhausted her. She sat down near the window with her hands folded in her lap—waiting for Wade.

As it happened, Trudy came in first, carrying a breakfast tray. The girl looked troubled when she saw that the guest had not eaten the food she had left the night before. "I'll just take this tray away, ma'am,"

"Thank you, Trudy. I was not hungry yesterday."

"But you will eat breakfast, won't you, ma'am?"

Caroline knew she could not swallow a morsel of food because her throat was hurting. When the girl left, she did reach for the glass of water.

A short time later Wade knocked on the door and called her name.

"You can come in," she told him, pinching her cheeks so she wouldn't look so pale.

He looked surprised when he entered the room. "I see you are ready."

With effort she held her head upright. "As you see, I am wearing the gown Dolly gave me. I hope I don't have to wear it as long as I did the trousers. I don't relish the thought of going into a river to wash it when it gets dirty."

He saw the stubborn tilt to her head that always meant trouble for him. "Dolly has purchased other clothing for you, so you can have several changes on the journey."

"You are kindness itself," she said in a tone that implied otherwise.

He wanted to tell her how sorry he was that the trip to San Antonio had been so rigorous, but he knew she would only throw his words back in his face. "Shall we go?"

She stood, wavering a bit, and grabbed on to a chair to steady herself. She was glad he had his back to her and didn't notice. "As always, I am yours to command."

"If only that were true." Wade was accustomed to her candid remarks, and he chose to ignore them this morning. He glanced at her breakfast tray and frowned. "You have not eaten anything."

She walked to the door. "The one thing I still have is my right to eat or not to eat. I do not choose to eat this morning."

He took her arm and escorted her downstairs. "Madame, in your present state of mind, I would deny nothing you say."

Dolly met them at the bottom of the stairs. "Caroline," she said, hugging her, "I have known you for such a short time, but I think we'll always be friends, don't you?"

"I feel that way, too. You have been very kind. If you don't mind, I will write you sometime."

Dolly's face brightened. "Please do. I hardly ever get a letter. I'd like to know how you're getting on from time to time."

Wade nodded at Dolly, and she patted his arm. "Let us see more of you. And take care of this lady."

Wade escorted Caroline outside and down the steps to the waiting carriage. He helped her inside, climbed in beside her, then nodded to the driver. "Take us to the depot."

Caroline turned to wave at Dolly, who stood on the front porch. "She is the one good thing that has happened to me since I've known you."

Wade looked down at her but said nothing.

Caroline could feel the heat crushing down on her, and she laid her head back against the cushioned seat. The world was spinning, and she closed her eyes.

"Are you ill?" Wade asked, noticing how pale she was. "You have been acting strangely the last two days."

She was afraid that if he found out how sick she was, he would take her back to Dolly's house. "Wouldn't you act strangely if you were put in my position? I only want to go home to Charleston as quickly as possible."

He clamped his jaw and said nothing.

They drove through town, but this time Caroline did not take the same interest she had when they first arrived in San Antonio. She wanted to lie down. She hoped the private car would have a bed where she could rest.

When they arrived at the depot, Wade helped her from the buggy and turned to give instructions to the driver. "See that the horse I left in the stable is sold."

"I will find a buyer, sir."

Caroline had grown accustomed to her little filly. She hoped that whoever bought her would treat her kindly.

Wade took her arm and steered her across the tracks. Even from a distance, she could see *Renault* painted in red across a black railroad car.

He assisted her up the three steps. "It will be cooler inside. I had the porter open the windows earlier. After we are on our way, there will be a pleasant breeze."

She only had the strength to nod in agreement.

"If you will excuse me for a moment, I want to see that my horse has been made comfortable in the boxcar stall. Make yourself at home. I will not be very long."

When he had gone, she glanced around the private car. Knowing Wade, she was not surprised to see that this was a man's domain. The walls were lined in tooled leather, and two cowhide couches had been placed along each wall. She saw several rifles displayed in a glass-front gun cabinet. In one corner a heavy oak desk was piled high with letters and documents. There was a small table with four chairs, and even a small kitchen.

Caroline was so weak she had to lean against a chair for support. After a while, she was able to approach the wide partition that served to create a private bedroom. The bed was large, and here, too, the walls were tooled leather. She saw two trunks at the foot of the bed. She imagined one of them would be Wade's, and the other, probably hers. She loosened the ribbons of her bonnet and tossed it on a chair before she was hit by another bout of dizziness and dropped down weakly on the bed. A feeling of helplessness washed over her, and she gripped a pillow fiercely to her chest, trying to call out to Wade.

She closed her eyes, hoping the tilting world would soon right itself. But when she opened them a moment later, everything was still spinning. She felt sick to her stomach and was glad she had had nothing to eat.

Blackness closed in on her, and she fought hard against it, but in the end she was swallowed by the darkness.

Chapter Fourteen

Wade had removed his jacket, unfastened his tie, and rolled up his sleeves before delving into the stack of papers on his desk. He could not seem to concentrate on his work; his mind was on more complicated matters. He was more sure than ever that he had made a blunder where Caroline was concerned. She was not the cold-hearted killer her brother-in-law had portrayed. She was innocent in every way.

Or was she? He was never quite sure.

He swiveled his chair around, propped a booted foot on a stool, and closed his eyes. "How long?" he whispered aloud. How long would this uncertainty nag at him? He had always been in command of his own thoughts and feelings, but not anymore. One moment he thought Caroline was innocent, and the next minute he could almost see her shooting her husband.

He broodingly stared out the window at the passing scenery as the train gathered speed and rocked over the rails. He thought back on the search that had led him to Caroline. She had left a trail that an amateur could have followed. He wondered why it had taken Brace Duncan three years to send someone to find her. Or *had* he sent someone before, someone who had returned empty-handed?

He had tried to be professional where Caroline was concerned, but it was getting harder by the day to pretend indifference toward her when all he could think about was holding her in his arms. He remembered how light she had been when he'd carried her out of the river. He did not want to turn her over to Brace—he wanted to keep her for himself.

He glanced back at the stack of work on his desk and shoved it aside. Every passing day would take them closer to Charleston. Could he really turn Caroline over to Brace Duncan, knowing she was so terrified of the man? He did not think so.

What would his life be like when she was no longer with him? He could not go back to his life the way it had been before he had met her. Knowing her had changed him somehow. The restlessness that had always stirred within him had been quieted, to be replaced by hot, burning desire—a desire he kept tightly leashed. But there had been times when he had almost lost the battle. Sometimes it could be just the turn of her head, the pursing of her lips. She was beautiful when she awoke in the mornings, with curls framing her face.

"Damn," he muttered, trying to think of something other than how her breasts pushed against her shirt when she stretched her arms over her head—a morning ritual that drove him crazy with need.

He unbuckled his gun and placed it on his desk. He had given up bounty hunting long ago because of a promise he'd made Anton before he died. He only took it up again when Brace Duncan had sent him a package with Caroline's picture and a letter informing him of her crimes. He had left two days later for Charleston to find out more about the woman whose face had begun to haunt him. The day he had agreed to find her and take her back to North Carolina was the day he had once again taken up his gun.

Damn that tintype! If only he had just thrown the package away without opening it. It seemed to him that all of his life he had been searching for something that was always just out of reach. Before he met Caroline, he had never realized how empty his life had been. She could be a hellion and dig her heels in stubbornly, insisting on having her own way, or she could charm him with the turn of her head or a smile from those lips.

He shifted in his chair and rubbed the back of his neck, ready to stake his life on her innocence. He just had to decide what to do about Brace Duncan.

He picked up a letter, opened it, and stared at it without really seeing it. He was thinking about his relationship with Caroline—looking at it from outside, he imagined she despised him. Who could blame her? She thought of him as mercenary and only interested in the reward money he would get when he turned her over to her brother-in-law.

With her, it had never been about the money, but he would never convince her of that. He had to think clearly, and that was the one thing that seemed to elude him at the moment. If he did not take Caroline back to Brace, the man would only send someone else to search for her.

He stood up and began to pace, swaying for a moment with the motion of the train. He braced his hands on the wall and lowered his head. Caroline was not the woman Brace Duncan had described to him. It seemed that she had loved her husband—still loved him, if he was any judge of character. But what did he know? Of late he had been lagging behind in the judging department.

His raised his head slowly as realization hit him hard. In his whole life, he had never deeply loved another human being. He had respected his adopted father, but he had not felt any deep emotion for him. Anton had been a hard taskmaster, but Wade had learned from him. The trouble was, he and Anton had been much alike, and neither one of them had known how to show love. Legally, Anton had been his father. But in truth, Anton had been a cold-hearted man; his only passion had been the acquisition of more wealth.

Wade came to another startling realization: In him, Anton had successfully created a son in his own likeness.

Wade had patterned his life after Anton's because of a promise, but that wasn't who he really was. He had taken the wealth Anton had left him and built an empire Anton would have been proud of. But the wealth meant very little to Wade; it never had. Bored to distraction with his life, he had been more than willing to revert to his past life when he had gone looking for Caroline.

* * *

Caroline felt as if she were fighting her way through a deep fog. She was so cold, and it was dark and dank in the place her mind dwelled. She was running from something frightful that was just behind her and gaining on her. She had the feeling that if she slowed her pace or slipped, the darkness would surely devour her. She tossed and turned, trying to run faster, but her legs would not move. She was lost and could not save herself.

The darkness seemed to clear a bit, and she could now see her pursuer. She tossed her head back and forth. The person chasing her was Brace, his hard eyes looking at her, his hands reaching out to capture her.

"Wade," she cried out in sheer terror, "help me!"

She felt herself being lifted into someone's arms, and she rested her head against a wide chest.

"*Mon amour, il n'y a raison pour craindre,*" Wade said, holding her tighter, and then slipping back into English. "My love, there is no reason to fear. I will let nothing harm you."

Her tears dampened his shirt, and she clutched at him, not willing to let him go. He was the only reality in a frightening world. "I am sorry," she gasped. "I don't seem to be feeling quite myself."

He could see that she was having trouble breathing, so he unhooked her gown and unlaced her corset so she would not be so constricted. While he gathered her close, he worked the pins out of her hair and let it flow freely across his arm.

"Is that better?"

She moaned and twisted her head. "He will find me

no matter where I hide. I don't want him to ever touch me again."

He brushed her hair away from her face, and the golden mass fell in curls down her back.

She was burning up with fever.

"Do not think about him," he told her soothingly, knowing exactly who pursued Caroline in her fever-induced nightmare.

She shook her head and nestled against him more securely. "Hold me. Hold me tight," she whispered.

He eased his weight onto the bed, leaned back against the headboard, then gathered her to him. There was an unfamiliar heaviness around his heart. "Sweetheart, why did you not tell me you were feeling ill?"

She opened her eyes, looking startled when she realized that she had not been dreaming that he was holding her, but she was actually in his arms. She tried to move away, but it took too much effort. She sobbed and sank back into the shelter of his arms.

"Why, Caroline? Why did you not tell me, or at least let Dolly know that you were unwell? You must have been ill for some time."

She drew in a shuddering breath. "I have to get home," she said in little more than a faint whisper.

He touched his lips to her forehead. "When you are with me, you *are* at home."

She took a deep, painful breath, not understanding his meaning. "I want to get back to Charleston even more than you want to take me there. I must confront Brace and make him admit his lies."

"Caroline," he said softly against her ear. "I am going to leave you for a moment. I need to get cool water so I can bring your fever down. I keep medical supplies in my desk drawer—I need to see if there is anything there that will help you."

She clutched his arm. "No." She gasped as if trying to catch her breath. "Don't leave me."

"Caroline, I have to get your fever down," he said as panic rose inside him. "I will only be a moment." He gently laid her down, looking into her fever-bright eyes. "I will need to remove your outer clothing so I can bathe you with water."

She grasped at his hand. "No."

His heart tightened, and he was hit with an emotion so hard and sharp that it left him stunned. "*Ma chère*, what have I done to you?"

His hands trembled as he bent over her, undoing her gown and unhooking her stays. When he had stripped her down to her petticoat, he went into the outer room to gather what he needed.

When he returned a moment later, he lifted her head, gave her a spoonful of cough elixir, and then applied a damp cloth to her forehead.

Guilt hung over him like a heavy cloud. She was so fragile, and he had driven her too hard. When she had spent most of her time at Dolly's resting, he should have known she was ill. He had wrongly thought she was just rebelling against him.

He dipped a cloth in water and bathed her arms, noticing how delicate they were. He could only imagine what hell she had lived through after her husband had been killed. She had endured stark panic hiding from Brace Duncan. And he had witnessed her fear when he had ridden into town that day.

"I'm so cold," she said, shaking all over. She clutched at the cover, trying to pull it over her.

He pried it from her fingers. "It would not be wise to cover you—I need to cool your body down."

"No."

"*Oui, mon amour*, it is necessary."

She became calm at the sound of his voice and allowed him to help her.

After he had bathed both arms, raised her petticoat, and bathed her legs, he straightened it around her ankles. With a worried frown, he watched her labored breathing. He imagined she had been sick even before they arrived in San Antonio. What concerned him most was her shallow breathing. He propped her up on the pillows and went in search of the conductor. He found the man two cars away, and informed him that he wanted his private car switched to the tracks that would take them to New Orleans. He also made arrangements for his horse to be shipped home at the next stop.

He had decided that he was taking Caroline to his home. He wanted her under his protection, and he wanted his doctor to look after her.

Later, as he sat beside her, he took her hand in his. He pitied anyone who might try to take her away from him.

It was after midnight when he saw the flashing lights of the switch tower. His car was unhooked from the passenger train and then left for over an hour in the Houston freight yard before being coupled onto a Louisiana-bound train.

Caroline had become more restless. Wade placed

his hand on her forehead and found her fever was higher than earlier in the afternoon.

He had never known real fear until now. He was terrified that she might die because he had been careless with her health.

What if he lost her?

He dipped a fresh cloth in water and ran it along her face and neck, moving to her shoulders, and then applied it to her forehead. He bathed her arms and legs several times, frantically trying to bring down her fever.

She fought him and cried out, "I am so cold."

After a while, her fever-bright eyes closed. Infrequently she would open them and stare at him as if she didn't know who he was.

Wade brought a chair to the side of the bed and sat down so he could watch her. "Rest, sleep. I will take care of you," he promised her.

She reached for his hand and brought it to her breast. "Stay with me this time."

He stayed at her side all night. Even in sleep, she would not relinquish his hand. It was nearing morning, and a cool breeze filtered through the opened windows when Caroline complained that she was too hot. So he bathed her once more.

It was around noon when Caroline suddenly began to thrash about on the bed, whimpering. "No, no," she moaned. "God, help! The blood—the blood all over my gown!" She turned and twisted her body. "Blood on my hands—Michael's blood."

Wade gathered her close, holding her against his chest. She was reliving her husband's death, and the things she said chilled his heart. Michael Duncan had died in her arms. Wade realized how important it was to keep her calm, so he spoke soothingly to her. "I have you in my arms. Nothing can hurt you while I am with you. Do not think about anything but the sound of my voice."

She buried her face against his neck. "I don't want to sleep—the dreams—"

"Hush, *ma chère*. You must sleep. Think about me holding you and standing between you and anything that might harm you."

The sound of his voice calmed her, so he kept talking to her softly. "You have been alone for a long time, and I know what that feels like. I think I touched your spirit before I even heard the sound of your voice."

She looked at him as if she didn't understand what he was saying.

He watched her eyes close, and she fell asleep. "I knew you from the likeness I carried with me."

He touched her lips with his finger, and she dragged her eyes open, then closed them again. "You will not remember anything I say to you after you awake, and I would never say these things to you if you were conscious."

She nodded, but he knew she wasn't understanding his words, merely reacting to his tone of voice.

He closed his eyes for a moment, blaming himself for what she was experiencing. How she must have suffered, knowing he was taking her back to the man she was so terrified of, and whom she had fled halfway across the country to escape.

"I promise you this, and I have never broken a

promise: I will right any wrong I have done you, and I will make certain that no one will *ever* hurt you again."

She moaned softly in response.

He touched his lips to her hand. "I will make it possible for you to return to your father and be safe, if that is what you want to do." One thing he knew for sure was that there was no way in hell Brace Duncan was going to get his hands on her. He would deal with the man in his own fashion.

It was late the next night when Caroline's fever finally broke. She tossed her head and grabbed hold of the headboard, her body drenched with perspiration.

Wade knew he had to change her into something dry and put fresh sheets on the bed, or she would catch a chill.

He stood up and stretched his cramped muscles, then left her long enough to ask a porter to bring clean linens for the bed.

When he returned, her eyes were open, and she stared at him in confusion. "I have been ill?"

His heart quickened. She was going to be all right. He felt joy!

Her golden hair hung limply about her face, but that did not detract from her beauty. "You have been ill, *oui*. You are much better now." He touched her hand. "I am going to change you into a dry nightgown. Are you able to sit up with my help?"

She made an attempt to rise but fell back weakly against the pillows. She licked her dry lips. "I'm sorry. I seem to be a little shaky."

He laid the dry sheets on the chair and opened the

trunk at the foot of the bed. He found the nightgown Dolly had packed for her. "Caroline, I am going to help you into this nightgown."

She grasped the sheet to her. "You can't do that."

"I have already seen more of you than you would be comfortable with. You have no choice but to accept my help."

She knew he was right and nodded reluctantly, her cheeks flushed with embarrassment. He raised her to a sitting position and worked the damp petticoat up over her head.

She did have vague flashes of him helping her with the most intimate needs. "How long have you been taking care of me?"

"We left San Antonio four days ago. I doubt that you remember much of what has happened since then."

"Only bits and pieces."

He drew in a deep breath and averted his gaze when she was naked. He did not want to embarrass her more than was necessary. He quickly pulled her fresh nightgown over her head and worked it down all the way to her ankles.

He took her by surprise when he lifted her into his arms. "You can lie on the couch while I change the bed."

She relaxed into the strength of his arms and allowed her head to fall back on his shoulder. He carefully laid her down, then brought her a pillow and a quilt.

"Thank you," she managed to say without looking at him.

He bent down beside her. "How do you feel?"

"Much better, thank you for asking. And thank you for taking care of me while I was ill. I must have been very demanding of your time."

"I had nothing better to do." His beautiful mouth slid into a smile. "I do not profess to be a doctor, so when we reach Baton Rouge I will have one come aboard to examine you."

She watched him move to the bedroom area. She breathed in deeply, and it felt good to be able to breath.

When he returned a short time later, she had fallen asleep. He touched her forehead and found it cool, and he could see that she was breathing much easier.

He moved to the window and watched a woman hurry from the train into the small Beaumont, Texas, depot. In only a few hours they would be in Louisiana—in two more days they would be home.

The train slowed and came to a stop, puffing out steam. They had reached Baton Rouge and would remain there long enough for one of the porters to bring a doctor aboard to examine Caroline.

When the short, stocky man arrived, he introduced himself. "I'm Dr. Goodman. I understand you have someone sick aboard."

After Wade had told him about Caroline's symptoms, he escorted the doctor to the sleeping quarters. The doctor stayed with Caroline for quite a while, and Wade paced the floor of the outer compartment. He heard the doctor asking Caroline questions, and her weak responses.

It was almost an hour before the man emerged to find Wade waiting for him. Closing his black leather bag, the doctor said in a serious tone, "Your wife is

it would do no good. "I will never eat potato soup again," she said defiantly.

He offered her the last bite. "Caroline, you can be such a child sometimes. You will eat well because you need the nourishment."

She fell silent. It wasn't the child in her that wanted to throw herself into his arms. It certainly wasn't the child in her that watched his mouth, wondering what it would feel like to press her lips to his. She watched that mouth softly curve into a smile. Her eyes quickly darted upward to collide with his golden gaze.

His voice was deep and his accent more pronounced. "There," he said as she finally took the last bite. "You have eaten it all."

"I am tired now. I want to sleep," she grumbled.

He stood up and placed the empty soup bowl on a tray as if he had already dismissed her from his mind. "And so you shall."

By the time they reached New Orleans, she was strong enough to dress herself. She moved to the outer room and waited for Wade to look up from his paperwork.

When he finally gave her his attention, he swept her with an inspecting gaze and nodded his approval. "You must have more suitable attire when you are settled in my house."

She wondered at what point their relationship had changed. He was not the same man who had put handcuffs on her and forced her to accompany him out of San Sebastian. She was seeing a softer side of him, although she knew he was still as dangerous as ever. Perhaps now she could make him see reason and persuade him that she was not the villainess he supposed her to be.

"Wade—" his name came easily to her lips. "I don't want you to buy me anything more." She started to say something and paused. "I am already in your debt." She paused again. "That is not exactly right, is it? I would not be in your debt if you hadn't forced me to be with you."

He rose to his feet and ran his hand through his hair. "I will make this all up to you somehow."

That was the last thing she had expected him to say. She was puzzled. "You owe me nothing. I will consider all debts paid if you will let me go."

He noticed that her gown was too loose at the waist: She had lost weight, and it worried him. "You are not well enough to travel on your own. You will have to regain your health before you can go anywhere. There is no need to discuss your leaving at this time."

Caroline heard the grating sound of the train disconnecting from the private car, and she swayed, keeping her balance by holding on to a chair. "I will be stronger, maybe in another week." She wasn't sure if he still intended to take her to Brace. She watched his face as she said, "If you will lend me money so I can go home, I will repay every cent. And," she added, hoping to sweeten the pot, "I will also give you the same amount of money Brace promised you."

He glanced at the ceiling, anger sweeping through him. She could not wait to get away from him, and who could blame her? He thought of the doctor's warning not to upset her and softened his tone. "We do not have to talk about that at this time." He took her arm and led her toward the door. "I believe Louis has the carriage waiting for us. Shall we go?"

He helped her slowly down the steps. Even though he kept a supporting hand on her arm, she was almost out of breath before they had gone very far.

Without hesitation, he swept her into his arms and carried her right past a crowd of people, who looked shocked.

"Put me down," she insisted. "Everyone is staring at us."

He glanced down at her. "Let them stare. What do I care?"

She had learned to recognize that stubborn set to his chin and did not say another word.

He carried her to a waiting coach with four high-stepping matched grays and deposited her upon the leather seat, then climbed in beside her. "Did you have to wait long, Louis?"

"Not at all. And welcome home, Monsieur Renault." The short Frenchman who addressed Wade had long ago lost most of his hair; what was left was whisky-colored. He handed Wade a small satchel and then turned his attention to Caroline, giving her a courtly bow. "Madame Duncan, welcome to New Orleans."

Wade was looking at one of the papers in the satchel and suddenly remembered his manners. "Caroline, this is Louis Dulong. He has worked for the family for longer than anyone can remember."

"That is true, madame. I was with this young rascal's papa long before he came to live with us."

Caroline was somewhat surprised by the familiarity the servant displayed toward Wade. It was proof that he was an old and valued retainer. "I am pleased to meet you, Louis."

He tugged at his cap and removed it. "The pleasure is all mine, madame." Then he turned to Wade. "Shall I get the baggage?"

"*Non*. Let us get Madame Duncan out of this heat. You can send someone for the trunks later."

The agile little man swung onto the driver's seat and took up the reins. As they left the depot behind, a cool breeze stirred Caroline's hair. It felt good to be able to take a deep breath. She glanced at Wade, who was studying a document. The breeze lifted his hair and rippled it across his forehead. He turned his head and showed his profile, so she studied him in detail. Her heart beat like a wild thing when she watched him compress his mouth and turn his attention to her.

"How do you expect me to do anything with you watching me so closely?"

"I wasn't—I didn't."

"You were, and you did. I am not the monster you think I am."

"No." She met his steady gaze. "How can I think that of someone who took such tender care of me?"

He reached toward her and then pulled his hand back. "It was no more than I would have done for anyone under the same conditions."

"I believe that about you."

He took up the document again, and she turned her head to look at New Orleans. The horses' hooves clipped along at a steady pace while she examined a tall brick building with iron grillwork. She saw a garden behind an iron fence and wondered about the lives of the people who lived there. "I have never been to New Orleans before."

"Then I must be your guide," Wade told her, putting his document back in the satchel. "If you will look far to your right, you can see the steeple of St. Louis Cathedral, which was built in 1795. We are on the side of the river that was first settled by those of Creole ancestry."

"That would be your ancestors."

"I believe so. There was a time when all Creoles looked down their aristocratic noses at what they called the 'unacceptable Americans' when the tide of settlers migrated to the other side of the Mississippi after the Louisiana Purchase."

"Dolly told me that you are Creole."

Knowing Dolly and how she liked to talk, he gave her a guarded look. "I am, however, not one of the aristocrats. I would have to be classed with the 'unacceptable Americans' had I lived back then, because I do not know my heritage, and I probably never will."

Caroline was glad that Dolly had told her about Wade's past because it allowed her to better understand him. "Tell me about your home," she said, switching the conversation.

"I believe you will find it comfortable, although it is nowhere as old or as large as your father's home in Charleston."

She quickly looked at him. "You saw my father?" She didn't wait for his answer before she posed another question. "You were in my home?"

He had not intended to let her know about his visit with her father until later. "I did have a short conversation with Mr. Richmond when I first began my search for you."

Her chin jutted out. "He would not have told you anything about me."

"He thinks you may be dead."

Chapter Sixteen

Tears gathered in her eyes. "My poor father—how he must be suffering." She did not want Louis to hear, so she lowered her voice and said in desperation, "You must understand that I have to go home as soon as possible. If for no other reason than to take care of him. My father has no family to speak of, just distant cousins in New York, whom he hardly knows. I'm all he has."

Wade became silent and turned away. It stabbed him deeply to see tears in her eyes. She was not the kind of woman who used tears as a weapon like some women he had known; if she cried it was because she felt something deeply. "Perhaps you would like for me to send him a telegram and let him know that you are all right."

She shook her head. "No. You can't do that. Brace might find—" She frowned and shook her head. "Of course, you have probably already informed Brace that you were bringing me here, so he knows where I am."

He turned to her so quickly it took her by surprise. "Do you really believe that?"

She caught the gruffness in his tone and raised her chin to a higher level. "It's what he hired you for, isn't it? You have been very clear about your intent."

He now knew the reason she had never contacted her father: She was afraid she would endanger him if Brace found out about it. The one thing Wade had not wanted to do was upset her and make her cry. "Let me tell you about my house. It is just outside the city. It is rather large with some wrought-iron grillwork. I think you will like the gardens."

She tried to concentrate on what he was telling her, but her mind kept taking her back to her father. "How was he when you saw him?"

He knew she was not going to let it go until she got some answers. "Since I did not know him previous to our conversation, I would be hard-pressed to judge how he was."

"Did he look well to you?"

He had sworn to himself that he would never be untruthful with her. "I thought he looked frail."

She lowered her head for a moment while she composed herself. "He was well the last time I saw him. Of course, that was three years ago."

"I know that. He told me."

It was too painful to talk of her father, so she switched the subject. "I suppose you have many servants?"

Wade was more than happy to talk about something else. "Actually, no. I do not like a lot of people around the house. There is Mary—I told you about her. She is the cook and housekeeper. She has two ladies who help her with the cleaning, but they go home at night. There is Louis, of course, and two gardeners. Of those three men, only Louis lives on the grounds. His place is above the carriage house."

"And what about Jonathan?"

"So," he said, crossing his legs and resting his hand on his boot, "Dolly told you about him, too."

"Yes, she did. Will I be seeing him?"

"Not at this time. He is away at school."

She could tell from his irritated tone that he did not want to talk about the boy. But Caroline was at her best when she was gleaning information. Her father had always said the troops could have used her during the war to ferret out information from the enemy. "He goes to school in the city?"

"Apparently, Dolly did not tell you everything," he remarked stiffly. "Jonathan attends a school in Baton Rouge."

At the present, they were passing out of the city and down a country lane. In the distance Caroline could hear the water of the Mississippi River as it lazily wound its way toward the Gulf of Mexico. The road curved, and they traveled beside the river. She craned her neck to get a better look. To her left, along the river road, she saw several large estates with very fine houses.

Louis turned between two huge wrought-iron gates and maneuvered the horses up a curved driveway. The house was a two-story red brick with a wide veranda sweeping across the front of the house, and a gallery that curved along the second story.

"Your home is very beautiful," she said, more puzzled than ever as to why he would revert to being a bounty hunter if he lived so well. He was definitely a man of prominence. "Just how much money did Brace offer you to find me?" she asked.

He stared down at her, his jaw muscle tightening, refusing to answer her question. "I have never thought of this as a home, but merely a place to live."

She thought it was a strange statement for him to make, and she wondered if his cryptic words had a deeper meaning. He was too complex for her to understand, and she certainly was too weary to verbally battle with him at the moment.

He disembarked and held his hand out to her. "Welcome to Renault Manor."

She looked at him and frowned. "Who are you? Are you the man who unfeelingly took me captive, or . . ." She indicated the house and grounds. "Why did you come after me?"

"Perhaps I will tell you some day."

As he led her up the walk and onto the porch, a cool breeze stirred the huge cypress tree in the front yard.

"This would be such a lovely place to raise a family," she told him, turning and looking at the Mississippi River curving around the bend.

Wade's clasp on her hand tightened as he momentarily envisioned children with her sky-blue eyes running and playing on the lawn. He opened the front door and ushered her inside. "Are you feeling all right?"

She gave him a tired smile. "I am fine. I wish you wouldn't worry about me." That thought suddenly took her by surprise—he really did worry about her. She realized that he was probably feeling guilty for the ordeal he had put her through. It suited her just fine to let him bear the guilt.

They entered a room that was so large it took up the whole front of the house. It was light and airy, filled with sunlight from the windows on both sides of the room. There were three lemon-yellow couches and chairs and several end tables set about the room. The wooden floor gleamed as only aged oak can when highly polished. There was a door to the right and an ornate staircase leading to the second floor.

She heard the ticking of a huge grandfather clock that seemed to preside majestically over the room. She glanced up at Wade and found him watching her as if waiting for her assessment. "It is very lovely," she said, turning around as she tried to get the complete picture of the room. "Lovely indeed."

His attention was drawn to the doorway, and a genuine smile curved his mouth. "Mary." He stretched out his hand to a woman who wore her silver-white hair in a tight bun. Her faded blue eyes danced with delight, and she rushed forward to grab him in a hug. It was the first time Caroline had seen him display genuine affection for anyone.

"Well, if it isn't himself, deciding to grace us with his presence once more," Mary said in a soft Irish brogue. "We'll not be letting you go so soon again."

"Home at last, Mary."

She turned, smiling at Caroline, and pulled her hand away from Wade, patting her hair into place and straightening her snowy-white apron. "And this would be Mrs. Duncan. We have been expecting you," she said, not giving Wade time to introduce them.

"I have heard much about you," Caroline said.

The housekeeper's gaze was guarded, and it seemed to Caroline that she was carefully measuring her. "If himself told you about me, you should take only half of what he said as truth."

Wade smiled down at Caroline. "I want you to meet the woman who runs my life. She boxed my ears when I was a lad, and I believe she would do the same today if she decided I needed it."

"Now, don't be taking anything he says to heart, and don't let him be fooling you, ma'am. He has had me right where he wanted me since the day I first laid eyes on him. I never could discipline him, and he needed it more than most." She smiled at him. "You know you did."

He was clearly amused. "Perhaps I still do."

Caroline could see that the housekeeper adored Wade. It was strange to see him in a domestic setting. This was still another side of him that didn't fit. She wondered what other surprises she would discover about him.

He immediately assumed the role of master of the house. "Mary, will you see Caroline to her room? The doctor says she needs plenty of rest."

"Everything is ready as you instructed in your telegram. I'll have Louis fetch the doctor as soon as I get Mrs. Duncan settled in." She waited for Caroline to precede her to the stairs.

But Caroline turned to Wade. He must have communicated with the housekeeper at the last stop the train made. Of course, he would never leave any detail to chance. "I'm feeling so much better, thank you. I don't really need a doctor."

"Do not distress yourself," Wade told her, his mind already moving to other matters. "The doctor may suggest nothing more than a proper diet to build back your strength."

A frown creased Caroline's brow. "I want to get well as soon as possible. I have to go home."

"Go with Mary so she can get you settled."

He watched her climb the stairs, seeing her strength wane when she was halfway to the top. He wanted to rush forward and carry her the rest of the way, but Mary sensed that Caroline needed assistance and took her arm, helping her to the landing.

The bedroom Caroline entered was so large it overlooked both the front and the back of the house. It served as a sitting room as well as a bedroom. The decor was striking, and the colors included every shade of blue she could think of. The Aubusson rug was a soft blue. The bed hangings and matching spread were in dark blue with cream-colored edging. A blue velvet couch and two chairs made a charming sitting area. Just off the bedroom was a large dressing room.

Mary pulled the drapes open, allowing sunshine to flood the room. "I have opened the windows on both sides so you will have a cool cross breeze. I hope you will be comfortable here, Mrs. Duncan."

She smiled at the housekeeper. "How could I not? This is a lovely room."

Mary moved to the double doors and threw them open wide. "Although it is a large room, I think you will find it cozy. I believe you will find the balcony equally delightful. What is unusual about this room is that it has two galleries—one looking north and the other south. The north gallery has stairs that lead down to the garden."

Caroline walked out on the balcony and caught her breath. She gazed upon a sweeping lawn, then spotted a tempting path that led past a tinkling fountain. To her left was a colorful garden with flowers of so many varieties she could not have put names to all of them. Oak, hickory, and dogwood trees vied for space in the huge area. She could only imagine how beautiful the grounds would be in spring when the dogwoods were in bloom. She decided that at the first chance she got, she would explore every corner of the garden.

She put her hand on a cane-bottom rocking chair, resisting the urge to sit in it and rock. She was startled when she noticed that another door also led to the gallery.

"Mary, whose room is that?"

"It belongs to himself, but have no worry about that. He had me move his belongings to a bedroom at the other end of the hallway so you would feel more comfortable here."

"I did not want to put him out of his room."

"He would have it no other way. He thought you might be uncomfortable if he were so nearby. He was always one to observe proprieties."

Caroline knew that about Wade if she didn't know anything else. Sometimes she thought he was too much of a gentlemen. "And no one will ever gainsay him," Caroline observed.

"No one I know of would ever dare," the little Irish woman replied with honesty.

Caroline felt a sudden chill as she remembered another house with two bedrooms leading to a gallery. Only in this house there was no fear. Wade would be nearby if she felt threatened.

She had grown accustomed to him, and she had begun to depend on him more than she should.

The housekeeper gave her a cheery smile and turned to leave. "The doctor should arrive within the hour."

Caroline dropped into the rocking chair and leaned her head back as she rocked. What was going to happen to her now?

Chapter Seventeen

Wade was waiting for Mary when she came downstairs. "Is she comfortable?" he asked anxiously.

"I believe so." It was a warm afternoon, and Mary fanned herself with her apron. She had watched Wade grow from a boy into a man under this roof with a father who demanded too much from him. She had hurt for Wade the day he had walked out of the house—the day Anton made it impossible for him to stay. She remembered when he had returned to watch his father die. And now she saw something in Wade that she had never seen before, not even on his worst days when Anton was so ill: She saw hopelessness.

She had never minced words with him and she didn't now. "How did you come to bring this young woman home with you?"

"It is a very long story." He propped his booted foot on the marble slab that jutted out from the fireplace. "And I fear the telling of it would not reflect well on me."

She eyed him carefully. "Then keep it to yourself, and I'll be thinking my own thoughts."

"What do you make of Caroline?" he asked, watching her closely because he always valued her opinion, and her impressions of people were usually correct.

"She seems to me to be a charming young woman. She's frail. It's easy to see she's been ill. But I knew about her illness because of your telegram."

He waved that aside. "What do you think about her as a person, Mary?"

"I don't know her well enough to judge." She was put out with him. He had been acting strangely since he'd received that package in the mail and had left directly for South Carolina. "If your reaction to her is any indication, I would be guessing that she will be mistress of this house before too long."

He raised himself away from the fireplace and straightened his coat. "Your leap from her being charming to my marrying her is most imaginative. Why do women always do that?"

Mary went right to the point. "I suppose it all depends on how charming *you* think she is?" She lifted her head and looked into his eyes. "What do you think of her?"

"I can tell you that she has the devil's own temper. When she gets a notion in her head, she can be fierce. I have never seen a woman like her before."

"She'll need to have a temper if she remains around you for very long. If she's going to continue handling you, she will need something more than a temper."

"Who said she was handling me?"

"I have known you most of your life. I see that

your concern for Mrs. Duncan goes well beyond mere politeness."

He rubbed his neck. "Sometimes, Mary, you see things that are not there."

The housekeeper let out her breath and broached the subject she had been dreading. "Jonathan is home."

He walked to the window and stared into the garden. "Dammit, Mary, you should have had Louis take him back to school. How did he get here this time?"

"By stage, the lad told me. Saved his money until he had the fare. We're lucky he came home and didn't run off somewhere like you did when you went to Texas."

"I was twenty when I left home. He's only eight. Anything could have happened to him."

"God preserves the fools of this world, and the little child," she said quoting Irish lore.

"He is going to need someone to protect him from me, this time. I have been very patient until now, but no longer."

Mary knew Wade had never raised a hand to the lad and he never would. "He knows you're home. Do you want me to bring him down?"

"I will not tolerate his disobedience. You know my views on his having a good education."

"He's so young, Wade. Did you ever think that he might rather be home with you than off in some strict school? He likes to be where you are, and he wants to grow up to be just like you."

"I will talk to him later. I'm too angry right now. But make no mistake about it, he will go back to the academy just like before."

She knew it would do no good to argue with him when his mind was set on something. "You have a telegram from Nate. I put it in on your desk."

He started for the study and said over his shoulder. "I want to see the doctor as soon as he has finished examining Caroline."

The housekeeper shook her head on her way to the kitchen. Himself was on a rampage, and Mary speculated that the woman in the master suite had a lot to do with it. She smiled at the thought of the firm grip that lovely young woman had on Wade's heart. She wondered if Mrs. Duncan was even aware of it. It was about time a woman got under Wade's skin. It was long past time for him to settle down and have a family.

Wade paused before entering the study, as he always did. He still had the feeling that the room belonged to Anton. He had even left most things the way they were when Anton was alive. A strange homecoming this had turned out to be, he thought, picking up the telegram and opening it. He scanned the page and slumped down in a chair. He reread it to make sure there was no mistake:

Richmond shot. Died two days later. Assailant unknown.

Time passed, and still Wade did not move. His thoughts were troubled, his mind on the young woman who had already lost so much and now must be told that she had lost her father. How would he ever be able to tell her that her father had been murdered?

He tried to think who might have something to

gain by killing her father. He just didn't know the family well enough to guess. He tapped the telegram against his hand. Caroline had once called him a fool, and that was what he was where she was concerned. If the truth were known, he was probably responsible for her father's death. It all fell into place in his mind—the killer was Brace Duncan.

And Brace Duncan had also killed Caroline's husband.

Wade could almost see how the man's mind worked. Brace had found out that Wade had questioned the father and had feared what he might have learned from Mr. Richmond.

Wade's eyelids came down over his narrowed eyes. Brace Duncan was the man he would have to go after, because Caroline would be his next victim. He had to guard her, to keep her safe at all times. He thought of the two Webber brothers who worked for him at the docks—they were men he trusted to guard the house. Of course, he could not let Caroline know what he was doing. If he did, she would give him trouble.

He stood up when the heavy knock fell on the door. "Come in."

Dr. Davis was heavyset with a boisterous laugh, and a voice to match. His gray hair was thinning now, and his shoulders were a bit stooped. Wade had known him since first coming to live in this house as a child.

"I'll take a drink of brandy if you're offering one."

"Of course."

Dr. Davis lowered his bulk onto a leather chair near the window. Wade moved to the sideboard and poured amber liquid into a snifter and handed it to him.

"How is Mrs. Duncan?" Wade asked.

"I'd say that young woman has been through a lot. A few of Mary's good meals would be of benefit to her. Her lungs are clear, no trouble there."

Wade leaned against his desk. "How strong is she?"

"I practice on instinct and have for years, and I'd say that Mrs. Duncan is troubled about something that has nothing to do with her health. It's more what she didn't say that caught my attention." He narrowed his bushy eyebrows. "Maybe you know what her trouble is, Wade."

"*Oui.* Some of it."

"If you know what it is, then maybe you can help her."

Wade glanced down at the telegram, not realizing he had crumpled it in his fist. "I just got word that her father has been murdered. Should I tell her or keep the news from her until she is stronger?"

The doctor's eyes widened before he took a drink. He nodded his head. "I don't think I'd tell her just yet. Perhaps you should wait a week or so." He took a last swig of brandy, placed the snifter on the side table, and rose. "Maybe someday you can tell me her story." He walked to the door. "Meantime, send Louis for me if you need me."

It was only moments after Dr. Davis's footsteps faded down the hallway that Wade heard quick steps coming toward the study. Jonathan poked his head around the door.

"Mary said I was to come see you."

The boy's blue eyes sparkled with defiance as Wade motioned him forward. His sun-yellow hair hung in his face, and he shoved it aside, his lower lip trembling. Jonathan was small for his age, and the headmaster of the school had said he took a lot of bullying from the other boys. Wade suspected that was the reason he had run away.

"Sit down."

The boy slumped into a chair, watching Wade pace back and forth before him. "You have broken the rules again. This time I am not sure I can convince Mr. Davenport to take you back again."

He rubbed his eyes. "I don't want to go back."

"Jonathan, I have planned for your future, and I will not stand for disobedience from you. This term is almost over, so I may be able to convince Mr. Davenport to let you start fresh when the new term begins in a little over a month."

"I want to stay with you. Why can't I go to school in New Orleans like other boys?" The child turned his face into the leather sofa to hide his tears. "You don't want me here—that's why you always send me away."

"That is not true." Wade took a deep breath. "I will always want what is best for you. I thought you knew that."

The boy jumped to his feet, standing stiffly before the man he loved like a father. "I don't know that! I just think you don't want me here!"

Wade was losing his patience. "You ran away from the academy because the boys tease you. There will always be someone who will want to tear you down. You must look an adversary in the eye and meet him on your terms, not his." He suddenly became quiet, his mind racing backward in time to when a similar scene had played out in this very room. Only before, he had been the child and Anton had said the words he'd just uttered. Anton had been angry with him for not wanting to work at the warehouse. That day was branded in his mind forever.

"I don't know what you're trying to tell me," the boy said, his head sliding downward.

Wade's tone was a little kinder as he remembered feeling the same anger Jonathan must be feeling. "Go to your room and reflect on what I have said, and I am sure the meaning will become clear. We will speak more about this tomorrow."

The boy stomped out of the room and up the stairs.

Wade let out his breath and opened the double doors that led to the garden. He stared into the distance, wondering how many more lives he could destroy with his good intentions.

There was only one sure way he could protect Caroline. He had to see that she stayed with him. He would eventually have to convince her that his plan was the best way to defeat Brace Duncan. She would fight him on this—but it was a fight he must not allow her to win.

Caroline could not resist going down the gallery stairs and walking out into the beautiful garden. She strolled down a shady lane that took her past a sweet-smelling honeysuckle vine clinging to a brick well house. She stopped short of the stables and took another lane that led her to a garden with brilliant red and pink roses. The smell was so sweet she dropped down onto a marble bench, overwhelmed by a bout of homesickness.

She hardly ever thought of her mother, because she had been only a small child when she died. But she always associated her mother with the scent of roses. Her mother's skin and hair had always smelled of the sachet she had made from the petals of her own garden.

Caroline leaned back against the hard bench and allowed memories to sweep through her mind and take her back home to a time of childhood when she had not known a care in the world. She missed her father. But she still didn't dare write to him.

Her musing was interrupted when a young boy bound out from behind the hedges and looked at her suspiciously.

"Who are you?" he asked.

Her brow knitted in puzzlement until she realized who the boy must be. He was smaller than she had expected, and his eyes were so blue it was almost startling. His hair was blond, and his features were fine. "You are Jonathan, aren't you?"

He was guarded as he stepped closer to her. "How did you know?"

"Dolly told me."

His face broke into a grin, showing a missing tooth. "I like Miss Dolly. Is she here with you?"

"No, she isn't. But I like her, too." He was wearing blue trousers with a plain white shirt, and she suspected it might be his school uniform. "I was told that you were away at school."

He looked behind him as if he expected someone to overhear. "I'm supposed to be, but I ran away."

"Oh?"

"I don't like school. I want to stay with Wade, but he won't let me. Don't you think that's mean?"

"Well, I don't really know." In her opinion, the boy was very young to be sent away from home. "I suppose your father has his reasons for wanting you to be in school."

"Wade isn't my father. I don't have one."

She could see the tears gathering in his eyes, and it made her sad. "Would you like to sit by me?"

"Uh-huh," he said, edging closer to her.

She moved her skirt so he would have room. "Tell me about the things you like to do." she said, trying to distract him.

He wiped his eyes on the back of his hand, and her instinct was to put her arm around him and give him comfort. But she knew that would be the wrong thing to do. He was like a small wounded bird, ready to take flight if anyone got too close to him.

"I like to read. And I like to draw, but I'm not very good at either."

"You are young to be a reader. You must be very smart if you can read at all."

"Can you?"

"Yes. I can."

"I sometimes go into Wade's study and look at all the books. I don't touch them, though. Mary said Wade might not like it if I did that."

"Perhaps we could ask him if we might look for a book you would like."

He sat down and scooted closer to her. "Would you like to read me a book? I don't know the real big words, so I don't always understand what I'm reading."

Her heart melted at the earnestness in his eyes. "Jonathan, I would be happy to read to you."

Chapter Eighteen

Caroline had been living under Wade's roof for three weeks, although in that time she had not seen much of him. He was usually working at one of his warehouses or going up the river on one of his barges. She had met him once on the stairs, and he had politely inquired about her health, and once in the garden when he was giving a workman instructions. He had given her permission to use his library to find Jonathan a book. She had chosen James Fenimore Cooper's *The Last of the Mohicans*, thinking Jonathan would like the adventure—she could always skip over the gory parts and he would never know.

Sometimes Caroline took her meals in her room, and at other times she would eat with Jonathan. She was growing stronger and more restless with each passing day. It was time for her and Wade to have a serious talk about her leaving.

As for Jonathan, he was simply bubbling with praise for his newfound friend, Caroline. The Webber brothers, Frank and Elliot, whom Wade had posted around the house as guards, reported to him that Mrs. Duncan walked in the garden every day and that she spent most of her time there with Jonathan.

This morning, Wade was having breakfast with the boy, who had not stopped talking since he came to the table.

"Wade, don't you think Caroline is as pretty as my mommy was?"

"I did not know your mother, so I cannot say."

"And you didn't know my papa, either?"

"I have told you before, I never knew either of them, Jonathan. Do you not remember when I found you and brought you here?"

Jonathan dug his fork into a slice of ham and held it up for inspection before he took a bite. "I remember being cold and hungry until you brought me here. I don't know much else." He paused and frowned. "I remember always getting lost in this house when I first came here. I don't do that anymore."

"You were very young then, so you cannot be expected to remember much. I did make inquiries right after I brought you here, trying to find your parents, but no one knew who you were. If you would like me to, I will begin a new search for your mother and father."

Jonathan shook his head, his eyes big and round. "No, don't do that. If you found them, they might want to take me away from you. I want to stay here with you and Mary." His eyes grew even rounder. "Don't let anyone take me away."

"We will let the matter of your parents rest for now. In the future, you may change your mind and we can start a search then." His thoughts turned inward, to the emptiness of his own past, when he had wondered who had given birth to him, and if his mother and father ever thought of him or wondered where he was. "Some people never know their parents, Jonathan. And that is all right."

"I would like it if you were my father and Caroline was my mommy. Why can't it be like that?"

"Do not talk with your mouth full," Wade rebuked the boy. "I am not going to think about what they let you get by with at that academy."

"I'm not ever going back there! If you take me back there, I'll just run away again. They don't like me there, and I don't like them, either."

Wade threw his napkin down on the table and stood. "You will do as you are told. How can a child know what is best?"

He walked out of the dining room, leaving Jonathan to stare after him. The boy took another bite of ham and shoved his plate away. He didn't like it when Wade was mad at him. When he grew up, he wanted be just like him. Why couldn't Wade see that and just let him stay home?

Caroline was hesitant to approach Wade in his study. It appeared to her that he had been avoiding her since he had brought her to his house, but she needed to talk to him, and today was as good as any day. She rapped lightly on the door, nervously smoothing her hair into place.

"Come in."

She slowly, almost hesitantly, opened the door and went inside. When Wade saw her, he came around the desk, took her hand, and carefully seated her on the leather couch.

"I understand you have all but recovered your strength. I can see there is more color in your cheeks."

She wondered if the color he saw had anything to do with the flush she felt working its way up her face. He wore black trousers and knee-length boots. The sleeves of his blue shirt were rolled up to his elbows in a casual manner. At the moment he seemed more like a stranger than the man who had nursed her back to health in the railroad car.

"I'm very well, and that is the real reason I want to speak to you. Are you busy at the moment?"

He leaned against his desk and folded his arms, giving her his full attention. "Not at all. Actually, I have been expecting you to ask for me."

She pressed an imaginary wrinkle out of her gown with the palm of her hand. "I don't know quite how to think of my position in your house."

His brow knitted. "What do you mean?"

"When you first took me, I was your prisoner and in handcuffs. Here, I am treated like an honored guest. It is a bit confusing."

He liked the way the sunlight made of her hair a halo. She was beginning to put on some of the weight she'd lost when she was ill. It made his chest tight to think of ever putting handcuffs on her delicate wrists. "Do not upset yourself—I no longer consider you my prisoner. And as for your position here, consider yourself a welcome guest."

Her gaze sought his. "Then I am free to leave anytime I want to?"

"*Non!*" His answer came hard and swift, and when he saw the uncertainty in her eyes, he softened his tone. "What I meant to say is that you are not well enough to travel at this time."

"But I am. I must get to Charleston as soon as possible—there is no time to waste. I need to see my father so I can ease his mind about my being safe. When I tell him everything, which I should have done rather than running away, he will know how to help me fight Brace."

Now was his chance to tell her about her father's death. "Your father . . ." His courage failed him, and he stared just above her head, unwilling to look into her eyes. He could not pile more grief on her delicate shoulders—she already bore enough. "Your father would not want you to travel until you are completely healed. Let us seek the doctor's advice in that matter."

She nervously gripped and ungripped her hands until she realized what she was doing; then she laced her fingers tightly together. Wade had started out being her enemy, but she now considered him one of the finest men she had ever known. "Am I right in thinking you no longer believe that I killed my husband?"

"I know with certainty that you are innocent of the crime. What I need to find out from you is what happened the day he died. You can trust me with the truth. I am willing to help you all I can."

She stared down at her hands as relief washed over her in waves. "It's not a matter of trusting you, Wade. What happened that day is a family matter, and it has nothing to do with you." She turned her gaze on him and said with conviction, "I must go home and see that justice is done for Michael's sake. I wish now that

I had stayed and fought for him and his good name." She shook her head and lowered it. "It was my first duty as his wife, and I failed him."

Wade pushed himself away from the desk and went to stand at the French doors with his back to her. "You will need my help more than you know before this is all over. Whether you like it or not, your troubles have become mine. I invited myself into your life, and I cannot seem to find my way out until you are free of Brace Duncan."

As he stood there, his head slightly bowed, he seemed such a solitary figure to Caroline. He had everything a man could want in wealth and possessions, and yet she knew in her heart that he was dying inside. "If you would just advance me passage money, I will take care of Brace myself. This is not your fight. I free you of any obligations you feel on my behalf."

His lips twisted sardonically. "I will never be free of you."

He sounded dispassionate as he turned back to her, but she saw anguish in his eyes before he glanced away from her. She wondered why he should involve himself in her troubles. Sudden panic and devastation swept over her. He was not going to let her leave. "You were never my prisoner, Wade—I was yours."

He stepped closer to her. "There are many different forms of prison—some are thrust upon a person, others we wall into ourselves."

He sat down beside her, not touching her, but near enough that she could see his nostrils flare. She did not know what had brought on the intensity that radiated from him. And she didn't know what to say. "If you would lend me the money I need to get home, I will send it right back to you."

"Where would you get money?"

"I told you that the money was hidden away so Brace would never find it—the morning I married Michael, I watched him hide it beneath loose bricks in the family crypt."

"I see." And he did. That explained why she had been forced to become a seamstress to make a living. "I don't want your husband's gold, but I am going to help you, Caroline." He rolled down his sleeves and fastened the cuffs. "Give me the details of your husband's death, beginning with when you decided to marry him and ending with the day he died."

Her lips trembled. "I don't like to think about that day. It was so awful, you can't even imagine."

"*Non.* I do not suppose I can." His hand suddenly covered hers, and she pulled away.

"Why would you want to help me?"

Now that he was closer to her, he saw the circles under her eyes that were so dark they almost looked like bruises. "Because I owe it to you."

"You owe me nothing but my freedom."

"I can see you are becoming upset. If you would rather, we can talk about this another day. But I will want you to tell me all about Michael's death as soon as you are able."

She tried to gather her thoughts, but he was so close to her she could not think clearly. "I would like to tell you what happened to Michael, but I wouldn't know where to start."

"Start at the beginning," he suggested.

"As I have explained to you before, I had known

Michael for most of my life—long before his father married Brace's mother. He was my best friend. I will always feel his loss within my heart."

The next question was difficult for him to ask, because he wasn't sure he wanted to know the truth. "And you loved Michael for all the years you knew him?"

"Yes." She stood up and started pacing. "He needed me. He was the brother I never had. I always . . ." She paused, thinking about what she had just said, then quickly corrected herself. "Not like a brother at all, but the man I wanted to marry."

"You wanted to be his candle in the darkness," Wade said, watching her face closely.

"Yes . . . no." She looked at him with pleading eyes. "You have to understand, Michael didn't have anyone but me. I couldn't turn my back on him as so many others had."

"I do not understand."

"I'm not sure anyone would. I can't tell you how often Michael stood between me and hurt. He was always there for me—but in the end, I let him down. You can't know what that feels like. I always wonder if I could have done anything differently to save his life."

She was becoming frantic in her pacing, and two different doctors had warned him to keep her calm. As much as he wanted to know the truth, now was not the time to press her further about her past. "Perhaps you would consider being the candle in my darkness."

"I . . . what?"

He stood and walked to her but did not touch her. "It is very simple. I am asking you to marry me."

Chapter Nineteen

She was astounded, speechless, and thought she must have misunderstood. For once, she could not even find her voice, so she merely stared at him as if he had lost all reason.

"I know how you feel about me," he said, taking her arm and turning her to face him. "If you will just hear me out before you say anything, I will attempt to explain my reasons for asking you to be my wife."

Still, she said nothing. He was the kind of man that girlhood fantasies were woven from. She defied any woman who crossed Wade Renault's path to not fall a little in love with him. She wasn't sure what she felt for him, but her feelings were strong and real, and they would not soon go away. The thought of leaving him, as she must, was almost more than she could bear.

"If you were my wife, you would have nothing to fear from Brace Duncan—I would have the right to protect you. Together we would bring him down and make him pay for what he did to his stepbrother."

Confusion rattled through her brain, and she frowned. "I . . . I don't understand."

"As you have probably already guessed, Nate is in Charleston trying to see what he can uncover about Brace. He has already found out some things, but we need to know more to bring him to justice."

Her thoughts were still in chaos. "You believed in my innocence as far back as when we were in San Antonio?"

"That was when I really started to question Brace's reasons for wanting you back. I came to the conclusion that you were guiltless and he was the killer."

"If that's the truth, why didn't you allow me to return to San Sebastian? Why did you bring me here with you?"

Instead of looking at her, he watched a breeze stir the maroon drapery. "It is difficult to explain, even to myself. I have done you a great wrong, and I want a chance to make amends."

In that moment she knew exactly why he had asked her to marry him—it was to appease his guilt. "So you think you can make it up to me by dragging me into a loveless marriage?"

He glanced down at her. "Many marriages have started out with less. I believe we would deal well together."

"Do you?"

"Otherwise I would not have asked you to become my wife."

Her chest rose and fell with the anger that now

drove her. "I am not flattered by such an outrageous marriage proposal. Nor am I inclined to accept it. I don't need your pity." She raised her head and stiffened her back. "I have men who would marry me for far different reasons."

Anger shot through him. "Your Captain Dunning being one, I suppose?"

"Yes, if you must know."

"Take me instead." He trailed his hand down her arm. "And I assure you I am not driven by pity. No one would feel pity for a woman as beautiful as you are." He raised his brow. "And with so many prospects."

"And those reasons are supposed to convince me to throw myself into your marriage bed?"

A smile tugged at his mouth. "I do find it an intriguing idea."

"I clearly see your reason for asking me to be your wife—you feel guilty about how you treated me." She met his gaze straight on. "I intend never to marry again."

"Just think about it."

"There is nothing to think about. I do not want to be the wife of anyone who would marry me out of a misguided sense of duty."

"Is that not what you did with Michael?"

He had hit too close to home, and he knew it. "The reason I married Michael is no business of yours."

He inhaled deeply. "What would you have me admit that would sway you?"

"Nothing. Everything has been said between us. I am going home to my father as soon as possible. If you will not lend me the money to get there, I have friends who will."

He watched her turn away with tears swimming in her eyes. He had handled it all wrong, but then, he had never asked a woman to marry him before. His eyes narrowed. Until now he had been a perfect gentleman, although it had been difficult at times to keep from touching her. It was time for him to stir her emotions, to awaken her passion, and make her want him as much as he wanted her.

Was it fair? *Non*, but he would do it all the same. He wanted her for now, tomorrow, and for the rest of their lives.

It was two days later when Caroline took a turn in the garden. It was that magical time of day when night had not yet fully descended and the sun had not relinquished its brightness to the night. Unhappiness tugged at her mind, and she kept remembering Wade asking her to marry him. She stopped near a crimson rose bush that was in full bloom and breathed in the sweet aroma, wondering if she would have said yes if Wade had professed an undying love for her—which, of course, was impossible, since he did not love her at all.

A slight breeze stirred the leaves of the lilac bush, wafting its delicate scent through the air. She had to impress on him the importance of her going back to Charleston. Every day she delayed would give Brace more reason to send someone after her. He must have guessed by now that Wade had either not found her, or was unwilling to turn her over to him.

Just behind Caroline, Wade watched her disappear down the path, knowing she was not aware of his presence. He had given her time to get used to the idea of becoming his wife; now he was ready to stop treating her like a fragile flower and show her how to respond to him as a man.

She spun around when she heard his bootsteps. "It's a lovely evening for a walk," she said, seeing something in his eyes that troubled her.

"It is. I am told that you come here often."

"I like to be in the open."

He moved closer to her, forcing her to look up to see him. "Then this garden was made for you."

She noticed that his French accent was more pronounced than usual, as it often was when he felt deeply about something. "I hope you are not here to ask me to marry you again."

His placed his hands on either side of her face and bent toward her. "Sweet Caroline, will you break my heart?"

She was dazzled and speechless as he laid his rough cheek against hers. She struck out at him with words. "You do not have a heart, Wade."

He touched his lips to her forehead. "Perhaps you are right." He whispered in her ear, "But I desire you, Caroline, and that can be a far more powerful emotion than love."

She realized that she should step away from him—this was a side of him that was far more dangerous than any of the other parts of his complicated personality. "How can you think that would be a good reason to marry?"

"Shall I show you, *mon amour?*"

She finally broke away from him and moved farther down the path, her heart beating so fast she could hardly speak. "I will not do it."

"Being married to me would not be so bad." He took her hand and pulled her back to him, suddenly feeling that if she rejected him, the rest of his life would mean nothing. "I have wondered how it would feel to kiss you," he whispered, bringing her face closer to him. He ran his thumb over her mouth. "Have you not wanted me to touch you?"

She could do little more than stare into his amber eyes: He was so near, she could see the brown streaks that gave them a catlike appearance. She had the impression that she was melting on the inside. She wanted him to kiss her so badly, she ached with need.

"Have you thought about me in that way, Caroline?"

"I have thought about it," she answered, being honest with him. "You are most certainly a man who knows how to get what he wants from a woman. I'm equally sure that few women could resist you for very long."

He was watching her with an unreadable expression. "What about you—can you resist me?"

All she had to do was remind herself how it felt when he had clamped those handcuffs on her and it made her answer easier to deliver. "I find that I can," she said, pushing against his chest and turning her face away from him.

He caught her hand, stalling her. "You are not still afraid of me, are you?"

"I was at first, but not now."

He stared at her lips, and watched as she shivered. He could so easily make her agree to anything he wanted—she was vulnerable, and she wanted him. "I have never asked another woman to marry me. I want only you."

"You of all people should know that my life is in a tangle, and no one can untangle it but me." She extracted her hand and stepped away from him once more. "The time for running away is over. One way or another, I'm going home to face my past. I would like to leave before the end of the week."

He knew what she did not. With her father dead, she had no ally waiting for her in Charleston; no one would stand with her against Brace. He would do anything he must to keep her from going back to the danger that awaited her there. Slowly he drew her to him. "You need me. You know you do."

Before she could protest, he brushed his mouth against hers, and a flickering flame fanned to life within her.

"Sweet Caroline, you have been ripping me apart inside. Before now, I was honor bound to keep my distance. But I am now free to tell you what I want, what I desire most in the world."

She gave a little sigh and moved her mouth closer to his, seeking the magic of the lips that lingered so near her own. She knew it was the wrong thing to do, but she wanted him to kiss her. Just one kiss and she would walk away from him—or so she thought.

Caroline's surrender was Wade's undoing. His arms slid around her shoulders, and he crushed her breasts against his wide chest. He was not gentle as his mouth ravished hers, molding and shaping it to fit his. He put all his frustrations in the kiss, and then he gentled it when he felt the rise and fall of her rapid breathing.

His lips moved over hers and then to the nape of her neck. "I have been wanting to do this for a long time."

When he raised his head, he stared into her passion-filled eyes. Without guilt he was using all his male prowess to his advantage, and it was working—he could see it in her eyes. "Say you will marry me," he demanded.

"No." Her voice came out in a painful whisper. She was confused and quivering inside, not knowing what she really wanted from him. But the one thing she doggedly held on to was the fact that she had to settle her own problems. She moved away from him, turning her back while she gathered her courage. "I can't marry you."

He went on the attack again. Pulling her against him so her back rested against his chest, he pressed his body tightly along hers, sliding his arms around her waist to bring her even closer. "*Oui*, you can. If a man ever needed a woman, I need you. All you have to do is say yes." He kissed the back of her neck and felt her tremble. "Agree to be my wife."

She dropped her head in bewilderment, wondering how her own body could betray her. She felt the swell of him pressing against her, and it was all she could do not to turn and press herself against him.

"But we don't love each other," she managed to say.

His eyelids lowered, almost covering his eyes. "Why should that matter?"

He twisted her around and touched his mouth to her throat, going further on the attack.

She tried to remember all the reasons she should run from him: But any objection she might have made was stifled when his mouth settled on hers. As fire streaked through her veins, and her heart skipped several beats, she could no longer resist him. For so long she had been alone in a world of danger and uncertainty; then he had come into her life. She could not imagine going on without him.

He raised his head and looked at her with an expression of inquiry. "Will you be my wife?"

Her lips tingled from his kiss, and she could hardly think of anything but laying her head against his chest and letting him hold her. "I am sure there must be some woman in your life whom you would prefer over me."

He laughed softly. "There is no one else."

"But surely—"

He touched his finger to her lips. "Say you will."

She heard her own voice as if from a great distance, as if the words were spoken by someone else. "I will."

He let out a long breath, his grip tightening on her. "I will attempt to make you happy." He smoothed her hair and tilted her chin. "I know you will make me happy. Now all you have to decide is what kind of ceremony you want and the date. I hope you will make it soon."

All of a sudden, he was all business and it was like a dash of cold water in her face. How masterfully he had manipulated her. All he'd had to do was kiss her a few times and she would have agreed to anything he had wanted. Even now she did not move away from the sanctuary of his arms. She didn't know what to say to him, but her head rested against his chest, and she was comforted by the sound of his heartbeat. "In truth, we hardly know each other."

"That can be remedied." He raised her face and gazed deep into her eyes. "I look forward to knowing you very well indeed. I dream of the night you will come to me as my wife."

She gave her head a shake. "I am not very good at being a wife."

He dropped his hand away from her shoulder—he had made her feel too much by taking advantage of her. He could have done much more to tear down her defenses completely, but guilt was already lying heavily on his shoulders for the way he had maneuvered her. He wanted her to come to him because she wanted to, and not because he had enticed her into it. But she would never have done that.

She was still dazed—it had all happened so fast. "I must write my father and invite him to the wedding. I believe he would want to be here." She took a deep breath. It would take time for a letter to reach her father and then for him to make his way to New Orleans. She would need that time to pull herself together.

Wade stared into the night. He still could not bring himself to inform her that her father was dead, but he would have to, and soon. If he told her, would she have a setback and become ill again? Would it not be better to tell her after they were married, so he could hold her and comfort her in his bed? "Let us keep this between the two of us for now. In good time we will let others know."

In a move that surprised him, she touched his face. "I wonder if I'll ever know who you really are. You do not share your deepest feelings with anyone."

He arched his brow and smiled. "You will know me better than anyone ever has."

"What will you be getting out of such a marriage?"

"A candle in my darkness."

Chapter Twenty

Caroline had slept fretfully.

It was now mid-morning, and she found herself restlessly pacing the bedroom floor, wondering why she had agreed to marry Wade. His powers of persuasion had been strong, and she had been unable to resist him. Under the same set of circumstances, what woman could have? Wade exuded an overwhelming force that knocked down every barrier between him and what he wanted. With him, she had been completely defenseless.

And yet she felt a certain anticipation. She sat down on the edge of the bed, thinking about what it would be like to be Wade's wife. She ran her hand over the blue coverlet, heat rising inside her—she would lie in this bed with him beside her. He had barely touched her, and yet she had been his willing slave. How would she react when he was actually her husband?

After she accepted his proposal, he had become a completely different man, not the tender lover he had been when trying to convince her to marry him. He had stepped back as if assessing her with those golden eyes of his. He had then kissed her softly on the mouth and remarked that he was happy she was going to be his wife. In that moment when she had wanted him to hold her in his arms, it had seemed as though a light had been turned off behind his eyes, and she had felt crushing disappointment.

She rose quickly to her feet.

She had made a terrible mistake.

It wasn't too late to rectify it, because no one else knew she had agreed to marry him.

She would just go to him and confess that she had changed her mind. As she gripped the doorknob, her gaze fell on the book lying on the side table, and she remembered promising Jonathan that she would read to him before lunch. Her meeting with Wade would have to wait. At the moment it was more important that she keep her word to Jonathan. Pushing all troubled thoughts to the back of her mind, she made her way out onto the gallery and down the stairs. With determined steps she walked toward the secluded garden where she had always met the boy.

When she arrived, he was already there, his eyes shining, a huge smile on his face. "I was waiting for you. I can't wait to see what happens in the next chapter."

She couldn't help smiling at the boy's exuberance. "Neither can I." She sat down on the bench with her finger marking the page where they had stopped the day before. "Did I tell you there are two more books about the adventures of Hawkeye? I would imagine that Wade has them all in his library, or if he doesn't, he will probably get them for you."

Jonathan surprised her by throwing himself into her arms, hugging her tightly. "I want you to stay with me and Wade forever. We could be almost like a family if you were with us!"

She hugged him back, thinking she could not love this child more if he was her very own. Jonathan was starving to be loved, and she had so much love to give him. She suddenly had a thought: Why shouldn't Wade adopt Jonathan? The boy needed the security of knowing he belonged to a family.

As his small hand clasped hers, tears formed just behind her eyes. "Do you remember the part where I left off in the story?" she asked, refusing to let him see her cry.

"Uh-huh. I could hardly sleep for wondering if Hawkeye and Chingachgook and Uncos were going to win in the battle."

She opened the book and began to read. Somewhere in the middle of the battle that Hawkeye fought with the Mohawks, Jonathan laid his head on her lap. She smiled down at him and placed one hand on his head.

She did love this little boy so. He was well cared for, and he wanted for nothing as far as money was concerned. The servants spoiled him, especially Mary. It was a very fine thing Wade had done in giving the boy a home, but he needed more. He needed to know he was loved and wanted.

Caroline didn't know how long Wade had been watching them before she became aware of him.

When she glanced at him, catching him unaware, she saw a softness in his eyes that was soon replaced by a look of bored indifference.

"Perhaps if I lay my head in your lap, you will read to me," he said, stepping forward and sitting on the end of the bench.

She glanced down at Jonathan and winked. "Shall we tell him that he's usually busy when we read?"

The boy sat up, looking as if he was considering the possibility. "You are busy most of the time, Wade. We have to read every day or we won't know what happens in the story."

Wade leaned against the back of the bench, his gaze on Caroline. "I am going upriver on one of the barges tomorrow, I thought you might enjoy the trip. We will attempt to make you as comfortable as possible."

Any thought she'd had earlier of telling him she could not marry him had now fled her mind. All she could think about at the moment was spending the rest of her life with him. "I would love to go with you!" She closed the book. "What do you think, Jonathan. Would you like to go up the river?"

"No." He shook his head while jealousy dulled his eyes. "I get seasick. Wade knows that."

"I know about seasickness, and it's not much fun." She smoothed the child's hair in place, much as a mother might have done. "I was once seasick for three whole days."

Jonathan's eyes lost some of their anger. "You were?"

"I was."

"Will you read to me when you get back?"

"Of course."

"You will have to be up early," Wade told her. "We leave the docks before sunup."

"I will be ready," she assured him. She looked into his eyes. "Will we see you at dinner tonight?"

"I am sorry but I have matters to attend to, and I will not be home for dinner."

"Oh," she said, trying not to show her disappointment; they hardly ever dined together. It was a situation she was determined to amend after they were married. "I understand."

"Well, then," Wade said, rising in a fluid motion. "I will see you at six in the morning, Caroline."

She and Jonathan watched him disappear, each lost in thought. "Shall we finish this chapter?" she asked at last.

"Yes, please," he said, but with little enthusiasm.

"What's wrong, Jonathan?"

"He would like me better if I didn't get seasick, and if I didn't let the boys push me around at the academy. He thinks I'm a weakling."

She laid the book aside and put her arm around him, drawing his head onto her shoulder. "I don't think that is true, Jonathan. He gave you a home and keeps you with him. He has to care for you a great deal. Besides, you are only a boy—your courage will grow with the inches you gain."

He glanced up at her with hope in his eyes. "Do you really think so?"

She opened the book. "You will remember that Hawkeye did not have a mother or father when Chingachgook took him for his son. And you know what a brave warrior Hawkeye became."

The boy looked disconcerted. "Could it be like that for me?"

"I'm certain that if you are ever called upon to prove your bravery, you will perform your duty admirably."

"Do you really think so?"

"I do. Now let us finish this chapter," she said, wanting to see the hurt disappear from his eyes.

Caroline stood on the deck, holding on to her straw bonnet to prevent the wind from carrying it away. Wade had explained to her that they were actually traveling on a flatboat instead of a barge because he thought it would be more comfortable for her. The flatboat was like a floating deck with large oars that were being plied by twelve men. There was a sudden whoosh as the sails unfurled to catch the wind and relieve the men at the oars.

She had been half afraid that the Mississippi River would be rough and she might get seasick: But it was calm, with gentle waves splashing against the boat. She stared at the muddy water as it lazily drifted seaward. She felt a sudden burst of happiness. For so long she had lived with uncertainty and fear. Now she was not afraid, and didn't have to look over her shoulder to see if someone was chasing her. And she owed her feeling of well-being to Wade.

He was conferring with the captain of the flatboat, and both their heads were bent over a ledger. When Wade suddenly glanced up at her and smiled, she felt warmth spread through her.

A moment later he came to her. "I thought you might like a diversion while the dockworkers go up the river to load their cargo. I have arranged a surprise for you. How would you like to have a picnic in the swamp?"

She watched the breeze lift his black hair off his forehead, and the sun seemed to be captured in the gold of his eyes. "Is that possible?"

"*Oui*. I can assure you it is." He stared at her lips, remembering how soft they had been beneath his. "If you will recall, I was cheated out of a picnic that day in San Sebastian."

"That is not true." She shook her finger at him, but her smile took the sting out of her words. "As I recall the incident, it was *you* who ruined the picnic for me."

He reached for the ribbons that had worked loose beneath her bonnet and retied them. "Did I? I remember wanting to draw my gun and shoot a certain Captain Dunning."

She thought he might be joking until she saw that unmistakable hardness in his eyes. "Whatever for?"

He ran his knuckle along her jawline. "I'll tell you some day. But for now," he said, smiling, "I am going to launch a small skiff as soon as the captain pulls up to that dock."

A short time later, he was helping her into a flat-bottom skiff. When she was seated, Caroline raised her parasol over her head to protect her fair skin from the sun. Wade set the picnic basket at her feet and took the oars.

The boat drifted away with orders to the captain to pick them up at the dock in three hours' time. Wade applied his oars to the water, and the skiff shot forward. He guided them down a small tributary with surprising speed. A seabird cried out overhead as the river disappeared behind them, and a white-tail deer dashed into a thicket and disappeared from sight.

"It is so beautiful here!" Caroline exclaimed as she watched a catfish leap out of the water and gulp down an unsuspecting dragonfly.

"It is as beautiful as it is hazardous. There are bogs in there that can swallow a whole boat and leave no trace. Then there is quicksand, poisonous snakes, and let us not forget the alligators." He stopped rowing for a moment and allowed the boat to drift as he studied her face. "But those who see the swamp for what it is are the ones who are greatly rewarded."

A fluffy cloud had passed beneath the sun, and Caroline closed her sunshade and laid it in the bottom of the boat. She removed her bonnet and let the cool breeze play across her face. "Well, I love it!"

"I thought . . . I hoped you would."

"This was a wonderful idea you had."

"Maybe I just wanted to get you alone."

"It seemed to me that on our journey to San Antonio, and the one here to New Orleans, we were alone quite a bit." She glanced at a misshapen cypress tree with green moss clinging to the trunk. "And we are not alone." She arched her brow at him. "Let us not forget the alligators."

He found her delightful. She was exactly the kind of woman he wanted. She was certainly the one woman he desired so much it hurt.

Caroline noticed he wore his gun belt, and she was momentarily reminded of his other profession—that side of him troubled her. But her gaze moved upward to his arms. He had rolled up his sleeves, and she watched his muscles ripple when he applied the oars to the water.

"I spent much of my time as a boy in these swamps. Anton once had all his workers out looking for me for two days. When they found me, I could not convince them that I had not been lost." He raised his eyebrows. "You can imagine how Anton curtailed my wandering for a long time after that. A whole year passed before I was allowed to come here again."

She trailed her hand in the water, making it swirl behind them. "Tell me more about the swamp."

"To me, it is a place of undisturbed beauty—man has not yet left his destructive scars upon this land. If you look closely, you will see that there is a constant struggle for survival between the hunter and the prey—it is the way of life everywhere, but nowhere more noticeable than here."

Her gaze dropped to his gun belt. "Like a bounty hunter and his quarry?" She hadn't meant to say that; the words had just slipped out. She saw his frown and was immediately sorry. But there would always be that part of their lives that stood between them like a wall.

As if he had read her mind, he drew in the oars and reached down to unbuckle the gun belt, allowing it to fall at his feet. "If you ask it of me, I will never pick this gun up again."

"I do ask it of you."

"Then that is the way it will be."

Her breath caught, and she wanted to touch his face, to spread her fingers through his dark hair. She wanted to feel his arms around her and have him hold her close. But she was still shy with him and dropped her gaze to the water.

"Now," he said, taking up the oars as if nothing important had just passed between them. "Around the next bend is my favorite place."

"You come here often?"

"Not in a long time." He paused for a moment. "I have never brought anyone here before. You are the first."

Her heart was drumming in her ears. He made her feel so many emotions, she could hardly separate them. She would have been satisfied to lie in his arms and just listen to the sound of his wonderful voice. She tried to concentrate on the scenery, but it was difficult with him staring at her so intently.

The boat caught a hidden current, and they rounded the bend in a rush. She gasped as she saw huge oaks with branches draped in veils of Spanish moss. Cypress trees stood like sentinels guarding this secret place against the unworthy. A heron circled above the secluded bayou that was home to a throng of creatures. She saw turtles sunning themselves on a fallen log, and several frogs raised their heads, looking for any unsuspecting insect that might come their way.

"This is wonderful!" she cried, joy spreading through her heart like slow molasses. "It is like nothing I could ever have imagined."

His voice was gruff. "I am pleased, Caroline."

No one had ever spoken her name the way he did: With his French accent it came out like a song. She watched him guide the boat toward a small, grassy island, then stand to offer her his hand. When they were ashore, he dragged the boat onto the grass so it wouldn't drift away. Then he reached inside and pulled out the picnic basket.

Caroline listened to the melodic sounds of swamp creatures. There were strange bird calls and other noises that she could not identify. Wade unfolded a quilt, and she helped him spread it underneath an oak tree.

She unloaded the picnic basket and looked amazed. "It seems Mary took you at your word to put weight on me. We have ham, chicken, corn, cheese, and some of her wonderful biscuits, and her homemade jam. And there are pastries—apple, I hope."

He took the ham sandwich she offered him and leaned back to watch her. "This is my grand scheme to fatten you up. If I must, we will have a picnic a day to put weight on you."

She nibbled on a slice of cheese. "You want me fat?"

"I want you healthy."

"I am." She suddenly needed him to understand something about her. "I have always been healthy and have rarely been sick a day. I don't know why I was so ill when we left San Sebastian."

She had his complete attention. "So you were sick as far back as that?"

"I don't think so. I was more terrified of you than sick."

Now he was watching her closely, and it was difficult for her to swallow.

Wade's guilt was growing by leaps and bounds. He fell into a brooding silence as he watched her wipe her fingers on a napkin. When she started to pack the basket, he caught her hand. "You have hardly eaten anything. That will not do." He picked up a pastry and took a bite. "You get your wish—this one is apple. You must have some."

"It seems to me that you are always trying to coax me into eating more than I want."

He took another bite and then held it out to her. "Come on."

She nibbled on the edge.

"That's not a bite."

She took a big bite and the apple filling oozed onto her lips. When she reached for the napkin, he took her hand and pulled her to him. She gasped when he brought her across his lap and held her to him. Her eyes were wide when he dipped his head, his mouth touching hers. He heard her sigh deeply when his tongue ran over her lips, tasting the apple tart.

"Mmm. You taste sweet like an apple," he whispered, nibbling at her lips and sending her heart rate soaring.

She could not have stopped him if she wanted to, and she didn't want to. He brought her head back and pressed his lips against hers while his hand moved over the bodice of her gown, lightly touching her breasts.

"Oh," she said, looking up at him and not wanting him to stop.

He reached for the blue ribbon that held the front of her gown together, looking at her as if asking for permission.

She did not stop him.

The ribbons slid through his lean fingers, and he gave them a quick yank. Again he looked into her eyes as if asking permission.

Caroline said nothing. She ached for him to touch her, to hold her, to kiss her again. She gasped when he pushed the gown open and slid his hand inside. "I don't think we should—"

"I definitely think we should." He halted her protest with his lips. While he kissed her, he moved her off his lap and stretched out, laying her beside him, molding her to his body. She felt the swell of him and pressed her body tighter against his, fanning the flame of his passion and hers.

When he raised his head, and when she could catch her breath to speak, she asked, "Can it be right to do this?"

"We are to be married," he reminded her in a raspy tone.

"Yes, but—"

He drew her face up to his, gazing deep into her eyes. "At any time you can tell me to stop, and I will."

Before she had time to think, his mouth moved down her throat, and she could not have spoken if her life had depended on it.

He pushed her gown off her shoulder and slowly undid the ribbon holding her petticoat together. "*Mon amour*, I have wanted to touch you like this for longer than you know."

Her eyes closed as he pushed the material aside and gently covered her breast. He ran his thumb around the nipple until it swelled, then he bent his dark head and touched his lips to the tip.

Her hands moved into his hair, and she threw her head back. Her body quivered when he ran his tongue over her nipple. "Wade, I can't . . . I need . . . I don't know," she cried, wanting something more from him. What he was doing to her was causing exquisite pain and waking a need in her that she could not understand.

He stopped and looked into her eyes. "Are you afraid of what I am doing to you?"

She shook her head and stared into his eyes, which were like storm centers. "It's just that . . . I never felt this way before. I don't know what to do."

He studied her face, her passion-bright eyes, her innocence shining through them like a beacon, and he knew—she had never been taken this far before. "Just how long were you a wife, Caroline?"

She pulled back a bit. "Why do you want to know?"

"How long did you share Michael Duncan's bed?"

Tears gathered in her eyes, and her head fell against his shoulder. "Michael was killed on our wedding day." She swallowed several times and shook her head. "I held Michael in my arms as he died. I tried so hard to stop the bleeding, but I could not do anything to save him."

"Dammit!" he swore, slipping her gown back in place and retying her ribbons with trembling fingers. "I am sorry—I had no idea. I believe you need to tell me just what happened that day—but not here—not now. Tonight I want you to tell me everything."

"Michael's death has nothing to do with you, Wade."

"It has everything to do with *us*."

"It is difficult for me to talk about that day. I try to forget about it."

"What a tangled web," he muttered, his manner turning suddenly cold. He helped her to her feet and folded the quilt, picking up the picnic basket. "I believe we should leave now."

Caroline noticed he avoided looking at her. Why

had the sky suddenly turned dark, and why had the joy left her heart?

He packed the skiff and helped her aboard, settling her on the wooden seat. When they reached the rendezvous point, the boat was just coming into view in the distance. She stood stiffly beside him on the dock, hurt and angry.

On the trip back to New Orleans Wade was strangely quiet. He stood as still as a statue, his arms folded across his chest, and he did not look in her direction at all.

The joy that Caroline had felt on the journey up the river had faded like the sun fading in the distance.

Chapter Twenty-one

When they arrived back at the house, Wade was just helping Caroline out of the buggy when a frantic Louis rushed up to them.

"There has been a fire at the indigo warehouse! It was contained before it could spread to the cotton storage, or we never would have been able to put it out. The workers did some looking around and concluded that the fire was deliberate."

With worry furrowing his brow, Wade led Caroline to the door. "You will have to excuse me tonight. We will have our talk tomorrow, if that is agreeable with you."

"Yes. Of course."

Wade was worried, but he gave her a warm smile. "Sleep well and dream of me."

Before she could answer, he had joined Louis in the buggy, and the team of horses raced down the curved driveway and through the gate. A fire, set deliberately, she thought. Who would do such a thing?

She entered the house and removed her bonnet. Mary was waiting for her.

"You have guests, ma'am. I put them in the morning room. Would you like me to bring in refreshments?"

Caroline frowned. She could not think who would visit her, or who would even know she was there. Her first thought was that Brace might have found out where she was staying. "Not at the moment. Did the visitors give you their names?"

The housekeeper saw Caroline's stricken face and wondered if she had done wrong to invite strangers into the house. "They said they were friends of yours. A Mr. and Mrs. Grady."

"Oh!" Caroline took a step forward, then another. By the time she passed through the formal sitting room, her footsteps were hurried. On entering the morning room, she could hardly contain her joy.

"Nelly! Yance! It is you!"

Nelly leaped to her feet and grabbed Caroline in a hug while a smiling Yance put his big arms around them both.

"I can't believe you are here. But," she said somewhat befuddled, "Mary told me that you were Mr. and Mrs. Grady—did I hear her right?"

Nelly clasped Caroline's hands and pulled her to the sofa. "We have been married for three weeks." She grinned up at her new husband, her eyes soft with affection. "Yance said the first thing we'd do after we got married was go in search of you. And he kept his word."

"I am so happy for you both!" Caroline took Yance's hand. "What tactic did you use to get her to say yes?"

"It was easy," he said, grinning. "That gal just found me too charming to resist."

Nelly gave him a mock scowl. "Humph. I find you to be nothing but trouble."

He grinned from ear to ear. "See, she loves me."

"And why wouldn't she?" Caroline stated, happy for both of them. "You are quite a catch, Yance."

"What we really need to know is if you are all right," Nelly said, seeing the dark shadows beneath Caroline's eyes. "And what are you doing here in that man's house?"

She didn't know where to start explaining. "This is going to take some telling. I am not sure how it happened myself. I was ill when Wade brought me here." She saw the frown on Nelly's face. "I am all right now. What I want to know is, how you were able to find me?"

Yance looked at Caroline carefully. "Mr. Gray saw you leave town with the bounty hunter, and we put the pieces together. Then when we went to your house, we read your letter and knew what had happened. Nelly knew you were in trouble, and she wouldn't rest until we could follow you. We followed your trail all the way to San Antonio, but from there, we completely lost it. Then we found out where Mr. Renault lived, and here we are." He looked at her guardedly. "I'm full ready to get you out of here."

"We didn't really expect you to be here," Nelly said, puzzled. She held Caroline's hand as if she were afraid to let go of it. "Are you really all right? Is the bounty hunter holding you here against your will? 'Cause if he is, honey, like Yance said, we'll get you right out of here. Yance will take care of Mr. Renault," she said, nodding up at her husband.

"I don't know where to start," Caroline said. "You are the truest friends I could ever have, rushing to my rescue like this. But I am not here unwillingly, although . . ." She drew in a deep breath. "It's a long story." And she proceeded to tell them about how she had gone to the boardinghouse the day of the picnic, and ended up explaining how she had come to be a guest in Wade Renault's home.

There were tears in Nelly's eyes, and she carelessly brushed them away. "I should have listened to you when you said he was after you. I am so sorry that I didn't believe you."

"You must not blame yourself. I will not have it. Even I was lulled into thinking that Wade had come to town looking for someone else. That is, until the day of the picnic."

"I thought you acted kinda strange that day. Didn't you, Yance?"

"I didn't notice. But I believed you when you said you noticed it."

"There's more." Caroline glanced from Nelly to Yance. "I am going to marry Wade Renault."

Nelly was immediately on guard, and she voiced her suspicions. "He's forcing you to marry him, isn't he?"

"No. I don't want you to think that. You must understand that Wade is a very fine man."

Yance was wondering if this was merely the romantic fantasy of a woman falling in love with the danger surrounding the bounty hunter. But Caroline had always been such a stable, levelheaded woman. "Are you sure this is what you want to do?"

"I do want to be his wife."

Nelly stood up and wandered about the room,

touching the back of a red velvet chair, looking at the marble fireplace that had been hand carved. She had never been in such a fine house. "A bounty hunter must make a lot of money." There was skepticism in her voice. "Yance, why don't you take a walk in that fine garden we saw out back? I want to talk to my friend."

He went directly to the door. "Not married a month, and already I'm thrown out." He smiled mischievously. "Just give me a loud yell when you want me to come back."

After he stepped outside and closed the door behind him, Nelly looked at Caroline. "You've lost weight."

"I did tell you that I was ill for a time."

Nelly sat down on the edge of a chair and concentrated on what she wanted to say, and how she would say it. "You can come away with us right now and know that we will not let him come after you, if that's what you want. Yance has a sister who lives in Sacramento, California, and we can take you directly to her. Wade Renault will never think to look for you there."

Caroline shook her head. "He would find me wherever I went—but I do not want to leave him." She wanted to make Nelly understand something she wasn't sure she understood herself. "I can't run anymore."

Nelly reached across and squeezed her friend's hand. "What in heaven's name are you running from?"

"If I tell you everything, you will only worry more."

"How could I worry more than I already am?"

Caroline took a deep breath and started telling her friend about her past life. She told her about the day she had married Michael and how he had died on their wedding day.

Nelly was horrified. "Hens' teeth, Caroline—you kept all that bottled up inside you? It's a wonder you are sane at all. Do you know who shot your husband?"

Caroline did, but she wasn't going to tell Nelly just yet. The less Nelly knew about Michael's murder, the safer she would be. Brace had a long reach, and Nelly would never understand how dangerous he could be. "Perhaps one day I will tell you the whole story, but not now. I want you to understand that my brother-in-law hired Wade to take me back to Charleston, and Wade understands that I would be in danger if I went home alone. When we are married, he will take me back to South Carolina."

"You don't have to marry this man just so he will take care of you. You have friends."

"I know. And you and Yance are the sweetest friends I could ever have. But I find I want to be Wade's wife. You must believe me when I tell you he is a fine man. If you only knew all that he has done for me."

"I was watching him the day of the picnic, and I thought for a moment that he was in love with you. But I talked myself out of that notion when he took you away with him." She looked doubtful. "If you change your mind, there is always Yance's sister that you can stay with."

"Thank you for all the trouble you went through on my behalf."

"I couldn't sleep until I knew you were all right." She finally smiled. "Yance has been very patient with me."

"What about his son and daughter?"

"That's the funny thing about it. After the picnic, Judy went to her papa and said it was time they had a new mama. She said I'd be as good as anyone else, and they wanted me for their new ma."

"So Judy changed her mind?"

"I swear it. I not only have a husband, I have a son and daughter, too. 'Course, if I don't get back to them, they may think they've been deserted. They're staying with the Grays. Wanda Gray said she wouldn't even notice two more faces at her table."

"Will you and Yance stay here for the night? I know Wade wouldn't mind, and I would love to have you with me."

"Thank you, but we're still on our honeymoon." She actually blushed. "We have a room at one of those fancy hotels in town. Now that I know you're all right, I'll pay more attention to my husband."

"Have you moved to Yance's ranch?"

"Not yet. But as soon as we get home, I'm going to sell the boardinghouse." She looked dreamy-eyed for a moment. "I want to be the best wife I can. He and the kids need someone to look after them. And I need someone to look after."

"Nelly, do you ever feel like you are betraying your first husband by marrying again?"

"No. Marty would have wanted me to be happy." She glanced at Caroline. "You aren't feeling guilty, are you?"

"Perhaps a little. Michael died so young."

"Then tell me this—do you love Renault?"

"I'm not sure. I don't feel the same way about him that I felt about Michael. Of course, I had known

Michael most of my life. But with Wade, my feelings are so intense. I can't explain it. I have never felt this way before." She looked up questioningly. "Does that make sense to you?"

Nelly chuckled. "That's the first sensible thing you've said to me. Wade Renault could make any woman's teeth rattle. He's so"—She tried to think of a way to put it delicately—"so male. And he's got a body like—" Nelly actually blushed. "I understand what you're feeling for him. But I'd feel better if you said you loved him just a little."

"Maybe love will come. But I trust him more than I trust anyone else. And I want to take care of him."

Nelly shook her head. "I can't imagine that man needing anyone to take care of him."

"He does, though. He needs someone badly, although he doesn't know it yet."

"When is the wedding going to be?"

"I don't know. We have not really had time to discuss it. It happened so quickly."

"He hasn't touched you, has he?" Nelly had her reasons for asking. Her friend was in a very vulnerable position. Renault would know exactly how to seduce a woman as innocent as Caroline—and no matter what, Nelly was not going to let that happen.

"No. But if he hadn't stopped himself, I probably would have." Caroline lowered her gaze and stared at the tip of her shoe. "As I said, he is very intense."

Nelly stood. "I see." And she did see. Renault had used his charm to get her to agree to marry him. "I see very well."

"Then tell me what I am feeling."

"It just may be the budding of love. I hope it is. I suspect that man is already in love with you."

"No. He isn't."

Nelly let the subject drop. "You will need to tell me what you want done with the belongings you left behind in San Sebastian."

"I hadn't thought about that. There is nothing there I really want to keep. I had so little." She thought of Archimedes and smiled, thinking she would like to have him with her.

"I'll box your things up and have Yance store them in his attic. You may decide later what you want done with them."

"You have already done so much. But I would ask one other favor of you. When you are packing my things away, I would like you to give all the books to Private McCaffrey. I think he would like to have them."

"I'll do that very thing."

"I don't know how I will ever thank you."

Nelly spread her hands and looked at her palms. "That's what friends do. I know because you've been that kind of friend to me."

Both women stood and hugged each other. "Thank you, Nelly."

"I'll be back tomorrow, if that's all right with you."

"I would love it. I would like you to get to know Wade."

Nelly looked doubtful. "I can never feel close to a man who makes his living with a gun."

"Nelly, he has not made his living bounty hunting for a long time. And he has given it up."

"Why would he do that?"

"For me."

Nelly stared at her for a moment and then nodded her head. "I can see him doing that." Then she gripped Caroline's hand. "I sure do miss you."

"My dear friend, I miss you, too."

"Well," Nelly said, gathering her purse. "It's late, and you look all undone. Me and Yance will be back tomorrow to see you."

"I look forward to it." She hugged her friend. "What about Archimedes—is someone taking care of him?"

"That cat rules the boardinghouse. He sleeps on the counter or anywhere else he decides to sleep. He goes into the guests' rooms and begs for attention, and usually gets it."

"Thank you. Thank you for everything. Oh, there's one other thing. Please tell Captain Dunning that I am to be married."

Nelly nodded. "I understand."

When Wade finally arrived home, it was long after midnight. With his keen hearing, he detected the presence of a stranger even before the man had stepped out of the shadows and approached him.

"Come forward," Wade said in a threatening tone. "Whoever you are, show yourself."

The stranger did not hesitate. "I just want to know what kind of shenanigans you are trying to pull with Caroline. And don't try to tell me that you came to San Sebastian looking for a wife, 'cause I won't believe you."

"Yance Grady. You are a long way from home."

"Nelly and me, we came looking for Caroline. I want to know what you've done to her."

Wade smiled to himself. This big man could break

every bone in his body if he chose to. "I am going to make her my wife."

"I've been told that. But what do you get out of it?"

"A wife."

"Smart talk will not get you out of this. I left Nelly back at our hotel room with a promise that I'd make you admit what your intentions are toward her friend. And I ain't going back to her without answers!"

"Nelly is with you?"

"Yeah, she is. We got married."

"Congratulations!"

"I'm not here to talk about us. I want to know what you feel for Caroline."

Wade's eyes narrowed. "My feelings for her are strictly my business."

Yance stepped in front of him, his broad shoulders blocking out the sky. "You'll tell me or I'll beat it out of you."

Wade gave a deep laugh and shook his head. "I believe you would. You can go back to Nelly and tell her that I want nothing but the best for Caroline." With a quick change of subject, Wade asked Yance, "Why did you marry Nelly?"

"We got married for the right reasons, but it's different with you and Caroline."

"What do you mean?"

"Hell, every man in San Sebastian would like to have had her, but she's a lady, and she's got lots of friends. She never knew that the young recruits she taught to read and write took turns watching her house at night to make sure she was safe. If you do anything to hurt her, you'll have the whole cavalry down on you."

Wade respected loyalty in anyone, and he certainly respected this big man. "If I can get Caroline to agree to marry me tomorrow, how would you and Nelly like to attend our wedding?"

Yance looked mollified for a moment. "We wouldn't miss it if it's what Caroline wants."

Chapter Twenty-two

The quarter moon unfurled a wispy illumination across the garden, leaving the pathways in shadows and casting an ethereal glow on the honeysuckle vine that twined around the base of the fountain. Dressed for bed, Caroline stood on the gallery dragging her fragmented thoughts together. So much had happened in such a short time, it was difficult to put all the pieces together. Her main concern at the moment was Jonathan and how her marriage to Wade would affect his life.

Somewhere in the distance she heard the lonesome sound of a ship's foghorn, warning other river travelers away from danger. The wind rustled through the cypress leaves, and she heard the musical sound of the fountain below her. It had been a very emotional day, starting with the swamp trip Wade had taken her on, and ending with Nelly and Yance charging to her rescue.

She smiled. Those two were the most unlikely pair of rescuers, and the most dear.

Wade had just returned from the stable to make sure his horse had been taken care of. The animal had just arrived home by a private stock car that morning.

He was thinking of Caroline as he moved past the fountain that sprayed water into the air, leaving a fine mist on his face. He paused to watch the small figure leaning on the railing of the gallery. Caroline was gazing at the moon, and he could only imagine where her thoughts were taking her.

He directed his footsteps toward her and watched her startled expression when she heard his steps on the stairs. She moved toward the safety of her room, halting only when Wade called out to her.

"It is only me. I saw you out here, and I thought we might talk if you are not sleepy." He came up beside her. "Are you too tired?"

"No. Not at all." She moved back to the railing. "Did the fire do any damage to your warehouse?"

"I was fortunate that my men reacted quickly and started a bucket brigade."

"Louis indicated that the fire had been set deliberately."

Wade leaned his arm on the railing, his elbow almost touching hers. "So it would seem."

"Fires are Brace's specialty." She curled her fingers until her nails dug into her hand. "Do you think he could be responsible?"

He looked down at her, noticing that her hair was unbound just the way he had often imagined it. Blond curls fell almost to her waist, inviting a man's hand to tangle in them. "I think it is more probable that it was some disgruntled employee taking out his spite on me. I cannot think what your brother-in-law would have to gain by such an act against me."

His shoulder brushed against hers, and her heart pounded as blood thrummed hotly through her veins. She had never been susceptible to a man's touch the way she was to his. She glanced up at him and felt trapped by the fire in his golden eyes.

"I had guests tonight," she said.

"*Oui*. So I learned."

She glanced up at him. "I suppose Mary told you?"

"*Non*. I have not seen Mary since I came home. I went directly to the stables before I came to you."

"Oh."

"Yance Grady was waiting for me when I came home." He smiled, remembering the incident. "I should say he was lying in wait for me."

She frowned and placed her hand on his arm. "He threatened you?"

Wade's laughter was deep and amused. "He threatened me with the entire cavalry from Fort Lambrick."

She covered her mouth to keep from giggling. "He didn't!"

"I can assure you he did. But," Wade added, reaching out and touching a strand of her hair and allowing it to sift through his fingers, "you might be able to save me from their attack."

The moonlight fell on his face, softening the hard planes as she asked, "And how can I do that?"

He wound the curl around his finger, then lifted it to his lips—the sensuous gesture made her gasp for breath. Could he know what it did to her when he did things like that?

"You can save me by agreeing to marry me tomorrow so we can invite your friends to our wedding." His eyes were dancing with merriment. "If it is all the same to you, I would rather not feel the points of fifty sabers at my back."

She returned his smile. "I think it can only be half that number who would come to my rescue."

"Do you need rescuing from me?" He asked the question lightly, but waited impatiently for her answer.

"I can leave any time I choose, and I choose to stay." She was wondering why he had set the wedding date for the next day, and she knew it wasn't for the sake of Yance and Nelly. "Tomorrow would be rushing things a bit, don't you agree?"

He turned her toward him, spinning a half lie and a half truth. "Caroline, you are an unwed woman living in my home without benefit of a chaperone. I do not want anyone questioning your virtue. Can you give me a good reason for us to delay the wedding?"

When he was so close to her, she could hardly remember her own name, let alone think of a reason not to get married the next day. "We have not told Jonathan, and he should be considered."

"We can tell him together in the morning."

"Wade, I have a favor to ask of you—well, two favors actually." She had been dwelling on this all day and had come to the conclusion it would be the right thing to do for Jonathan's sake.

"I believe you could ask anything of me, and if it were in my power, I would grant your wish."

The sound of his deep voice ran through her like

quicksilver. "When we are married, I want us to adopt Jonathon. I want to be his mother, and he already loves you like a father."

He was quiet, thoughtful, and she was afraid he was going to say no.

"Is that all that is bothering you?" he asked tenderly.

"It is my utmost consideration."

"That is easily granted, *mon amour*. We will bind our marriage by taking Jonathan as our son." He laced his fingers through hers. "You said there were two things you wanted."

"Yes." She lost her voice when he touched his lips to her fingers.

He looked at her tolerantly. "What could it be?"

"Jonathan doesn't want to attend the academy in Baton Rouge."

His answer was short and swift. "He needs the discipline."

She placed her hand on his arm. "He needs a mother and a father. He is so loving and in need of love. He has no feeling of importance. Can't you find a day school for him to attend in New Orleans? Perhaps a good private school?"

Wade's chest rose and fell, and he wondered if she knew how beautiful she was to him at that moment. He could almost see her heart through her eyes and was touched by her concern for Jonathan. Too many others in her life had disappointed her, and he did not want to be among them. "I will see what I can do, if it is that important to you," he told her.

She threw her arms around him and pressed her body against his. "That is the best wedding present you could give me! You are a kind and thoughtful man."

No one had ever called him kind before. He laughed against her ear, her happiness flowing through him like fine wine. "The moment you accept me as your husband, you will be delivered an eight-year-old son."

She pressed her cheek against his chest. "Thank you. You won't regret this." She drew back and looked at him. "How do you know Jonathan is eight years old?"

"It is merely an age that Mary in her wisdom attached to him."

"Has he ever had a birthday party?"

"We do not know when the boy was born."

She smiled brightly. "Then we must decide on a date for him. Everyone needs to have a birthday."

A feeling he could only label as happiness swept through him like a cleansing wind, and he wondered how he had managed to get through each day before he had met Caroline.

"What about you, Wade? When is your birthday?"

"Like Jonathan, I do not have an official birthday."

She beamed up at him. "That is perfect! You and Jonathan can share the same day as your birthday."

He held her to him. She was the most perfect creature he had ever met—she filled his heart until it overflowed. "You can set the day for us both," he remarked gruffly.

She suddenly remembered that she wore only a filmy dressing gown over her nightgown, so she slipped out of his embrace. "I should go in now."

He gently brought her toward him. "Please stay a moment longer."

His words were almost like a plea, and she felt as if she had just touched his soul. With a little cry, she buried her face against his chest and felt his strong arms go around her.

"I am a little frightened," she admitted.

"Why is that?"

"Because of the way I feel about you. Sometimes when you touch me, I feel like I am melting inside. Do you understand that?"

He breathed in slowly and let his breath out before he could speak, and then his voice came out as a groan of despair. "I understand better than you do. You have never been intimately touched by a man, have you?"

"Michael kissed me several times. But not the way you do."

"I suspected as much this afternoon when we were in the swamp." He could not explain the joy that shot through him. He would be the one to teach her about the desires that flowed through a man and a woman. "Caroline," was all he could manage to say.

She glanced up at him and saw his jaw muscles tightening. "I am sure you thought I was more"—she grappled for the right words—"more experienced than I am. Will it make any difference to you?"

His head descended, his breath brushing against her lips. "*Mon amour*," he said, his lips moving along her jawline. "*Je sais gré le cadeau que vous m'amenez.*"

As sometimes happened with him, he had reverted to French.

"I don't speak or understand French, Wade."

"I merely said, I am grateful for the gift you bring to me."

"Are you sure you want to marry me?" She looked into his eyes to search for the truth.

"*De tout mon coeur.*"

"You are speaking French again."

A smile curved his mouth. "I said, with all my heart. But you must not always hold me to what I say when I am about to kiss you, because I sometimes lose my head."

She turned her face to offer him her lips, and he took the offer. His lips were warm, drawing emotions from deep inside her. She sighed as he untied the sash of her dressing grown and slid his hand up to cup her breast through the thin material of her nightgown.

Her body shook so violently that he absorbed the tremors by bringing her closer to him. "Caroline, tomorrow you will be mine."

"Yes," she whispered, feeling that sudden burst of joy that she so often felt when she was with him. "I will."

He suddenly swept her into his arms and carried her into her room. She secretly hoped he would take her to bed and do all the wonderful things she could only imagine. But he set her on her feet and pulled her covers down.

"I will leave you for now." He raised her hand, brushing his mouth against her inner wrist. "Sleep well, *mon amour*."

She touched his face, and he closed his eyes. "What does it mean when you call me that?"

He focused on her eyes. "It is merely an endearment meaning 'my love.' You will find that we Creole are very passionate people, Caroline."

"But you always hold back, keeping your deepest thoughts to yourself," she said with an insight that surprised even herself.

He gripped her shoulders, and there was that leashed intensity that he kept tightly reined. "You will never understand what it has cost me to honor you." He slowly brought her to him, dipping his head to kiss her breast through the thin material of her nightgown. "But tomorrow night," he said, pulling her robe together, "there will be no need for me to hold back."

Her heart rose to her throat. Before she could reply, he had released her and walked through the door to the gallery. She ran to the balcony, but he had already gone down the stairs and disappeared into the night.

"Tomorrow night," she whispered, pressing her hand against her pounding heart, "I will be his."

Wade walked in the garden with Caroline's sweet scent still clinging to him. He was aching with unsatisfied desire. He had come so close to laying her on that bed and taking all that she had been so willing to give him. But he had stopped himself just in time. One more night—he could wait one more night.

For so many years he had felt dead inside: Each day would pass much like the one before it. But then Caroline had stormed into his orderly world, stirring everything up and tying him in knots. Now when he awoke each day, his life had meaning. The days were long when he could not see her face, and the nights were longer still.

In the past when any woman had caught his fancy,

he had merely taken what she offered, and let her go with no regrets. But it was different with Caroline. Knowing her had taught him to be patient. Although he wanted her more than he had ever wanted any of the others, he had the strength to hold back.

He raised his head in the dim moonlight, wondering if he was doing the right thing by her. He had gone to her tonight with the express intention of telling her about her father's death and finding out what had happened to her the day she married Michael Duncan. But when he had seen her looking so adorable, and worrying about Jonathan, he could not bring himself to hurt her.

Tomorrow night, after making love to her, and while he held her in his arms, he would tell her about her father, and then he could comfort her.

He was sure he had done the right thing. Had he not?

He walked down the path to the bench Caroline and Jonathan always used when she read to him. Warmth spread through him when he thought how kind she had been to Jonathan. She had sensed right away that the boy needed tenderness in his life, and she had responded to that need. He wondered what it would feel like to watch her stomach swell with a child he had planted in her.

She was making him crazy, thinking about things that had never mattered to him before. But the thought of having a child by her rocked his world to the core.

There were going to be troubled times ahead. He was not sure what her reaction would be when he told her that he had withheld the news of her father's death from her. Would she understand that he had not wanted to hurt her when she had been so weak and ill?

He exhaled, feeling his heartbeat settle into a natural rhythm. He glanced up at her window and saw the light go out.

Tonight she slept alone, but tomorrow night she would sleep in his arms.

Chapter Twenty-three

The weather was bright and clear and seemed to smile on Caroline's wedding day. Strangely enough, she had slept the night through with no nightmares to haunt her and no worries to keep her awake.

It had been her intention to rise early enough to have breakfast with Wade. She didn't want to eat another meal from a tray in her room. She wanted to be the kind of wife who takes care of her husband, sees to his needs, and is a good companion to him.

She slid out of bed and quickly got dressed. She paused when she looked in the mirror to pin up her hair. She had not felt this same joy on the day she had married Michael. She backed away from the mirror as if it had given her an insight she did not want to examine too closely. Wade was a man, Michael had been only nineteen, and she had been seventeen the day they had married. She was now a woman with a woman's needs.

She wondered what their marriage would have

been like if Michael had lived. She glanced back into the mirror, staggered by the truth. In the back of her mind, she had known all along that she had married Michael in the hope of supporting him against Brace. But she had failed in that.

At the moment, her joy was being suffocated by unwanted memories that settled on her mind like cobwebs from the past. She remembered not wanting to be Michael's wife, but his friend as they had always been to each other.

Caroline was glad when Mary's knock on the door brought her back to the present.

"Good morning, ma'am," the housekeeper greeted her, smiling. "I wonder if it would be all right if Louis came in. He has an armload of packages for you."

Caroline nodded. "Yes, of course." She wondered what was in the packages and boxes that were stacked in the little Frenchman's arms.

"You can put them on the bed," Mary instructed him.

Louis did as he was told, then he nodded and backed toward the door. "This is a happy day for us all, madame. A very happy day indeed. You are welcomed by all."

She smiled at him with warmth. "Thank you, Louis. I appreciate that."

He left with a wide grin on his face.

"Louis says what we all feel, ma'am." Mary opened one box and removed silken stockings. "This house has not had a mistress in over twenty years, and it sorely needs one."

Caroline was gratified by the housekeeper's approval. "Thank you, Mary. What have you in all those boxes?"

"It's every kind of finery you can think of. Himself went to Madame Sophie's, the finest ladies shop in New Orleans, and Madame Sophie herself chose everything for you—with himself's approval, of course." She opened a long box and lifted out a soft pink gown with tiny rosebuds embroidered on the sleeves.

"He thought you might like this for your wedding gown."

"It's lovely," Caroline said, running her hand over the soft silk. "However could he have managed to purchase such a beautiful creation in such a short time?"

Mary paused with a stiff petticoat in her hand. "When he wants something done, it gets done. The people of New Orleans will stumble all over themselves to accommodate him."

"Yes. I can imagine that they would. Wade Renault can be very persuasive when he wants something."

Mary smiled as she nodded. "I knew the day you entered this house that you would be the mistress here."

"How could you have known? I certainly had not given it any thought at the time."

The housekeeper could have told her that Wade had never shown such concern for any other woman, but she kept her thoughts to herself. "There are many more boxes in the morning room. I'll have them brought up and packed in trunks for your trip."

Caroline did not want to admit she knew nothing about a trip. "Thank you for all your help. Has Mr. Renault already had breakfast?"

"Yes. Hours ago. He said I was to be asking you to join him in the study at your convenience."

* * *

After Caroline had eaten a light breakfast, she walked toward the doorway of her bedroom while Mary was instructing a maid to draw her bath.

"I shouldn't be long," Caroline said, stepping out of the door. Her footsteps were light as she descended the stairs and hurried toward the library. The door was open so she stood in the archway for a moment.

Jonathan was seated on one of the leather sofas, looking uncertain. Wade was seated at his desk, and he rose to his feet when she entered.

"Caroline," the boy mumbled. "Wade said you had something to tell me. I've been waiting for over an hour."

There was accusation in his tone and fear in his expression.

She would have gone directly to him, but Wade motioned for her to approach his desk. "Jonathan, you will soon learn that it is a privilege to wait for a woman." His gaze went to Caroline. "Especially when she is the right woman," he explained laughingly.

Caroline glanced at the document he pushed in front of her and saw that it was Jonathan's adoption papers. Wade's bold signature was already on the document.

He spoke quietly so Jonathan would not overhear him. "This merely says that you and I have adopted Jonathan, and that you are legally his mother and I am his father. You will need to sign your name as Caroline Renault. Louis will file the documents right after the wedding. Everything is as you wished it to be. The deed is all but done."

She glanced quickly up at him. "How did you accomplish this so quickly? We only spoke about it last night."

The warmth in his eyes spread over her. "I rose early." His hand settled on top of hers, and he gave it a squeeze. "I could not sleep last night for thinking about you."

He moved back a pace and handed her the pen. "Sign this, and you will have a son."

He saw her hesitate when it came to the last name. But she gripped the pen and signed her name as his wife.

"Congratulations," he whispered near her ear. "You are now a mother."

She beamed up at him and then turned to the forlorn child who sat with his chin resting on his chest. She went forward and seated herself beside him. "I am sorry to be late. There is so much to do this morning."

"She will repeat those same words many times through the years, Jonathan," Wade said, coming around his desk and sitting on the other side of the boy. "Women always have something to do, and we let them."

The child lowered his head even more. "I know why we're all here." He looked up at Caroline with tears clinging to his lashes. "You want to tell me that we can't read anymore because I have to go back to that old academy in Baton Rouge."

"Jonathan, how would you like to attend school in New Orleans?" Wade asked.

The boy looked up suspiciously. "You mean and come home to you and Caroline every night?"

"That is exactly what I mean."

He was still untrusting. "Why would you let me do that when you said I couldn't before?"

Wade looked at Caroline. "You will have to ask your mother."

His little face crumpled into a frown. "You found my mommy, and she's going to take me away? No, I won't go with her. I won't—I won't!"

"I have not found the mother who gave birth to you, but I hope you will like the one I have chosen for you." Pain shot through Wade's heart when he watched the confusion in the child's eyes. He remembered wanting Anton to love him like a father and knowing that he never would. This child would have a better chance at happiness than Wade ever had.

"Caroline and I are going to be married."

The boy's eyes brightened. "And she will stay with us forever?"

Wade's gaze went back to his bride-to-be. "I hope she will never want to leave us."

Jonathan threw his arms around Wade, taking him completely by surprise. He was awkward at first, but then he patted the child's back.

"You did it! I hoped you'd marry her so we could keep her."

The sound of a genuine laugh came from Wade. "Caroline has something to tell you." He nodded at her. "I hope you will be pleased, Jonathan."

The child turned inquiringly to Caroline. He thought the two adults were acting very strangely.

She took his face between her hands and looked into his eyes, her own were already brimming with tears. "Wade has arranged for us to adopt you,

Jonathan. As of today, you will be our son, if that is your wish."

For a moment, Jonathan did not quite understand what she was saying. But as the truth finally became clear to him, all doubt left his eyes and he smiled widely. He was crying and laughing at the same time. He jumped off the sofa and danced around in a circle. "I knew it—I knew it! Mary told me if I wanted my wish to come true, it would help if I wished upon a star." He blinked back tears and shook his head. "I had such a big wish, so I had to wish upon the moon and the stars!"

Caroline held her arms out to him, and he rushed to her. "And your wish came true," she said.

He pulled away from her, looking first at Wade and then back to her. "Shouldn't I call you Mommy now?"

"I would like that," she told him.

He looked hesitantly at Wade. "And what do I call you?"

Wade's voice was husky when he answered. "I believe it would be appropriate for you to call me Father."

Jonathan ran to the door and then back again. "I'm going to tell Mary. And I want to tell Louis and—" He stopped to catch his breath. "I want everyone to know." In his exuberance he ran back to Caroline and gave her another hug. "Mommy."

He ran out of the room, his light footsteps disappearing in the direction of the kitchen. Wade slid his arm around Caroline. "Have I made all your wishes come true?"

For a moment, she wondered if he had gone through with the adoption merely to please her. She hoped not. She wanted him to love Jonathan as much as she did. "What I want from you now is not the fulfillment of a wish, but more of a promise."

"You have only to ask."

"No matter whether we have children of our own, and I'm sure we shall, I always want Jonathan to feel that he is our eldest son with all the privileges that go along with that claim."

He pulled her to him. She had a way of saying the unexpected and taking him completely by surprise. He swallowed twice before he could answer her. "The law allows and upholds that fact," he assured her. "We both signed the paper to set it in motion."

She rose and walked to the double doors that led to the garden, allowing the breeze that came off the river to cool her face. She was too overcome to speak. When he came up behind her and slid his arms around her waist, she leaned her head back against his shoulder.

"It is a good day, *mon amour*. I want all your days to be good. I wait for the day when you no longer fear anyone."

She could have told him that she was never afraid when he was with her. His strong presence had given her hope for the future, and she no longer looked over her shoulder in fear that Brace would be there.

"You have made Jonathan very happy. He is a very lucky little boy to have you for a father. Of course, you have taken care of him for years, but it isn't the same as giving him your name, is it?"

"Would that all your requests could be so easily granted."

"I ask for nothing more than what you have already given me."

He held her hand, looking at the delicate fingers.

"Someday I will ask something of you. I hope you will grant it."

"What can it be?"

He shrugged and changed the subject. "I believe we should talk about the wedding. I have invited Mr. and Mrs. Grady, and, of course, Jonathan and the servants will attend. Do you mind that the ceremony will be an informal affair with only a few guests?"

Because of his standing in the community, she imagined that there would be many people who would want to attend the wedding. She was glad he had chosen a private ceremony. "I prefer it that way."

"Then I did right in choosing the rectory? If you have no objections, the ceremony will take place at four o'clock this afternoon."

He had suddenly grown solemn and methodical—no detail was too small to escape his notice. She wondered if she would ever understand this complicated man. "I have no objections."

"I have also made arrangements for us to go up the Mississippi on a riverboat, the *Cotton Maid*. Will that meet with your approval?" His voice deepened, and he reached for her hand, raising it to his lips. "It will give us a chance to be alone."

She laughed up at him. "How can we expect to be alone on a boat with other people?"

He stared at her lips for a long moment before he said, "By remaining in our cabin."

Her heart started beating faster, and she felt her face flush. "I have never been on a riverboat."

He laughed softly and rested his chin on the top of her golden head. "You have many new experiences awaiting you."

"You are right, I do." In true woman fashion, she asked, "When did you decide that you wanted to marry me?"

"I believe a hint of the notion came to me even before we met."

"That is not possible."

He guided her toward the hallway. "I am sure you have things to do. This day will be long for me."

She turned away from him. "I do have to get ready." She stood on her tiptoes and kissed his forehead. "Thank you for the lovely wedding gown."

"It is my pleasure."

He thought as he watched her rush from the room, *Fly away, little bird. You have been running for so long, you do not know I am about to end your wandering.*

Nelly arrived at the house early so she could help Caroline dress. Mary had brought pink roses from the garden, and Nelly wove them into Caroline's hair.

The filmy pink gown came floating down over her head, and Nelly hooked it up the back. Caroline slid her feet into the pink satin shoes and glanced into the mirror.

"How do I look?"

Nelly came up beside her, noticing the flush in Caroline's cheeks. "Like a happy bride. I think you love this man."

Caroline bit her lip. "Perhaps. I just know I want to make him happy and never to cause him pain. I want to help him come into the sunshine."

Nelly looked skeptical. "And you think you can rescue *him?*"

Caroline remembered another husband she had not

been able to help. "That would be presumptuous of me. But, yes, I would like to try."

Nelly straightened the gown and watched her friend in the reflection of the mirror. "Now is your time to run if you are going to."

"No more running."

"Well then, we had better leave for the church. Yance has gone with your groom, and a carriage is waiting for us."

As they left the house, Caroline's heart was suddenly filled with happiness. Today she would not only have a husband, but a son as well.

She would have a family.

Louis helped Caroline and Nelly out of the carriage and escorted them to the back of the church where the rectory was located.

Jonathan stood beside Wade and the bishop, watching the back door open. Nelly took her seat beside Yance, and Caroline continued to walk toward Wade.

Wade could see his future in Caroline's shimmering blue eyes. Her gown was a mere whisper against the polished wooden floor, and he had never seen a vision as beautiful as she was to him in that moment.

Jonathan, dressed in a fine blue suit, stood solemnly beside his new father. When Caroline drew even with them, Wade took her hand and felt it tremble. When they knelt before the bishop and each gave the appropriate responses to the age-old ceremony, Caroline was so overcome with emotion, she could not look at Wade—but she could feel his eyes on her the whole time.

Wade's mood was serious, and Caroline's was hesitant. She had been in this position before, on her knees repeating the same vows.

But this time it was different.

A revelation hit her when the bishop asked them to lower their heads in prayer. "Dear God," she prayed silently, "here in Your house I realize that I love this man with my whole heart and soul. I pledge that I will do all in my power to make him happy." The truth of what she was feeling was like opening a floodgate, and she was afraid to look at Wade because he might read the love in her eyes.

It somehow seemed unreal when the bishop pronounced them man and wife. Wade seemed oblivious to anything but her. He swept her into his arms for a slow, lingering kiss.

Well-wishers pressed in around them, everyone laughing and offering best wishes.

Caroline hugged Nelly, and her friend assured her that she and Yance would be returning to New Orleans to make sure everything was running smoothly in Caroline's life.

Jonathan elbowed his way forward and beamed up at them. Caroline bent down to him, and he threw his arms around her neck. "We are a family now," he said, grinning.

She kissed his cheek. "I was just thinking that myself. Yes, Jonathan Renault, we are a family. No one can take you away from us."

"Not never?"

She laughed and kissed his cheek again. "Not never!"

She took the child's hand, and he walked beside her

and Wade through the door of the rectory. When Louis pulled up with the buggy, Caroline once more bent down to the child.

"You do understand that we are going away for a short time? You are not to worry, because we will be back very soon."

He nodded. "Mary said you were going to the moon."

"Not to the moon, Jonathan," Wade said in amusement. "We are going on a honeymoon." He bent down to the boy. "You will look after things at home until we return, will you not?"

He nodded. "I'll take care of everything."

Nelly came forward and took the child's hand while Wade helped Caroline into the carriage.

His hand slid across the seat, and she felt excitement building inside her. She was still trying to accept the fact that she had fallen in love with Wade.

When had it happened?

How had she gone from being terrified of him to loving him so desperately?

"I have you now," he said, pulling her head to his shoulder.

"Yes," she whispered. "And I have you."

Chapter Twenty-four

On the carriage ride back to the house, Wade took her hand in his. "This is all new to me, Caroline." His smile was warm with amusement. "I have never shared a room with anyone before."

He was so near she could smell his clean male scent, and all she could think about was later that night when she would be in his bed. "Perhaps you will want separate bedrooms."

He pulled her roughly to him and said, "I want you in my bed so you will always fall asleep with my kiss on your lips and wake up in the morning ready for me to make love to you."

Heat rose through her entire body as she thought about his words. "I have always slept alone as well," she reminded him.

He looked at her strangely, and he suddenly became silent and withdrawn. Her hand still rested in his, but she could tell that his mind was on other matters, leaving her to wonder what had caused his abrupt mood change.

When they arrived at the house, miraculously Mary had arrived ahead of them and was waiting on the veranda. "Mr. and Mrs. Grady asked if they could take Jonathan for a carriage ride along the river. He was excited about going with them, so I agreed that he could. He wanted Mr. Grady to tell him all about Texas and his ranch."

Wade led Caroline inside the house. "He will barely finish one question before he will fire another at them. He has a very curious mind."

"Is that your way of saying my son is very intelligent?"

"*Oui*. He is."

"I have prepared a special meal for the two of you, and I took the liberty of choosing the smaller private dining room," Mary said, her face reflecting her happiness. "Your trunks have been taken to the dock," she told Wade. "I laid out your traveling gown for you," she told Caroline.

Caroline moved toward the stairs. "I will just go upstairs and change. I won't be long."

Her hands were shaking as she slipped out of the filmy pink gown and into the more suitable gray silk. She patted her hair into place and went downstairs to join Wade. Her heart was in her mouth as he walked across the polished floor toward her, looking more handsome than a man had a right to. With those glorious golden eyes focused on her, she felt her heart leap.

He raised her hand to his mouth. "Mrs. Renault, you have made me a very happy man today."

But he wasn't happy. When he seated her at the table and sat beside her, he was unusually quiet.

Something was definitely wrong.

Of course, he had married her for the wrong reason—guilt. That would make any man pull into himself, she thought with an aching heart.

"Jonathan seemed to be enjoying the wedding and the attention from Nelly and Yance," she remarked, at last breaking the silence that hung between them like a heavy fog.

Wade was silent for a moment, and then smiled and nodded his dark head. "He was telling everyone who would listen that he has the best mommy in the whole world." Her hand was resting on the table, and he stared at the ring he had slid on her finger a few hours earlier. "And I must say that I agree with him."

"Wade, I feel I should tell you I do not expect you to cater to my every whim. You do not have to make all my wishes come true."

"Is that not what a husband does?"

"Not for this wife. I do not expect to be treated like a porcelain doll. I am strong, and I can take care of myself." Her gaze dropped to her plate. "I know you must think I am delicate because I was so ill—but I'm not."

He had a faraway look in his eyes. "You may very well be in need of that strength before the night is over."

She wondered what he meant by his cryptic remark. But Mary entered carrying a large lamb roast, so Caroline's question was never uttered.

His eyes once more filled with warmth. "Nelly has been a very good friend to you, Caroline."

"Yes, she has. I don't know many people who would

take time from their honeymoon to go dashing across country to rescue a friend."

"Nelly and Yance seem to be ideally matched."

Caroline frowned. "In what way?"

"She is impulsive and forward, while he is calm and adores her."

"That is exactly right. How could you know what they are like on so short an acquaintance?"

"It was my profession to be able to read people. My life often depended on how well I knew my prisoner."

Her head dropped a notch. "And you think you know me so well, don't you?"

His gaze met hers. "You are the only one I was wrong about."

This was not at all the conversation Caroline would have expected on her wedding day, and she turned the topic back to her friends. "Yance and Nelly have loved each other for a long time."

"Tell me something, Caroline. Before I came along, was your life happy in San Sebastian?"

"Why do you ask?"

"I am just trying to understand what your life was like there."

"When I first arrived, Nelly was my only friend. I took in washing and ironing in those first few months because I didn't have any money. Then, with Nelly's help, I became a seamstress and life was better." She thought back to her time in San Sebastian. "I was as happy as I could have been under the circumstances. I left behind some very good friends." She started to take a bite and then said, "I hope someone will take my place in teaching the young recruits to read and write."

He remembered a time when he had thought she was giving the cavalrymen more than reading lessons. But he would never tell her what those first impressions had been. To do so would only be courting folly. "If Yance is to be believed, the whole cavalry is devoted to you."

She laid her fork down and laced her fingers together. "Not the whole cavalry. Just a few young men who were far from home and needed a friend. They were always very respectful to me."

He shoved his plate aside, the food uneaten. "Do you really believe that they only came to your house so you could teach them to read?"

His words had come out like an accusation. "I don't understand. What are you implying?"

"How could you be expected to understand how a man reacts when he is near you?"

"I don't think that is a fair assessment of the situation. And your making such an assumption does no credit to me or the young men who wanted so badly to learn."

"I ask your pardon. Of course they had an apt teacher in you." He ran his hand over his closed eyes. "Please forgive me. I have had a lot on my mind," he said, thinking of her father and wondering how he would find the courage to tell her about his death.

"I am finished," she said, placing her napkin beside her plate.

He rose to his feet. "Then Louis can drive us to the docks. It is not long until the riverboat leaves port."

She was almost relieved when they left the dining room. Shouldn't a wedding day be happy? He had reverted to the brooding stranger that she had been afraid of when they had first met. She had not understood him then, and she now understood him even less.

What was he keeping from her? She did not know.

When they boarded the *Cotton Maid*, there was a festive mood onboard. Music was filtering out of the lounge, fireworks lit up the sky, and streamers were flying through the air.

Wade escorted Caroline through the crowd to their suite and then allowed her to precede him inside. The whole cabin was decorated in white and gold. The bed cover and curtains were white fringed in gold.

The sheer gaudiness suddenly struck Caroline as funny. Wade, with his strong male persona, could never feel comfortable in such surroundings.

He shrugged and shook his head. "I should have inspected the cabin myself. I asked Louis to book the bridal suite."

She was still trying not to laugh. "I'm sorry, it's very lovely, but how will you abide all this fringe?"

"This will not do," he said, taking her arm to keep her from going any further inside. "I will have the purser change rooms immediately."

She slid her hand up his arm. "You will do nothing of the sort. How else will we ever know how it feels to live in a sultan's palace?"

"I know your tastes are more refined than this."

"But what does it matter?"

He smiled down at her. "Are you sure you do not mind?"

"Not at all. It will give us something to tell our grandchildren."

He watched her approach the bed, where she batted at one of the many velvet balls that dangled from the bed hanging. She covered her mouth to keep from laughing. "Poor Louis. You are not to say a word to him about this—do I have your word on that?"

"*Oui.*" Most women would have insisted on being moved to another room, but Caroline was more concerned about Louis's feelings than the ridiculous decor. Wade liked that about her.

"Happy wedding day, Madame Renault."

She gazed back at him, wishing she could interpret the many secrets that were hidden behind those golden eyes. "I hope it will be." She hadn't meant to say that, it just slipped out.

He averted his gaze. "You will find everything you need in the brown trunk." He moved away and paused in the doorway. "I believe it is customary for the groom to give the bride time alone. I will return shortly."

She watched him leave and then turned to the trunk. With Mary's efficiency, she knew everything would be appropriate. She stepped out of her gray gown and draped it across a chair.

Opening the trunk, she found a delicate white muslin nightgown with blue satin ties at the neck. After undressing, she pulled the nightgown over her head and slipped into the blue dressing gown, belting it at her waist. Her hands were trembling when she sat before the vanity and unbound her hair, brushing the golden curls until they crackled.

Not knowing what to do next, she sat on the bed, leaning against the white velvet headboard, and folded her hands in her lap.

Waiting.

The *Cotton Maid* swayed gently on the calm river, and she could hear the distant sound of the paddle wheel splashing against the water. She was momentarily lulled into a sense of serenity. But when Wade entered a short time later, he jolted her calmness.

His eyes sought hers as he bent to blow out the lantern. As her vision adjusted to the faint moonlight that streamed into the compartment, she could still see the vividness in his golden eyes.

She watched his hand go to his belt, and she waited as he bent to remove his boots.

Her heart was pounding, then drumming against her breasts as he removed his shirt, allowing it to slide to the floor. She did not look away when he slid his trousers down. Her eyes widened when she saw his arousal, and he came toward her.

Gently he swept her long hair off her shoulders and bent over her, brushing a kiss across her forehead. She was breathing fast when he laid his face against hers.

"I have waited a long time for tonight," he said, lifting her to her feet and untying her sash, kissing her while her dressing gown dropped in a clump at her feet. She was hardly aware that he had pushed her nightgown off her shoulders until a cool breeze from the open window touched her skin.

He stepped back, his gaze moving slowly over her naked body. His voice was thick when he said, "You are a rare beauty, Caroline."

Her eyes closed because she felt so much she could not speak. When he gently touched her breasts, she felt a hunger she could not explain.

"You are mine now," he said, touching his lips to hers. "All mine." He moved forward, his hard body touching hers. "*Mon amour*, come willingly to me."

And she did.

She flung her arms around his neck, and he lifted her onto the bed. When he came down beside her, she thought she would die from wanting him.

There was nowhere on her body that Wade did not kiss, caress, and explore. She was mindless and ready to submit to his every desire. He used the allurement of seductive words to draw her to him, sometimes speaking in French, sometimes in English. She was sure that his prowess was so strong that no woman could resist him.

Certainly not she.

His hungry mouth devoured her, and she was almost in a frenzy. She threw off her inhibitions and ground her lower body against his, and she heard him hiss through his teeth.

A cry of longing escaped her throat when he dipped his head to kiss her breasts. His tongue slid around one nipple, then his mouth covered it while she squirmed beneath him. She had not imagined anything more exquisite than what he was doing to her—or anything so painful as wanting him to do more.

His desire was unleashed at last, and it tore through him. He explored every inch of the soft body that had kept him awake many nights. His hand moved over her hips, pulling her closer to him, forming her to his shape.

He moved his hand down and touched her intimately. He drew in a quick breath when she arched against his hand, inviting him to do more.

He could not wait! There was no time to woo her into accepting him. If he did not have her now, he would explode. He covered her body with his and eased inside her, gritting his teeth at the intense pleasure that shattered through him. She had been untouched, and her tightness stopped him. He did not want to hurt her, so he pulled back. Slowly, his finger slid into her, and she cried out.

"I know what you are feeling, my love. I know this is new to you. Trust me?"

"Yes."

She bit her lip but still groaned when he touched a certain spot on her, and she almost came off the bed.

He touched his lips to her ear. "*Je t'attends depuis longtemps*. I have waited a long time for you."

He nudged her legs wider apart, and his eyes drifted shut when he experienced emotions so acute that they were like pain. He wanted to remember the moment her body was finally joined with his.

She opened to him, her arms going around his neck, touching her lips to his throat.

He quaked and trembled, and he sought her mouth, partaking of her sweetness. He tried to control his movements, to still his heartbeat, but he was on fire.

Caroline's emptiness filled with his warmth as he slowly pushed forward inside her. When he probed deeper, she sighed with even more pleasure.

"Forgive me," he said as he drove into her, unable to contain his torrid passion. With a quick jab he tore through the barrier that had proclaimed her a virgin.

When he heard her sharp breath and felt her stiffen, he stopped and held her tightly.

"The pain will not last long."

She could not utter a word as he eased farther into her. Her eyes widened in wonder when he slowly rocked back and forth.

In a haze of passion, she watched him bare his teeth, and she stared into those wonderful golden eyes that were like flames of fire. She had the feeling he was drawing her inside him, and the sensation was beyond anything she had ever imagined.

He seemed to know instinctively what would please her, and he masterfully conquered her.

When she arched against him, drawing him deeper, Wade whispered roughly, "*Mon amour*, do not."

His lovemaking opened the door to so many new emotions. One new feeling had hardly struck before another took its place to leave her gasping for breath.

The two of them trembled together as they reached satisfaction at last. They clung to each other while their spirits seemed to soar free.

Then Wade sank against Caroline, and she joyfully bore the full weight of his body.

Long moments passed as his fingers interlocked with hers, and he raised her hand to his lips. She slid her hand from his and pushed his hair back, kissing his mouth.

She sighed—he took a deep breath.

Reluctantly he moved off her and turned her to face him, pushing a sweat-dampened curl from her face. He traced her arched brow with a finger and drew it down to her swollen lips.

"I was sure it would be powerful between us, and it was," he admitted, pulling her head against his shoulder. "I do not think my mind has ever been this clear before."

She ran her fingers up his arm. "I want to be a good wife to you." She lowered her lashes coyly. "I certainly want to try."

His laughter was deep and sexual. "Caroline—" he touched his mouth to hers. "You have just given me your purity and sweetness, and I would definitely call that gift being a good wife." He took her face in his hands and made her look at him. "I believe I knew we were meant to be together before I met you."

She pulled back and raised herself up on her elbow. "You said that before. What can you mean?"

He hated to bring anything ugly into such a perfect moment, but he had to tell her about her father, and he had to go slowly. "Brace Duncan had sent me a picture so I would recognize you when I saw you."

She disliked the thought of Brace having a picture of her. He must have taken the one that she had given Michael. "I did not know he had my likeness."

"I want you to understand what I have to say to you. I want you to know how I feel about you so there will be no doubt later on." He forced her to look at him. "Caroline, I would never have taken the assignment to go after you if I had not first seen your likeness. I cannot explain it, but I felt compelled to find you wherever you were."

"And you did."

He drew her back into his arms, holding her tightly. "There is so much we have to say to each other. We do not know each other all that well, although my heart spoke to yours long before you answered."

His words were enticing, the meaning just out of her reach—he was as much a master with words as he had been with a gun. "You are keeping something from me."

"I admit that I have been. I want you to realize that I could not tell you this before now because you were so ill. The doctor warned me that I must not upset you."

She suddenly went cold inside, and she wasn't sure she wanted to hear what he had to say. The passion that had flared between them was just below the surface, and it would take only a touch of his hand to bring it back into flames. "I don't understand."

Wade wanted to make love to her again so he could avoid telling her about her father. He was about to make the hardest confession he had ever faced in his life, and he dreaded the outcome. Would she hate him for keeping the news from her for so long?

"Even before I start," he said, moving his mouth over hers, "I will remind you that I once told you that I would soon ask something of you. I ask it tonight. I ask it now."

"What can it be?"

"I ask for your forgiveness."

She felt her world crumbling and falling down around her. Something was dreadfully wrong, and he was about to tell her what it was.

Chapter Twenty-five

She rolled away from him and propped herself against the headboard, tossing her hair behind her. "Are you about to tell me that you are handing me over to Brace?"

"Never. How could you think that?" He moved toward her so he was sitting beside her, but not touching her. In the soft moonlight he was familiarizing himself with the face that had haunted him even before he met her.

"First, Caroline, will you answer some questions for me? Even if you think they are ill-timed for a wedding night?"

Her hand fell onto his leg, and she jerked it away. His eyes begged her for something she did not understand. She felt defenseless in her nakedness.

And she needed to be in control. Whatever he was about to tell her was going to be very bad. She slid out of bed and pulled on her robe and moved away from him. "If I can answer your questions, I will."

He stood up and slipped into his trousers, then moved closer to her. "Tell me about your mother and father."

To Caroline the moment took on a feeling of unreality. Why was he asking these questions tonight?

"My recollections of my mother are really just impressions. When I think of her, I remember that she loved me. I think of her as a very gentle and kind person. And she always smelled of roses."

"And your father?"

Perhaps he was asking the questions because he wanted to know what her life had been like as a child. She remembered the questions he had thrown at her that day in the swamp—maybe this was more of the same.

"My father is a planter, although he lost everything in the war and the fields around my home are now dormant. You have been to the platation and spoken to my father; you must have noticed the ruin and how run-down the house was."

"A lot of the South has not yet recovered from the war. I thought your home was better preserved than most."

She tightened her belt. Her body still tingled from his lovemaking, and it would only take a touch of his hand to bring her back into his arms. Why was he so distant now?

"I suppose so."

"You said your father objected to your marriage to Michael?"

"Yes, he did. Fervently." She lowered her head, but just for a moment, and then she met his gaze. "My father told me that he would never see me again if I married into the Duncan family."

"What did he have against them?"

He was grilling her hard, and she felt exposed by his questions. But he seemed insistent, so she answered his questions.

"The Duncan family did not have a good reputation—not good enough for my father. Michael's father did not put all his assets into Confederate funds like my father thought a true patriot should have done when the war came along. Instead, Mr. Duncan bought Yankee gold. I believe our neighbors who lost everything in the war resented Mr. Duncan for it. But he did not live long enough to rue the day."

"In retrospect, it sounds like he made a good business choice."

"That was what Michael always said. But my father's main objection to the family went deeper than that. He despised and mistrusted Brace, who had a reputation for bullying anyone who didn't think the way he did. It was suspected by some, although never proven, that Brace had set fire to the Jamiesons' house because of an argument he had with Mr. Jamieson over a horse." She clasped her hands tightly together. "The Jamiesons' five-year-old daughter died in that fire."

Wade noticed that her whole body was trembling, and he cursed himself for being an insensitive fool. But in a few moments he would have to say even more cruel words, words that would tear her heart out. He wished there were another way, but there was not. The thought of hurting her made him feel sick inside.

She watched the emotions play across his face, and she felt a deep sadness in him.

"Wade?"

At first she resisted when he reached out to gather her in his arms, but then she laid her head against his chest.

"Caroline, I wish there were some way I could spare you this, but I cannot."

She didn't want to know what he had to tell her. She spoke in a rush, trying to ignore what was to come. "My father did not go to the wedding, and our last meeting was a very painful one."

"Do not say any more. There is no need."

She felt like crying, but she held back her tears. "I know my father is sorry now. I know he would want to see me. It is painful for me to remember that his last words to me were spoken in anger." She felt a tightening in her chest as a premonition hit her. "I will want to see him as soon as possible." She clutched at Wade's arm, already knowing what he was about to tell her. "Say that I can see my father very soon."

He took her hands and captured them in his. He could not stand to look into her eyes as he began to speak. "And if it is not possible to see him, then what?"

She shook her head as dread settled over her. She turned an uncertain gaze up to him. She freed her hand from his clasp and moved across the cabin to stand at the window. "What are you trying to tell me?"

He went to her and eased her toward him. It seemed that she could not hold herself upright, and her head fell against his chest.

"Tell me what is wrong with my father."

"Caroline, I wish there were some way I could spare you this. You have been through so much."

She burrowed her face against his skin and allowed his arms to go around her. "What happened?"

"I received a telegram from Nate. He said your father had been shot."

He waited for her to react, but she said nothing. He had expected her to cry and carry on, but no sound came from her lips. Then he felt the violent trembling that shook her slight body.

"No! It cannot be. My father is not dead. If he were, I would have felt it in my heart."

He caught her hands. "Caroline, it is true. Do you think I would fabricate something like this?"

She stumbled away from him and threw herself down on the bed, burrowing her face into the pillow and sobbing so hard her whole body shook with the intensity of it.

He sat on the edge of the bed and gathered her in his arms. "*Mon amour*, I am so sorry." He kissed her tear-wet face, his heart hurting for her. He had never seen such complete devastation in anyone before.

At last the crying lessened, and he ran his hand up and down her back, trying to comfort her.

"I remember my father laughing and strong. I remember him teaching me to ride a horse. I remember his personality changing when he lost my mother. He was sad for so long. But I will always remember that he was angry with me when I last saw him."

"*Non, non*, do not think that. When I saw your father, he had only concern and love for you."

"You said he was shot?"

"That is what Nate's wire said."

"But who would do such a thing?"

"Perhaps you can guess."

"Brace!" She fell across the bed like a wilted flower. "When did it happen? How long ago?"

This was the question he had been dreading. "The telegram was waiting for me when we arrived in New Orleans from Texas."

She sat up and looked at him as if she didn't understand. "If you knew then, why didn't you tell me?"

"I was not sure you were strong enough to hear such tragic news."

"That was not your decision to make. We are talking about my father. You had no right to withhold the news from me."

"Do you forget how ill you were at the time? The doctor thought I should wait and tell you when you were stronger."

Her grief had suddenly turned to anger. "And who was to decide when I was stronger? It was not for you or the doctor to say what I could hear and what I should not be told."

"I made the decision to wait."

Her eyes were gleaming with anger. "What right did you have to decide for me? I am not your prisoner now."

"You have every right to be angry with me. But I wanted only to take care of you. I owed it to you because it was my fault you became ill."

She scrambled away from him as he spoke the words that crushed her heart. "Did you owe me when you forced me to leave San Sebastian? Did you owe me when you handcuffed me to the horse? Did you owe me when you married me today? Or did you just feel guilty because you tortured an innocent woman?"

He reached out to her and clasped his hand around her wrist. "I hope you will one day find it in your heart to forgive me. What I did to you was reprehensible. I would do anything to make it up to you."

"So you married me, thinking you could make amends for what you had done? I salute your sacrifice on my behalf."

"It was not like that at all."

When he reached out to her, she batted his hand away. "Don't touch me! How could you do such a thing? I had a life, and you took it away from me. Since the first day I saw you, you have been controlling me."

"Caroline, do not think that."

She moved to the long sofa and sat down, folding her legs beneath her. "What am I to do?" She buried her face in her hands. "My dear, sweet father, dead."

He knelt down beside her. "Caroline"—his hand slid up her arm—"I do feel guilty for the way I treated you at first. But guilt was not my motive for asking you to be my wife."

She flipped her hair out of her face as she tried to gather her fragmented thoughts. "Then what was your reason?"

The hand that touched her arm became caressing; he was so near, she could feel his breath on her cheek. The news of her father's murder had been a terrible blow, and her heart was shattered—and yet, at the moment, she wanted to be in Wade's arms, and she saw in his eyes that he sensed it.

He opened her robe, his hand moving across her thigh.

She bit her lip and caught her breath.

His hand moved between her legs, his finger easing into her while he lowered his head, molding his lips to hers.

Frantically she pressed her lips against his, fighting to bring him closer, needing to feel him inside her. She wanted to forget the sadness that swamped her. She wanted only to feel the wonderful things he could do to her. Her hands slid down his stomach, undoing his trousers.

He left her only long enough to undress; then he moved into position and gripped her hips, plunging into her in a rage of passion.

She touched her lips to his and took his groan into her mouth. She closed her eyes and turned her body over to his masterful lovemaking.

Afterwards, neither of them spoke. His hand tangled in her hair, and he lifted her face, kissing her, plunging his tongue into her mouth.

She whimpered, her body ready to receive him again. He carried her to the bed and lowered her onto the mattress. He could see her passion-glazed eyes in the moonlight, and he knew she was trying to think of anything but her father. She was not offering her body to him out of passion—she was giving herself to him out of desperation.

He spread her legs and eased into her, watching her eyes widen and then drift slowly closed. He plunged deeper and whispered in her ear, thinking her anger would be better than her grief. "I married you for this."

Her hips struck back at him. "Then take it—it's yours!"

Chapter Twenty-six

Wade was awake to watch the sunrise advance into the dark corners of the cabin, washing them in a soft light. He glanced at the golden head resting on his arm and studied her as she slept. He had hurt her badly last night. He had demanded a response from her body while he told her of her father's death. Could he have done anything worse?

He touched his lips to her cheek, wanting to hold her until her hurt went away and she could think about her father without crying.

She sighed in her sleep and nestled closer to him. He found himself wanting to possess her thoughts, her mind as well as her body. He had never cared about what was in a woman's mind until he met her.

Before now, he had always preferred to sleep alone. But he found he liked waking up with her beside him. His gaze wandered to her breasts; one was pressed against his chest, the other he touched softly. Like a fist slamming into his heart, a strong possessiveness hit him. She belonged to him, and no one was going to hurt her again.

He watched her eyes flutter and her breathing become shallow. She was slowly waking. He dreaded the moment she would remember that her father was dead. He also dreaded the accusations that she would probably hurl at him again. He deserved whatever she said to him.

She stretched like a sleek cat, and blood rushed through his body. He had never felt with any other woman what he had found with Caroline. He wanted her even now, but he would have to harness his passion for her sake. He was accustomed to that where she was concerned.

Caroline was just coming out of a deep sleep, and she groaned, dreaming that she had been riding astride a horse on her way to San Antonio. She was sore, and her body ached.

"No more liniment," she said, her eyes snapping open at the sound of her own voice.

The first sight she saw was soft golden eyes, staring back at her. "*Non*, *mon amour*, what is aching now cannot be helped with liniment."

She remembered now.

His hand moved down to gently massage the place where she really ached. "The pain will pass very soon." There was sorrow in his gaze. "I should not have been so greedy for your body. Forgive me."

Her hand slid up his arm, and she brought his head down to her. "You did this to me."

He rubbed his mouth against hers. "I am guilty, sweetheart. And I have a great need to have you again.

But I will control that need." He muttered under his breath, "I have done it before with you."

"Have you?"

"You have no idea."

"When?"

His lips skimmed hers. "Every time you wiggled that beautiful body at me."

She punched his shoulder. "I never did that."

"You were born to please a man. To please me."

He had no clothing on, and now in the light of day, she could see the entire length of his magnificent body. He was lean and tall. Black hair curled on the leg that touched hers. "I like the way you look."

He grinned. "Do you now?" He was doing some looking of his own, and she realized that she wasn't wearing anything either. She reached for the sheet, and he caught her hand. "It would be a shame to hide such beauty, especially from your husband."

She was shy, thinking about her outrageous actions of the night before. "What must you think of me?"

He turned her so her body fit against his. "I think you are the perfect wife for me. Most women are taught to act as if they do not like the intimacy between husband and wife, but you are not ashamed of your feelings, and you have delighted me with your honesty." His mouth gently touched her lips, and he kissed along her throat. "Never change. Always show your true feelings with me."

Caroline suddenly remembered about her father, and she pushed against him. Sliding out of bed, she recovered her robe from the floor and pushed her arms through the sleeves. "I need to find out what happened to my father. Will you help me find out how he died?"

"Of course I will. I expect Nate to be in New Orleans by the time we get back. He will have more information for us at that time."

Wade pulled on his trousers and shirt, tucking the shirttail into his waistband. "We have many things to talk about, Caroline."

She dropped down at the vanity, picked up a hairbrush, and began taking her anger and sadness out on her hair. She tugged at the tangles, pulling out strands of hair while tears washed down her cheeks. "How could I let you make love to me while my father lies dead?"

"You needed me last night, and I knew that." He sat down on the edge of the bed and pulled on his boots. "I am going to help you find your father's killer. Remember, I am good at hunting the guilty."

"And the innocent," she reminded him, tangling her hair in the brush. In her frustration she yanked harder.

He took the brush from her and gently unwound her hair from the bristles. Then with long strokes he brushed the golden mass. "Caroline," he said, meeting her gaze in the mirror, "you will need to trust me and tell me everything you think I should know."

There was a commotion at the door, and Wade went to see who was there. A waiter greeted him with the breakfast cart. Since Caroline was not dressed, Wade rolled the cart into the room. He uncovered the serving dishes, and then held a chair out for her. "They have sent us every kind of breakfast delicacy known to man." He placed her plate in front of her. "What takes your fancy?"

"I'm not hungry."

"You always say that." Without ceremony, he filled her plate and handed her a fork. "You must eat to keep up your strength."

She gazed at him through half-closed eyelids. "You used up almost all my strength last night."

He laughed. "And it took all my strength to satisfy you," he stated, raising his dark brow and taking a bite out of an apple muffin.

Her spontaneous laughter took him by surprise. "Are you likely to collapse at such times?"

"Very likely." He swept her onto his lap and urged her to take a bite of his muffin. Before he was finished enticing her, she had eaten a boiled egg and a slice of ham and drunk a cup of tea, while sitting on his lap. When he offered her a biscuit, she shook her head.

"I can't eat another bite."

He slowly turned her around so she was straddling his legs and brought her head forward so he could have access to her lips.

At first she was hesitant, but his hand went beneath her robe and settled over one of her breasts. Her eyes closed, and she gave him her lips.

She was fairly panting by the time he raised his head. Her hand slid over the fasteners on his trousers, and she opened them while he watched her with impatience.

He almost shot out of the chair when she pushed the material aside and touched him intimately, feeling him swell in her hand.

He lifted her in his arms and murmured something in French. He tossed her on the bed, shed his clothing, and went to her.

"What did you say?" she asked, meeting his flaming gaze.

"I was giving thanks that I found the only woman in the world who could satisfy my hunger," he muttered, jerking her forward and pressing his mouth against hers.

It was late that evening when Caroline stood at the railing watching the shoreline in the distance. She wondered if she would ever be able to think about her honeymoon without remembering her father's death. The two were linked together in her mind, and they always would be.

"What made you choose the *Cotton Maid* for our honeymoon?"

"I had a very good reason. But you may not agree with me."

"And that was?"

"You could not very well leave me if you decided that you wanted to swim away. The San Antonio River cannot be compared with the Mississippi River."

She smiled up at him. "As I recall, it was you who went swimming in the San Antonio River—I was merely drowning."

He tucked her hand into the fold of his arm. "So you were."

Her thoughts turned inward. If he had known her better, he would have recognized the danger signs in her eyes.

"You should have told me about my father before the wedding, Wade."

"I may have been wrong in that."

"We should not have married."

He glanced down at her. "I do not agree. I will make you happy, Caroline."

She thought of how angry Brace would be when he heard about the marriage. Brace was not right in his mind, and he had been obsessed with her from the beginning. He would come after Wade with a rage that could only be guessed at. Even Jonathan would not be safe from Brace's need for revenge upon her.

Wade noticed that he was drawing several envious glances from some of the male passengers. Instead of being pleased that they admired Caroline, he felt irritated. He imagined he had just felt the first pangs of jealousy. He pulled her closer to him, and his cold stare settled on the man next to Caroline. The man abruptly left without Caroline ever being aware of the drama that had just played out around her.

"The deed is done," she said, not realizing she had spoken aloud. "How much longer until we are back in New Orleans?"

"Three days."

She shivered as a cool breeze drifted off the water. He removed his coat and put it around her shoulders. "Are you ready to go to our cabin and listen to what I have to say?"

She nodded. "Yes, I am."

Moments later, he sat at the table with a pen and paper before him. "Let's make a list of your father's enemies."

"I am not aware that he had any enemies."

"What about Brace?"

"Well, yes. He was my first thought when you told me about my father's murder. If there was such a list, I would put him at the top. But Brace never does anything without a reason. What would he gain by killing my father?"

"That I cannot say, but nonetheless, Brace stands alone on our list of suspects."

"It has to be him." Anger surged through her, and she wanted to hit out at someone. No one but she could bring Brace to justice. It was a debt she owed her father and Michael.

"What if I inadvertently led Brace to your father?" Wade asked, voicing the question that had nagged at him ever since he'd heard of Mr. Richmond's death.

"In what way?"

"I do not think Brace Duncan intended for me to question your father. He directed me instead to the Lowell family in Savannah to ask my questions."

"But you went to my father first, didn't you?"

"I like to be thorough."

"I have often wondered what the Lowell family must have thought when they returned home and found me gone. You see, they were out of town when one of Brace's hirelings broke into the house. I barely escaped with my life that night. I had very little money, but it was enough to get me to Texas."

"The family was unsure what had happened to you. They found you gone, and your room in a shambles. They thought you might have met with foul play. They alerted the authorities, but no one could find you."

"I'm sorry about that. But I could not write and tell them the truth. Brace leaves nothing to chance when he wants something, and if they had known where I was, he would have done anything to make them talk. It probably saved their lives when they reported me missing to the authorities."

"And what does he want from you exactly?"

"He wants Michael's money, and he wants me."

"He cannot have you."

"If I thought he would leave me alone and never bother me again, I would consider giving him the money."

Wade could almost understand the man's obsession for Caroline: she was beautiful, intelligent, and the most desirable woman he had ever known. He had been drawn to her by just looking at her tintype. But he said none of that to Caroline.

"That will not stop a man like him. Looking back, I should have seen his obsession with you," he said.

Caroline sighed. "At least we know where he is for the moment. I don't think he has found out about us yet."

"He will. And when he comes, I will be waiting for him."

"If I could only talk to his mother, Lilly, she might help me. I know she is afraid of Brace. But she helped me escape him the first time."

"I do not want you involved in this. It is too dangerous. I want you at the house, where you will be protected."

She gave him a disgruntled glance. "I have had just about enough of you protecting me!"

He shrugged as if her outburst meant nothing to him. "You will just have to endure it."

She seated herself on a chair, her back straight, her hands folded in an elegant arch. "The estate Brace and his mother live on belongs to me now," she said in irritation. "It isn't that I want any part of it. I just don't like Michael's killer living in his house."

He was tapping the pen on the table, his eyes on the paper before him. "Hmm," he said as if he had not heard her.

"You know a lot about me," she said, standing and moving across the room. "Do I also have the right to ask you questions?"

He had been scribbling on the paper and paused to glance at her. Laying his pen aside, he gave her his full attention. "What would you like to know about me?"

"Whatever you want me to know."

He glanced at the floor as if editing his thoughts. "Caroline, I believe Dolly told you some of my background. My earliest memory is of living on the streets of New Orleans. If I had a mother and father, I do not remember either of them. But I do not want you to think that is important to me—I hope it is not to you."

"I do not care about your past."

"There was a woman, Maude Blackman, who ran a bakery—she was toothless, had frizzy gray hair and a stooped back. Many people shunned her because they thought her a witch. But I loved that old woman. She took me in at night and saw that I was fed. I slept in the back room of her shop."

Caroline realized that he was sharing information with her that very few people were privy to.

"I hung out with a rough gang of older boys who were always in trouble. They would rob people, sneak into houses and take things. Maude saw me with them one day and dragged me into her shop. I have never had a thrashing like the one she gave me that day. She said I was not to hang around with those boys, because I was going to grow up and be somebody. She made me work in her kitchen, scrubbing floors and washing pots and pans."

"She must have been very kind."

He shook his head. "Maude was never kind to anyone. She spoke broken French, she was crude and always said exactly what was on her mind. But the only time I have ever cried in my life was the day she died."

"How old were you?"

"I do not know my true age. Maude swears I was six when she took me in—that would have made me seven years old when she died."

"So young."

"Younger than Jonathan was when I found him."

"What did you do after Maude died?"

"My life was very different from yours. My earliest memories are of always being hungry."

She could not stop the tears that swam in her eyes. "But see what you have become. You are a man hundreds of people look to for their livelihood."

"I owe a great deal to Maude and to Anton. After Maude died, I moved to the docks, because I had learned that I could sneak into one of the warehouses and find a warm, dry place to sleep on a cotton bale. And I could always find food there. I had been living in Anton's warehouse for three months when he discovered me. The rest you know. He took me in and made me his heir."

"He was a father to you."

"Not in the true sense. He was a hard man, and it was not in him to show affection, but that was all right with me. I did not know how to give affection either. He sent me to one of the best schools, and I looked forward to class every day. Until I went to that school, I spoke very little English. Anton did not approve of my speaking French, so I tried to please him. But as you have probably noticed, when I feel deeply about something, I revert to my native language."

"Maude would have been proud of you today."

"Caroline, just as you quarreled with your father, I quarreled with Anton. He had a passion for guns. We had a country home at the time, and he would take me hunting almost every weekend. Not because he liked my company, but because he discovered I could shoot straight and fast. He taught me everything he knew about guns."

"So when you quarreled with him, you ran away and became a bounty hunter."

"I had no money of my own, and I did not want Anton's. The one thing I could do well was use a gun. I remember the day I went into a sheriff's office, in Abilene, Texas, and took a wanted poster off the wall. I then went after the man. As time passed, my reputation grew, and so did the price to hire my gun. I was a bounty hunter for nine years."

"Dolly told me your father became ill and sent for you."

"*Oui*. By the time I arrived in New Orleans, Anton had only hours to live. He told me that he had left me everything in his will, and that I must promise to lay down my gun and take care of the people who worked for him."

"And you did."

His gaze met hers. "I kept my promise until Brace

Duncan wrote me. Then I went in search of you."

She didn't want to talk about Brace. "What was Jonathan like when you found him?"

"The day I found him, it was raining. He was huddled between two buildings trying to stay warm and dry. He was ill and feverish, so I carried him home with me, and Mary took care of him. I had no intention that day of letting him live with me. But when his health improved, I could not bring myself to put him in an orphanage, and he did not ask to leave. I wanted him to have a suitable future, so I eventually enrolled him in a school in Baton Rouge. At the time, I thought it was the best thing for him. You made me understand that I was wrong."

"And you made me understand how much you cared for him. He is a wonderful boy. I have seen him grow and change every day."

"It is because of you that he is so happy now."

"I believe you understand him better than anyone, because you grew up much the same way."

"You now know as much about me as anyone, Caroline. I am a man who does not know his parentage. I am a man without a past. Will that ever matter to you?"

"Of course not. Why should it? I am more interested in the man you are today."

"When you agreed to marry me, did you think of me as one of your noble causes? Did you think you could help me like you tried to help Michael Duncan?"

"You are nothing like Michael."

"In what way are we different? We both wanted you. I want to know about the man who came before me."

She did not understand his mood. "Actually, the two

of you are very different. You will never really need anyone, Wade. Michael could never stand alone."

He rose to his feet and offered her his hand. "How would you like to eat in the dining room tonight?" he asked, deciding it was time he learned to live with the fact that other men admired his wife.

Chapter Twenty-seven

It was their last morning on board the *Cotton Maid* when Caroline stood alone at the railing, her mind wandering as she watched the mud-colored river being churned up by the paddle wheel.

Wade was in their cabin going over some documents he needed to finish before they docked. This was the first time she had been alone since coming on board, and she needed this time to think about what she was going to do about her father's death. She had not been able to go to his funeral, so she would have to mourn him in her heart. There would probably be debts to settle, and paperwork to be tended to.

There was no doubt in her mind that Brace had killed her father. She shuddered, hoping he had not suffered before he died. She had been a coward when she ran away after Michael's death—she should have gone to the authorities and told them everything. If she had, her father would still be alive.

She had to stop Brace before he killed again. She could not allow his evil to touch the ones she loved.

She had to go to Charleston before Brace decided to come to New Orleans. If Wade knew what she had in mind, he would stop her. She would have to be careful that she did not give her plan away.

A wedding vow was forever or until death. What Wade did not understand was that Brace would come after him, he would come after Jonathan, and he would come after anyone she loved.

She glanced across the smooth river to a place where the water drifted into a small tributary. In the distance she could see a grove of cypress trees and wished that she could just get in a skiff with Wade and Jonathan and disappear into the swamps where Brace could never find them. But that was not possible—life and reality would soon encroach on her world, and she had to protect the two people she loved the most.

This time, she would not run.

When they arrived in port, Caroline and Wade were jostled by the crowd as they made their way to the gangplank. Wade took her arm and hurried her out of the crowd and to the waiting carriage.

The little Frenchman was beaming, and Jonathan stood beside him, jumping up and down with excitement.

"Welcome home, Wade, madame," Louis called.

Jonathan's greeting was less formal and much more energetic. He jumped into Wade's arms and reached out to hug Caroline. "I missed you both so much. I'm glad you're home now."

Wade grinned at the boy. "You little scamp. I suppose you gave Mary and everyone else a difficult time while we were away," Wade said, depositing the boy onto the leather buggy seat.

"Not much. I did fall into the fountain with my Sunday clothes on. And I broke a plate, but it wasn't my fault. It just slid right off the table when I was reaching for a biscuit. I did break a window, but I wasn't aiming at it with that rock I threw."

Caroline's laughter spilled out like a fountain. "What were you aiming at, Jonathan?"

"A tin can I put on the window ledge. If that man hadn't sacred me, I wouldn't have broken the window or fallen into the pond."

"It would seem, Jonathan, we arrived home just in time to salvage the house."

The boy grinned, looking up at Caroline and then Wade. "I couldn't wait for you to get back home. Mary let me check the days off on the calendar."

They were chatting happily when something Jonathan had said registered with Caroline. "What man scared you?"

"I don't know who he was. He didn't say his name. I was all wet and climbing out of the water when I asked him what he was doing in our garden. He said he was looking for a friend."

Wade was speaking to Louis, so he hadn't paid attention to what the boy had said. He did not see Caroline stiffen when she took Jonathan's arm and lowered her voice. "What else did the man say to you?"

"He asked who I was and who owned the house. So

I told him my parents were not at home. He asked me if there was a woman living in the house, but before he could tell me her name, Mary came out."

Her insides tightened. "And what did you tell him?"

"Nothing. Mary was real mad because I broke the window, and she came to get me. When I turned back to talk to that man, he was gone. Just disappeared. Mary said I was making it up 'cause she didn't see anyone. But I did see him—I really did."

Caroline felt the same blind terror that she always felt when she thought of Brace. She knew his cunning mind, and how far he would go to get to her. If the stranger had been Brace, she shuddered to think of the evil that had come so close to Jonathan. Her heart gave a lurch when she thought what could have happened to this child if Mary had not appeared.

Mary was a marvel. While they were dining, the housekeeper got them both unpacked and the master suite prepared for them.

Wade was meeting with some men in his office, so Caroline went to Jonathan's room to tuck him into bed. She moved a chair to the side of his bed and opened the book they had been reading before the wedding.

He yawned and said as if it were the most natural thing in the world, "I'm sleepy, Mommy."

"Then close your eyes while I read to you." Before she was halfway though the first page, he had already fallen asleep.

She closed the book and watched him for a time.

He was a beautiful child, and smart. With Wade to direct him, his future was assured. She wanted Jonathan to be happy, to grow up strong and to be a man of honor—there again, with Wade as his guide, that was sure to happen.

She bent to kiss his cheek and then blew out the lamp. "Good night, little son." She left the door half open when she tiptoed into the hallway.

She walked through the master suite and out onto the gallery. There was a chill to the night, which meant that the wind was coming from the direction of the river. Someone had lit a torch, and she could see the light ripple across the water in the fountain. Deeper into the garden, the light faded to shadows and then into ominous darkness.

Should she tell Wade what she suspected, or would he merely laugh at her and accuse her of having an overactive imagination?

Her troubled musing was cut short when strong arms slid around her waist and a warm mouth nibbled on her neck.

She shivered with delight as Wade's mouth moved to her earlobe.

"Did you finish your work?"

He led her into the room, watching how the lamplight cast golden light onto her skin. "I sent everyone home." He closed the double doors and pulled the curtains. "Nate was here."

She spun around to face him. "Where is he? I want to talk to him and find out what he knows about my father."

"He will return tomorrow." He ran his finger around

the neck of her gown. "He did tell me more bad news." To Wade, it seemed he was always the one who had to deliver ill tidings to her. "Your father's home was burned to the ground."

She sucked in her breath. "No! Why would Brace do such a thing? Why, why, why?"

"You know him better than we do; perhaps you can guess."

She slumped down on the bed. "He did it because he wanted to hurt me."

"That is what I think."

"Not only my father gone, but the memories—everything that was my mother is now ashes."

He knelt down beside the bed and gathered her in his arms. "Keep the memories in your heart and be glad you have them."

She touched his cheek, and the grief on his face cut into her heart. "You have no memories of your mother and father."

"That is not what I meant. I need no memories, I have you and Jonathan and the future. But your memories can never be taken from you—they belong to you alone."

She touched her lips to his. "I will always be with you."

He rolled her backward on the bed without taking his mouth away from hers.

"If you are with me, there is nothing more I need."

He left her to blow out the lamp, then came back to her. His mouth recaptured hers, and he sank down onto the bed.

All thoughts of Brace were wiped from her mind as

Wade kissed and touched her. She sighed when he molded her to him, and she pressed her face into his neck when he made love to her.

The shadowy form of a man detached itself from the darkness to stand by the fountain. He crushed his hands into fists as he watched the light go out in the master bedroom.

"That bastard is touching her," his raspy voice choked out. "He has soiled her purity, and for that they will all die!"

He paced back and forth, anger building inside him like lava in a volcano ready to erupt. "I will bring him down—I will bring them all down and her with them."

He stalked toward the stairs that led to the gallery, reaching into his pocket to make sure the gun was still there. When his foot hit the first step, he heard loud voices and the sound of running footsteps.

"I saw someone," Brace heard one man call to another. "You go around the front of the house, and I'll go this way!"

Brace melted back into the shadows, moved quickly into the garden, and attempted to climb the high brick wall. He was not a tall man, so he made several tries, falling back into a muddy flowerbed that had just been watered. After several more attempts, he finally made it over the top and dropped to the other side. His hand darted into his pocket, and he cursed aloud: He had dropped the gun in his scramble over the wall.

He moved along the wall until he came to the neighboring house. He boldly cut through the yard and found his horse where he had left it tied to a tree branch.

There would be another time. He smiled to himself. He would not stop until Caroline had paid with her life for betraying him.

Frank and Elliot Webber met at the front of the house. Both of the brothers were dockworkers, but Wade had pulled them off their jobs to guard the house. Frank, the elder, had been employed by the Renault family for twenty years, and Elliot almost that long.

"When Mr. Renault asked us to watch the house, I didn't think we'd see anything. Until tonight it's been as quiet as can be."

"No one could have got past me," Frank said, raising the lantern so he could look behind a neatly trimmed hedge.

Elliot looked disgusted that he had let the man get away. "I tell you, I saw someone! He was sneaking toward the back stairs until I called out to you. Then he must have run off."

"What if he went over the back wall?" Frank said, knowing his brother was not likely to exaggerate. If he said he'd seen someone, then he had.

"Let's check and see," Elliot said, already walking in that direction.

When they got to the back wall, they saw muddy footprints. Elliot bent down and picked up the gun, holding it out for his brother to see.

"Just look what we have here. A double-shot derringer. Looks like a toy, but deadly. Now, how do you suppose it got here?"

"Yeah, a derringer," Frank said, taking it and flipping it open. "And it's loaded. Even if Mr. Renault is asleep, I think we'd better wake him up for this."

Chapter Twenty-eight

Wade had just made love to Caroline, and he now held her close to him. She had been dealt another blow today. He smoothed her hair out of her face. "*Mon amour*, give me one more week, and then I will take you to Charleston, and we will settle all your affairs."

She rose up on her elbow. "There is no need to go to South Carolina. Brace is here."

Wade gave a half shake of his head. "I do not think so."

"He is! I know it. And if he's here, it is for only one reason. He wants to see me dead."

He pulled her to him. "You must not think that way. You are protected as long as you are in this house."

"You don't know him like I do," she said in frustration, wishing she could make him understand. "You have never understood his evil. I am not safe in this house, and neither is Jonathan—and neither are you. Brace was here in this yard."

Wade gave her a skeptical glance. "He could not

possibly have gotten into the yard. I was not going to tell you this, but I have men on guard."

She shook her head and sat up. "Jonathan said he talked to a stranger while we were away. I haven't questioned him too much for fear I would make him afraid." She shook her head. "I should caution him about Brace. He must be careful."

Wade had every reason to believe that Brace Duncan was a madman. But he also believed that Caroline was just overreacting to something that could easily be explained. She had been running and hiding for so long, she saw danger everywhere.

"You are allowing your fear of Brace to make you suspect everything that happens and to see trouble when there is none."

"Why won't you believe me?"

Wade glanced toward the door when someone knocked. He frowned and pulled the cover over Caroline. "It must be important, for someone to disturb us at this time of night.

"Just a moment," he called out, getting out of bed and drawing on his trousers. He grabbed his shirt, pulled it on, and went to answer the door without buttoning it.

"Mary?" he asked, opening the door a crack. "Is something wrong?"

"I'm sorry to bother you. Frank and Elliot Webber are downstairs. They say it's important."

"Let them know I will be down directly."

He buttoned his shirt and tucked it in his trousers. Then he pulled his boots on and leaned over to place a lingering kiss on Caroline's lips.

He saw the fear in her eyes and realized just how upset she was. "This is just business. I should not be long." He gave her another kiss and allowed his hand to drift across her breasts. "Wait for me."

When Wade went downstairs, Frank and Elliot Webber were waiting for him in the entry. It was easy to see that they were brothers, because each had a shock of brown hair and deep-set gray eyes. Big and heavily muscled, they were a force to be reckoned with. Each of them looked as if his nose had been broken. It was reputed that the Webber brothers liked a good fight, especially after consuming too much whisky. But they were men Wade trusted, and that was why he had enlisted their help to protect Caroline.

"Sorry, sir," Frank said, jerking his cap off and digging his elbow into his brother's ribs, reminding him to do the same. "I thought you might want to see what we found."

Wade shook hands with both men. "What have you there?"

Elliot held the derringer out to his boss. "Someone was lurking about in the yard. He ran off when he realized I'd seen him. He's a sly one—we couldn't catch him. But he left footprints where he went over the back wall, and he dropped this."

Wade took the gun and turned it over in his hand. "Did you get close enough to describe him?"

"No, sir. I'm sorry. It was too dark, and he was too far away. If I met him in daylight, I wouldn't even know him."

Wade valued their opinions, so he asked, "What do either of you make of this?"

"I think someone was up to no good. I can't say who, and I can't say why, but maybe you know, since you have us looking out for Mrs. Renault."

Wade had almost made another grave mistake with Brace Duncan. The man was in New Orleans just as Caroline had warned him. He should have trusted her instinct. Because he had been careless, evil had come close to her tonight. And unless Brace was apprehended, he would not stop until he got even closer to Caroline.

Frank watched his boss check the gun to see that it was loaded. "What do you want us to do, Mr. Renault?"

Wade's mind raced ahead to what must be done to keep Caroline safe. "I want the guard doubled—no, tripled. Choose whomever you trust so you men can work in round-the-clock shifts. I want the house protected at all times."

"I agree, sir," Frank said.

Elliot looked confused. "To cover such a big area, we'll have to use five or six men at all times."

"Do whatever you have to. I want one man watching every door."

"And when the missus is in the garden?"

Wade clapped Elliot on the back. "I'll leave it up to you. I owe both of you for tonight. You may have saved Mrs. Renault's life."

"This man is trying to kill her?" Frank asked, attempting to sort it all out in his mind.

"He has killed before, and he will not hesitate to do so again."

Wade didn't realize he was pacing as he described Brace with the perception of a bounty hunter.

"The man's name is Brace Duncan. He is of

medium height, has dark hair, and wears stylish clothes. He had a mustache, but he could have shaved it off. He wears a gold ring on the little finger of his left hand with the letter D inscribed on it."

Wade stopped pacing and looked from one man to the other. "You must understand and make the others understand—this man is dangerous. Make sure you are all armed."

"We won't let you down, sir. You can depend on us."

"I do. You must not allow any strangers on the property, is that understood?"

Frank answered for them both. "Yes, sir."

Wade walked toward the stairs. "Have Mary give you something to eat. I will want the two of you to stay here at all times. Tell her to find you a room in the house."

Wade quietly entered the bedroom and placed the derringer on the dressing table. He knew that Caroline had fallen asleep, because he could hear her slow, even breathing. He quietly undressed and slipped into bed beside her and took her into his arms.

Mon amour, he thought, pressing his mouth against hers. She barely stirred in her sleep.

At what point had she become his life, his reason for being? If anything happened to her, he would find no joy in existence. He pulled her tightly to him and spread kisses over her face. So this was what it felt like to love someone to the exclusion of everything else, to put another's life before one's own? He felt as if his heart had been ripped to shreds because of the hurt she had been forced to live through.

He touched his lips to her ear and whispered

softly, "I cannot go back to what I was before you came into my life. I was dead inside until you breathed life into me."

She opened her eyes and blinked as if coming out of a deep sleep. Seeing the fire in Wade's eyes, she reached up and stroked his cheek.

"I tried to stay awake but I was sleepy."

The emotions pouring out of him were so strong, he was staggered. He could not talk or think clearly. "Go back to sleep, sweetheart."

"You will stay with me this time?" she asked sleepily, burrowing herself against him.

"I will be right beside you always."

Brace entered his dark hotel room, not bothering to light a lamp. He fell back on the bed, thinking how near he had come to being caught tonight. It looked like Renault was keeping guards at his place, which would make it harder to draw Caroline out, but certainly not impossible.

He rubbed his hands together. He had scraped them on the brick wall, and he had torn his trousers when he climbed over it. Rage lingered in his heart. No brick wall would keep him away from Caroline.

He had to think of a plan, something the bounty hunter would never expect. He had to find someone who knew details about their daily life. There would be a hole somewhere in Wade Renault's defenses, and Brace was determined to find out what it was.

At first he had thought he would just shoot Renault, but that would be too easy. He wanted Renault to suffer—wanted him to cry out in agony knowing the woman he loved was dead!

He should have realized that Renault would fall in love with Caroline when he sent him after her. He'd thought he had selected well by choosing a dispassionate man with a reputation for being cruel and detached.

He had been wrong.

The blood ran cold in his veins when he thought of Caroline lying beside Wade Renault.

"You will be sorry, Caroline. You will learn that you belong to me, and no one else."

Caroline opened her eyes, feeling calm and rested. She turned her head, and her face bumped against Wade's wide chest. She propped herself up on the pillow and watched him as he slept. With his intense spirit, she could only imagine the warmth he could pour into a woman if he loved her. She wanted badly to be that woman, but he had married her for a far different reason.

His dark lashes lay like silk against his tan cheeks. She loved the way his ebony hair fell across his forehead. His mouth, she could hardly resist kissing. She lightly touched a lock of his hair and jumped when he grabbed her hand, coming instantly awake.

For a moment, she saw the adversarial look of the hunter in his golden eyes until he realized who had touched him. His mouth moved into a smile, and he stretched slow and long, then pulled her toward him.

"So you want to play," he taunted, rubbing his thumb over her lips.

"I was just watching you sleep. Did you know that you are a very handsome man?"

His smile was lazy and sensual. "I am glad you think

so, although I have not heard any woman say that to me before."

"They were probably too frightened of you to tell you how they felt. Besides, I don't want to think of you with other women."

He studied her face, looking for the truth in her eyes. "You have nothing to be concerned about, Caroline. You have erased them from my mind."

She gave him her most seductive look. "Perhaps you need more reminding that I am your wife."

He pulled her on top of him, yanking up her nightgown so her bare flesh touched his. She felt him swell against her, and caught her breath. Leaning slowly toward him, she touched her lips to his. "Mmm," she breathed, flicking her tongue out and touching his mouth, bringing a groan from him.

He rolled her over, pinning her beneath him. "I hope you intend to wake me this way every morning." He nudged her breast, then ran his teeth over the swollen nipple. "I can think of no better way to start my day."

His mouth ground against hers, and she was lost to the flowing emotions that passed between them.

"I want to hold you forever," he muttered, sliding into her.

"And I want you to," she answered, trembling, sighing, biting her lip, and then surrendering.

It was sometime later, when Caroline was curled up next to him, that Wade broached the subject he dreaded. "You were right about Brace. He is in New Orleans."

"God help me," she whispered. "I felt certain that

he was here, but I had hoped I was wrong." She felt sick inside, and bile rose up in her throat. "How did you find out?"

"He was here, just as you said. I am sorry I did not listen to you when you warned me."

She trembled, burrowing closer to him.

"So it was him that Jonathan saw in the garden."

"It would seem so."

"Then we must send Jonathan away so he will be safe. Send him to Nelly and Yance."

Wade could feel the panic rising in her, and he gathered her close. "It is best for Jonathan to remain here with us. I have good men guarding the grounds, and Brace will not be able to slip past them. I want you to remain in the house and keep Jonathan with you."

"My first instinct is to run, but I promised myself I would never do that again." She looked into his eyes. "I know you will keep us safe. It's just that Brace is a destroyer of lives. He destroys without feeling guilty about it."

"Caroline," he breathed her name into her hair. "I could not go on without you."

She drew back and stared at him—was he admitting he loved her?

"I have never heard you say that before."

"I guard what belongs to me. You and Jonathan are mine."

She closed her eyes, knowing that was as close to a declaration of love as he had ever made.

"Our son and I are very fortunate to be under your protection."

He felt her relax against him, and he knew she was drifting off to sleep. Had he done enough to protect her? For the first time doubt nagged at his mind. Caroline knew the danger, he reassured himself. If she stayed within the safe boundaries he had made for her, Brace could not get to her.

He shifted his weight, but she did not move. Could there possibly be anything he had overlooked? He pressed his lips against her cheek and heard her steady breathing. Life was just so damned good now—but there was always the threat of Brace hanging over them.

He had men searching the town and many of the outlying areas, looking for the man. So far, there was no clue to where he was staying. But he was nearby and he was a determined killer.

Brace would have to surface sooner or later, and when he did, Wade would be waiting for him.

Chapter Twenty-nine

Brace had searched for days to find a deserted place where he could lure Caroline to him. He was anxious to get his hands on her, so much so, he had considered storming the house and taking his chances. But reason returned when he discovered the house in the swamps; it was perfect for his needs. It was far enough away from everything that he would draw no attention to himself. The house was in pitiful condition, damp and dark. The cane-bottom chairs were wobbly, and the bed sagged in the middle; the blankets he had thrown on the mattress were already musty and dank.

But the derelict house suited his purpose just fine; nothing would dampen his spirits now. Caroline was as good as in his hands.

He smiled as he mounted the horse he had acquired from the livery stable. He would find Renault's weakness and use it against him.

* * *

It was late afternoon when Brace rode past the Renault estate, gauging the number of men on guard there. If he hadn't stirred things up by almost getting caught, Renault would not have brought in so many men. One of them was clipping the hedges at the side of the house, and another was just standing under the shade of a tree, keeping vigil. They were all fools if they thought they could stop him.

One of the guards looked his way, and Brace waved as if he were out for a leisurely ride. The man waved back. No suspicion there.

He had decided that there was no way he could enter the estate at the front. And he had very little doubt that there would be even more men watching the back of the house.

He had to talk to the boy he had spoken with. He had no notion how the boy figured into the lives of Renault and Caroline, but he had to find a way to draw the child's attention. He needed an ally on the inside. He didn't know much about kids, but he figured they could be bribed easier than an adult.

A plan was forming in his mind. He would hide behind the back wall until either Caroline or the boy came along. He certainly wasn't foolish enough to tangle with Renault: he couldn't beat him unless he outsmarted him in some way. But the day would soon come when he would have his revenge on the bounty hunter, one way or another.

He heard someone coming down the path, and he ducked behind the wall, listening carefully. The footfalls were light, so it had to be the boy.

He edged himself halfway up the wall and called out, "Lad, come over here. I want to talk to you."

Jonathan went to Brace without hesitation. "Sir, what are you doing on our wall? Why don't you come to the front of the house if you want to see us?"

"I found this lying in that field over there," Brace said, holding out a gray and yellow striped ball. "I thought it might be yours."

"No. My ball is red."

"What's your name?"

The boy took a bite of an apple before he answered. "I'm Jonathan Renault. What's your name?"

The hated name of Renault twisted in Brace's gut, but he managed to smile. "My name is a secret. Can you keep a secret, Jonathan?"

"I can if I want to." He took another bite of his apple.

"Do you know Caroline?"

"Sure I do. She's my mommy."

Brace was taken aback. He had been asking questions around New Orleans about Renault, and no one mentioned that he had a son. "Are you sure she's your mother?"

"Of course. I guess I ought to know who my mommy is. And Wade is my father." He had finished his apple and threw the core toward the pond, missing it by inches. "What's your secret?"

"I know someone who lives in your house—someone who is a good friend of mine."

"You know me. You saw me before, but I don't think we are friends."

"I know Caroline."

The child frowned, sensing that something wasn't quite right. "No, you don't. She would have told me if she knew you."

"But she does. You see, we have been friends for a long time. I'm from far away where she once lived. I came here because I want to surprise her."

The child swung onto a low-hanging branch so he could be even with the man. "Why would you want to do that?"

"Don't you think that your mommy likes surprises?"

Jonathan thought about that. "I guess so. I guess everyone does."

"Why don't you come with me, and we'll ride into town, and you can buy her a little gift. You'd like that, wouldn't you?"

"You mean I could ride on a horse with you?"

"That's exactly what I mean. Just climb up here, and I'll lift you over the wall. You'll have to hurry."

At that moment Frank called out to the boy. "Jonathan. Where are you hiding? You're wanted in the house."

The boy's face crumpled into disappointment. "I can't go with you right now." He hopped down from the branch. "I guess Mommy wants me."

"I'll be here the same time tomorrow, if you decide you want to go with me into town. Remember, tell no one about our visit—let this just be our little secret."

Jonathan nodded. "I won't tell anyone. I gotta go now."

Brace smiled to himself. He had found Renault's weakness.

It was the boy.

As it happened, it was over a week before Jonathan again made his way to the back wall. In that time, Brace had been there waiting every day, ever vigilant for a chance to draw the boy to him, his temper mounting. He had been forced to hide like a coward when the guards patrolling the grounds came his way. His anger was almost more then he could swallow, and he was beginning to lose all reason. He had even considered making a run for the house and shooting anyone who got in his way. It really didn't matter what happened to him. All he could think about was seeing Caroline dead.

He could hardly believe his good fortune: The boy was coming down the path in his direction. He took a deep breath and tried to smile.

"Boy . . . Jonathan, over here," he said as quietly as he could so he would not be overheard by the guards.

Jonathan casually walked toward him. "Are you here again, mister?"

"Of course I am," Brace bit out. "I told you I would be, didn't I?"

"I forgot all about you."

Brace's anger shot up—he didn't like anyone to forget about him. But he could not show his anger until he had the child in his grasp. "Do you still want to come with me to get your mommy a surprise?"

Jonathan glanced back toward the house and then to the man. "I'd like to, but my father might not like it."

Brace reached into his coat pocket. "Just put this letter on the bench, and come back here so I can lift you over. Your mommy will be so surprised by what I have in mind."

Jonathan took the letter and turned it over in his hand. "What's this for?"

The boy was beginning to annoy him. "Do you

have to question everything I say?" Then realizing his anger had startled the boy, he softened his tone. "This is for your mommy."

Jonathan blinked at the man's harsh tone, but he carried the letter to the bench, propping it against the back. "Can I still ride on the horse? Can I guide it?"

"Yes. You can ride in front."

Jonathan held his arms up, and Brace lifted him over the wall. Once he had the boy in his grasp, he kept a hand on his arm, half dragging him forward as he walked away.

"You're walking too fast. I can't keep up with you."

"Keep your mouth shut and quit whining."

Jonathan halted, knowing something was wrong. "You aren't going to buy my mommy a gift."

"What a smart boy you are." Brace's heart rate accelerated. The moment the boy had come with him, he had won this game between himself and Caroline. He knew her—she would do almost anything to get the boy back. "You are my gift to me," he told the now frightened boy.

Caroline was waiting for Jonathan on the veranda. Since she had discovered that Brace had been lurking about, she insisted that they read on the veranda in sight of the guards.

She heard the tall case clock chime two times. It wasn't like Jonathan to be late—he was always so excited about reading another chapter. Uneasiness settled over her as she entered the house. First she went into the kitchen, where she found Mary bent over a copper kettle with a polishing rag in her hand.

"Have you seen Jonathan?"

"No. Not since lunch. He was supposed to be with you, wasn't he?"

Caroline could not keep the worry out of her voice. "He's not. Where do you suppose—"

Mary paled, setting the kettle aside. "I'll just search the upstairs. He may have gone to his bedroom."

With growing concern, Caroline nodded. "I will search the downstairs."

When Mary returned a short time later and shook her head, Caroline's concern deepened. "He's not in the house. If you will speak to the guards out front, I'll go into the garden and look for him," Caroline said, running for the back door. She was still running when she reached the path that led to the place where she and Jonathan had first met. Perhaps he had misunderstood her instructions and was waiting for her there.

As she approached the bench, her heart stopped when she saw the letter. She snatched it up, already knowing whom it was from. Ripping it open with trembling fingers, she read:

Caroline, if you are the one to read this, I have Jonathan. If you want him back alive, you must follow the map I drew on the back of this page—come alone or I will kill the boy. You know me well enough to realize I do not make idle threats. You also know that if I give you my word, I will keep it. If you come to me, I will let the boy go. But if you tell Renault, and he shows up, they will both die. Come as quickly as you can and come alone. I am most impatient to see you again.

She clamped her hand over her mouth. Brace had Jonathan! She suppressed a sob. The child must be so frightened—she had to get to him as soon as possible. She turned the letter over and memorized the directions. There was no time to lose—if Brace said he would kill Jonathan, he would do it. She heard a guard coming in her direction, and she hurried toward the house. There was one thing she needed before she left.

"Good day, Mrs. Renault. Mary said you were looking for Jonathan," Frank said.

She shook her head and stared at the ground so Frank would not see how upset she was. "It's all right. I know where he is."

"Good. That little scamp keeps us all busy."

"If you will excuse me," she said, hurrying toward the back steps that took her to the bedroom.

"Wait, Mrs. Renault, you dropped—"

She didn't hear him; she was already halfway up the stairs. Frank glanced down at the paper and saw the map sketched on the back. With a worried frown he turned it over and read what was written there. In the next moment he was running toward the front of the house, where he found Louis hitching the horses to the carriage so he could take Mary into town for her weekly shopping.

"Louis, get me to town and don't spare the horses—I have to see Mr. Renault!"

Caroline found the derringer on the dresser where Wade had left it. She checked the chamber and saw that it was loaded before she dropped it into her pocket. With quickened steps, she ran down the back stairs and made her way to the stable.

She had wanted Wade's gelding because it would be the fastest of all the horses, but his stall was empty. Wade must have ridden the horse into town. She grabbed a bridle from a hook and went to the next stall, where a frisky gray mare tossed her head. She quickly slipped the bridle over its head and, not bothering with a saddle, hauled herself onto the mare's back.

She kicked the horse into a gallop as soon as they left the stables. She heard Elliot calling out and running after her, but she did not slow her pace. She had to get to Jonathan before Brace hurt him.

As it happened, Frank met Wade returning to the house not a mile down the road. He leaped out of the carriage and handed him the letter. "We've got real trouble, sir."

Wade read the letter while trying to control his spirited mount. "God help me!" he exclaimed as fear tightened in his gut like a vise. "Where did you leave my wife?"

"She went into the house. I thought she would be safe there. He's got the boy, though."

Wade's eyes narrowed, and his jaw tightened. "She will go after the boy. You should have stayed with her so you could have prevented it."

"I didn't think she would—"

"Let me have your gun," Wade said, his voice trembling with emotion.

Frank unbuckled his gun belt and handed it to his boss.

"I'll come with you."

"No. This I have to do alone." He buckled the gun belt around his waist and kicked his horse into action, his heart in his throat. "Caroline," he said, grief tearing at him. "Let me get to her in time."

Chapter Thirty

A feeling of growing desperation tore at Caroline. She kicked her mount to a faster pace. She could only imagine how frightened Jonathan must be. Brace would have made threats—she just hoped he hadn't hurt the boy.

Dust rose behind her as she bent lower over her mount. According to the map Brace had drawn, the place should be just around the next bend. The mare ran as if she were still fresh. Caroline rode beneath drooping willow trees, the branches snagging her hair, tearing it loose from the chignon. Finally, in the distance she saw the house. There was no reason to sneak up to the place, because Brace would be watching for her.

She dismounted, looking about with her hand resting on the derringer in her pocket. She was as frightened as she had ever been in her life, but she was more afraid of what Brace would do to Jonathan than she was for her own safety.

It was an eery place with moss hanging from dead cypress trees; it looked as if it had been abandoned for a long time. The house sat on stilts, the paint chipped away from years of neglect. Rickety steps led to the front porch, where the door hung on one hinge. There was no one in sight. The sounds coming from the swamp were almost deafening: Then silence fell around her, and a shiver went up her spine.

The hand that held the derringer trembled as she stared at the two front windows, wondering if Brace was there watching her. He probably was. She reminded herself that she was doing this for Jonathan, and for Michael.

"Jonathan! It's Mommy. Are you in the house?"

She heard a small cry from somewhere inside the dwelling and she clutched the derringer tighter. There was no doubt in her mind that she could shoot Brace stone-cold dead if she got the chance.

"Mommy. I'm scared!"

She ran in the directions of the child's voice, praying Brace wouldn't hurt him before she got there. He was perfectly capable of hurting a child, and he would do it just to spite her.

"I'm here!" she cried, a bit breathless from running. "Don't be afraid."

She had just reached the bottom step when the door creaked open, and Brace stood there, his face twisted, Jonathan under one arm. A rifle was slung over his shoulder, and a slow smile curved his lips. He was the same as she remembered him except his hair was a little grayer now. His eyes were still cold and cruel, and he was still her worst nightmare.

She took another step and then another—there

were seven steps before she reached the porch. "Let my son go."

"You have no son."

"Jonathan, remember the book we were reading—remember about being brave?"

He nodded, but his eyes were fraught with fear, and his small body trembled.

Caroline glanced back at Brace. He was capable of any crime if it would get him what he wanted. He had come all the way to New Orleans, worked out a plan to get his hands on her. She knew there was nothing she could say that would deter him, but she had to try. "I told you to let my son go."

He rubbed his stubbled cheek against the stock of his rifle. "All in good time."

"Do it now."

"My, my, my, but you seem to have found courage since I last saw you. How have you been doing, Caroline?"

"Don't speak to me about that. Tell Jonathan that you do not intend to hurt him—you're frightening him."

"It's not the boy I want, and you know it." His voice came out in a hiss. "You know what I am here for."

Caroline reached out to Jonathan. "He doesn't mean any harm to you. You heard him—he has come for me. Please do not be frightened."

"I'm sorry," the boy said, wiping tears on the back of his hand. "He said we would get you a present and it would be a surprise you would like. It's all my fault."

"No. You must not think that. None of this is your fault."

"He wants to hurt you, Mommy—he said so. I don't want him to."

She stared openly at Brace. "Allow me to put him on the horse and send him back home. You have me—that's all you ever wanted."

"This boy can't ride that horse," Brace said scornfully. "He could hardly stay astride the one I was holding him on."

"I would rather have him take his chances on that horse than to let him see what is going to happen here."

"The boy stays." Brace smiled cruelly, and Caroline knew in that moment that she had shown him her weakness—her love for Jonathan—and he would use it against her. He was good at that. She had given him the power to hurt her by hurting her son.

"What do you have in mind?" she asked, moving up another step, inching closer to Jonathan.

"I'm going to have the pleasure of watching you die today, Caroline. You never listened to me when I told you that you belonged to me. You married Michael, and I had to get rid of him. Now you've gone and married Renault, and I'll soon take care of him, too. But you won't be around to know, so don't worry about it."

She probably would die today, and just when she had so much to live for. Her gaze went to Jonathan, who was squirming and trying to pull himself free. "Don't fight him, Jonathan. You will only make it worse."

Brace yanked painfully on the boy's arm. "Listen to her, and I just may let you live." He glanced at Caroline. "I can do that one thing for you if you will sign the papers leaving me Michael's estate."

"If you will allow Jonathan to leave, I will tell you where the gold is hidden."

"Do you think I am a fool? You could tell me anything you wanted to, just to free the boy."

Jonathan kicked at Brace. "You leave my mommy alone! I'm not going to let you hurt her!"

With a sudden jerk, Brace flung the boy against the porch railing, using such force that Jonathan crumpled onto the warped boards.

Caroline climbed another step so she could go to him, but Brace raised his rifle, aiming it at her.

"You don't know how long I have waited for this moment. I dreamed of you crying and begging me to let you live."

She raised her head. "I'm neither crying nor begging. I will not sign the papers giving you Michael's estate. I despise you for you are evil. You killed my father."

"I'm not evil," he said, looking surprised by her words. "I'm just a man who loves a woman too much. You did this to me, Caroline. I had to kill your father. He wouldn't tell me where to find you."

Tears sprang to her eyes. "You fool. My father didn't know where to find me." She was crying openly now. He had blatantly admitted killing her father with no more feeling than if he had swatted an insect. "You have left a trail of destruction and broken lives. Even your own mother is afraid of you."

"Do you think I care? I don't let anyone come between me and you." He flipped the rifle forward and centered his aim at her heart. "I give you one more chance to sign the papers."

She knew that even if she did as he demanded, he would kill her anyway. Her only satisfaction would be in knowing that Wade would hunt Brace down and end his evil life. "Never."

"That's what I thought you would say." He gave a feigned expression of sorrow. "Too bad."

Caroline pulled the derringer out of her pocket. "You can do what you will to me—but I can't let you hurt my son."

He glanced at the gun. "So you found that where I dropped it." He cocked the rifle, the sound resounding through the swamp. "That's nothing more than a popgun you've got there."

She pulled back the hammer on the derringer, surprised at how calm she felt. If she was going to die, she would take the man who'd destroyed so many lives with her. Regretfully she thought of Wade. If only she could see him one more time before she died.

"This 'popgun,' as you call it, is aimed right at your black heart. Did you know when you got out of bed this morning that you were going to die today, Brace?"

He merely smiled and shook his head. "Caroline, Caroline, you will be dead long before you can ever pull that trigger."

Wade had dismounted several hundred feet away from the house and cautiously made his way forward, keeping to the cover of the bushes. He was close enough to see Caroline and hear what was being said. His blood chilled when he saw Brace's rifle aimed at her.

Caroline was in his way, so he could not get a clear shot at Brace. He drew his gun, feeling panic rise inside him. He had to work his way around to the left, but there might not be time. He could hear Brace threatening her, and he heard her speak to him, sounding so unafraid. She was his life—he could not lose her.

He heard when Brace cocked his gun. If he raced across the opening between him and the house, could he distract the man, or would his actions make Brace fire the gun?

It was at that moment that Wade saw Jonathan in a crouching position inching in Brace's direction. Dear God, he could not lose them both! Then he saw the boy dive at Brace, taking him off guard and throwing him off balance. It was the distraction Wade needed. He did not have to take aim, he just fired.

Wade covered the distance to Caroline in no time at all. She was staring down at Brace as if she were dazed. She saw the bloodstain widening on his shirt-front, just as it had with Michael the day he had died. The derringer dropped from her numb fingers—she had not fired the gun, and yet the fatal shot had come from somewhere.

She reached out, scooped Jonathan up in her arms, and took a step backward, her gaze never leaving the horrible scene before her. She tried to shield her son from the awful sight.

She was suddenly surrounded by strong arms, and she sobbed, shaking all over as Wade gathered her to him, his hand on Jonathan's head.

"Thank God, I was in time," he said, his body trembling with raw emotion. "I could have lost you."

"Is he dead?" she asked, not wanting to look back at Brace.

"He was dead the moment I fired the shot."

Tears slid down Jonathan's face, and Caroline held him tighter.

"He was going to shoot Mommy."

Wade took the boy from Caroline. "I know, son. You helped save her life. If you had not slammed into him when you did, I would not have been able to get the shot off in time."

Jonathan wriggled out of his arms, his eyes filled with pride. "You came after us! I knew you would, and I told that man so. He didn't have a chance against you, Father."

Wade folded Caroline into the shelter of his arms. She looked ready to collapse. "Let's get you away from here," he said, not wanting to linger at the scene of death.

Frank and Louis had arrived with the buggy, and Wade lifted Caroline into his arms and carried her toward it, while Jonathan hurried beside them.

"Do not fret, *mon amour*. It is all over. You will never have to worry about him again."

"All I could think about," she said, resting her head on his shoulder, "was that I would never see you again."

He halted, his golden gaze sweeping her face. "Was that what you were thinking?"

"I love you so much," she said, tears swimming in her eyes.

"When did you come to that conclusion?"

"The day we were married."

He held her tightly to him, unable to say a word. Louis came up to them, but Frank drew him away and nodded toward the porch at the dead man.

"He won't be bothering the little missus anymore,"

Frank stated, kneeling beside Brace's body. "The boss shot him clean through."

"You knew he would," Louis observed. "This man was as good as dead the moment he threatened Mrs. Renault."

"He should never have gone for the boss's woman. His days were numbered when he did that." Frank stood. "We'll have to get Mr. Renault's horse back to the stable. Then I'll go into town and report what happened here."

Louis nodded. "Tell them that justice has been done today."

In the buggy, Jonathan sat between his mother and father, his little body shaking. Wade's strong hand came down on his head. "I was proud of you today, son. You did a brave thing."

Jonathan's eyes were bright as he looked at his mother. "I wasn't brave—I was scared."

She smiled at him. "You were Hawkeye."

The child looked pleased. "I was, wasn't I?"

Caroline touched Wade's cheek. "You saved our lives."

"*Non*," he said, his accent growing thick. "If I had protected you both better, this would not have happened."

"Do not be hard on yourself. Brace would have found a way to get to me sooner or later."

She saw a flash of anger in his eyes and she knew what he was going to say.

"You should not have gone to the swamp."

She nodded at Jonathan. "I had to."

Chapter Thirty-one

When they reached the house, Mary was waiting for them on the veranda; she rushed forward with a worried frown.

"Saints preserve us all, you are safe!"

"Yes, we are," Caroline said, sinking deeper into Wade's supporting arms.

Mary caught Jonathan's hand and brought him into the light so she could see him better. Brushing his hair aside, she saw a bruise on his cheek. "You have been hurt, lad."

"Not so much." He grinned up at her. "I'm a hero."

Mary glanced at Caroline in astonishment. "What happened?"

"We will talk about it later," Wade told her. "I want to get Caroline upstairs."

Caroline's legs felt so weak, she could hardly stand. "Mary, Jonathan may have other bruises or even cuts. I want him to have a warm bath and to be put right to bed." She looked up at Wade. "Do you think we should send for the doctor?"

"Yes, I do. Mary, have one of the men fetch Dr. Davis immediately. Although Jonathan has not complained of pain, I want to make sure nothing is broken. He took quite a tumble. I want a warm bath for Caroline, and she will have her meal on a tray. Make a big pot of tea."

"Will someone tell me *now* what happened? I have been worried sick," the housekeeper demanded.

"Let me get Caroline settled; then I'll come downstairs and tell you everything."

"I can tell you," Jonathan spoke up, his eyes shining.

Wade led Caroline toward the stairs, and she smiled listening to Jonathan's version of what had happened.

When they reached the landing, she looked around at everything that was dear and familiar; the tall case clock chimed the hour, and she sighed. "I never thought I would see home again. I was planning to shoot Brace, but I am not sure I could have pulled the trigger."

"What does that matter now?" Wade swallowed hard and pulled her against him. "Caroline." It took him a moment to speak. "I thought I had lost you today."

She brushed the hair off his forehead. "I am not so easy to lose."

The house was quiet as Caroline moved down the hallway toward Jonathan's room. The authorities had arrived at the house earlier and Wade had gone downstairs to explain what had happened at the swamp cabin. They'd already heard most of what had occurred from Louis and Frank.

The shock of facing Brace hadn't hit her yet, but she knew it would. It was difficult for her to understand that he was dead and she no longer had to fear him.

Her thoughts turned to Michael. He had been avenged and could now rest in peace. She would have to make a trip to Charleston very soon—a mountain of details needed her attention there.

She wanted to ask Wade's advice on whether she should sell her father's land. Of course, there was nothing left on the land but the charred remains of what was once a beautiful house. Her life was here now, and she wanted to cut all ties with Charleston.

She paused at Jonathan's bedroom door. So many thoughts swirled in her head—of things she wanted to do: She wanted to put flowers on her father's grave, and she wanted to have Michael's body moved to the consecrated ground of his family crypt. She wanted everyone to know that Michael had not taken his own life, but had been murdered by Brace.

She thought of Lilly. The poor woman had no one to look after her. Caroline was determined to see that Lilly had everything she needed. Of course, Michael's father had provided her a home, but Caroline wanted more than that for her. Lilly had been lonely and friendless—she deserved so much better than she ever had.

Jonathan's door was open a crack and she pushed it wider. He was asleep. She approached him on tiptoes and stooped to press a kiss on his cheek. He turned over and snuggled down into the soft mattress, but did not awaken.

"My little hero," she whispered. "Sleep well."

* * *

Wade was in bed when she returned. He looked tired, although he would never admit to such a weakness. It must have been difficult for him to witness Brace's cruelty firsthand. It would have been even more difficult for him to watch Brace making his threats, knowing he might not be able to stop him. He would have no regrets about shooting Brace. He had been a man protecting his family.

She slipped into bed beside him, and he took her into his arms.

"Are you all right?"

"I am now."

"I am still angry with you for facing Brace alone. You should have waited for me."

"I couldn't. Brace would have killed Jonathan if I had not gone to him." She slipped closer to him. "Don't be mad at me."

He touched his lips to her brow. "I could never stay mad at you."

She grinned. "I'll remind you of that in the years to come."

He watched her closely. "Did you mean it today when you said you loved me?"

"With all my heart. I never knew love could be like this."

He was quiet for a moment, and when he spoke, his accent was heavy. "Neither did I, Caroline. I did not even know what love was until I met you."

She touched her lips to his shoulder. "You love me?" She already knew he did, but it would be nice to hear him say the words.

"How could you ask? You are my heart and soul, *mon amour*."

"I think of that day when you rode into town and how terrified I was of you. If I had known how I was going to feel about you, I would have jumped over everyone to get to you."

He laughed and shook his head. "I cannot see you doing that."

She frowned, her mind going back to the scene that had played out with Brace. "I was afraid for Jonathan today. He is so young to have witnessed such evil."

"He saw bad things when he was abandoned on the streets of New Orleans."

"When I think of him living on the streets at such a young age, it makes me sad." She pressed her cheek to his. "And then I think of you living the same way when you were a boy. I cannot bear to think of either one of you being cold and hungry."

"That was a long time ago for me, and Jonathan has all but forgotten about it."

She rose up on her elbow. "An idea has been forming in my mind this evening. I wonder what you will think of it."

He tangled his hand in her hair. "What is it?"

"Do you need money, Wade?"

"What?"

"Do you need money?" she repeated. "If you do, I have plenty."

"*Non*, I do not want your money—I have more than we will ever need. But where are you going with this, Caroline?"

"Michael had a great fortune. But I do not feel that

any part of it should belong to me. Will you mind if I do something with it?"

"I prefer that you live on what I provide for you. Do what you want to with Michael's money."

"Would it bother you if I used most of his money to build a home for boys who have nowhere to live?"

He frowned. "Is that what you really want to do?"

She laid her head against his chest, listening to the steady beat of his heart. "I believe every young boy should have a chance in life. I don't want to think of any of them being cold and hungry. I want them to know there is a place they can go where they will be welcome, where they can find sanctuary."

He closed his eyes, thinking he had just caught a glimpse of her soul. "That is a beautiful thought."

"Will you help me?"

He slid his arms around her. "I will see what can be done."

"Wade, I want to make you as happy as you make me."

He tugged at her gown. "I can think of a way."

She laughed and wriggled out of her gown, easing her body next to his. "If that is all it takes, I will always make you happy."

As he fitted her against his body, his hand sweeping down her back, she could tell there was something on his mind. She looked at him questioningly. "Is something the matter?"

He trapped her face between his hands. "Do you forgive me for what I put you through?"

She was speechless for a moment. She'd had no idea that his guilt was still bothering him. "Of course I do." She touched her lips to his. "My darling husband, how can your conscience bother you over a deed that brought us together?"

She felt the tenseness leave him. "You do not know how many nights I lost sleep worrying about what I did to you."

She pretended seriousness. "I release you from any guilt. It is a wife's duty to make all things right for her husband."

He kissed her deeply and long, and when he raised his head there was a gleam in his eyes. "Duty, *mon amour?* I will make you pay for that."

She was captivated by the look in his eyes. "How will you do that?"

His hand swept across her stomach and his mouth shaped itself to hers.

Nothing more needed to be said.

Epilogue

Caroline removed her bonnet and tossed it on a chair. It was spring in New Orleans, and the dogwoods were finally in bloom. She had snipped off several small branches and was now arranging them in a tall crystal vase, thinking about the letter she had received from Nelly—she, Yance, and the children would be coming for a visit after spring roundup.

Caroline felt a fluttering in her stomach as the baby she was carrying quickened inside her for the first time. She slid her hand over her slightly rounded stomach, impatient for the birth of the baby that was due in early September.

Because of the baby, she had had to postpone her trip to South Carolina. But Nate had gone in her place, and he was a man who could make things happen. She was learning why Wade valued him so much.

She jumped back, startled, when something furry rubbed against her ankle. Staring down at the floor, she cried, "Archimedes!"

She scooped the cat into her arms, so glad to see him again. "How did you get here?" She ran her fingers through his soft fur and rested her cheek against him. "I have missed you so, you lazy cat."

The tabby purred and settled in her arms, as if to say he forgave her for leaving him behind in Texas. She turned around at the sound of familiar bootsteps coming down the stairs.

"Wade." Her heart was in her eyes as she watched him walk toward her. "How did you get Archimedes here?"

He came up beside her and ran his hand over the cat's fur. "I own a private railroad car," he reminded her. "And I could not leave my partner in crime behind in Texas."

It did Wade's heart good to see Caroline happy. Her joy and goodness had spread throughout this dwelling like a warm wind, healing everything in its path and making the house a real home. He looked into her beautiful face and noticed, not for the first time, that she was blooming with health.

His hand went down to her rounded stomach where his child was nestled. She had brought light to all the dark corners of his life, and she now carried his baby. Sometimes he was so filled with thankfulness that he could not speak of it—like now—so he spoke of other matters. "I have some papers for you to sign. Come into my office, *mon amour.*"

When he touched his lips to the back of her neck, she smiled at him, assuming the papers had something to do with her father's estate. With her hand clasped in his, they went into his study, where he led her to his desk and pushed a document in front of her.

"What have you here?" she inquired.

"Read it for yourself."

She placed the cat on the floor and picked up the document, quickly scanning it. "It says here that—" She looked at him puzzled. "I do not know what this is. What does it mean?"

"It means that you will soon be the proud mother of twenty-seven young boys. And no doubt before the year is out there will be even more."

"An orphanage for young boys?"

"*Oui, mon amour*. As the paper states, 'The Caroline Renault Home For boys.' As my gift to you, I will also be building one in Baton Rouge."

He had taken her at her word when she had told him that she wanted Michael's money to go toward building a home for the many homeless boys who roamed the streets of New Orleans. She had not expected the deed to be accomplished so soon, and she had not expected him to go one step further and build a second home in Baton Rouge. She should have known that he would move heaven and earth to please her.

"And you also arranged it so Lilly will have plenty of funds to live on for the rest of her life?"

"I sent Nate to Charleston to tend to the matter. He writes that he hired a competent woman to stay with Mrs. Duncan as her companion, and a housekeeper and cook as well. Nate assures me that she is doing quite well, and that she sends you her gratitude."

Her eyes were shimmering when she looked at him. "Thank you for helping me. I believe Michael would have approved of what I have done with his money."

There was no jealousy in his heart for the man who

had once been Caroline's husband. He was secure in her love for him. Michael had been only a boy when he died, and no ghosts of his presence lingered in their lives. Wade slid his arm around her shoulders and pulled her closer. "It is more than a pleasure to do anything that will make you smile."

She stared down at the paper where she had just affixed her signature. "Will the school serve nourishing meals, have good teachers and comfortable beds?"

He smiled at her. "I have purchased the land, and the architect only awaits your approval of his sketches before we break ground. You can personally choose the teachers and the cooks if you want to. It is entirely your project."

She threw herself into his arms while he laughed delightedly. She closed her eyes, basking in the joy that burst through her. She could see the warmth shining in her husband's golden gaze, and she felt love so strong it surrounded her like a fortress.

The baby chose that moment to move inside her, and Wade looked at her, startled.

"Did you feel that?" he asked, his eyes widening in amazement. "What just happened?"

"It's the baby trying to get your attention."

He had been happy about the baby, but until that moment it had not seemed entirely real. A feeling of fierce pride hit him hard, and he placed both hands on her stomach. If it was a son, Jonathan would have a younger brother. If it was a daughter—that thought rocked him even harder—a daughter with Caroline's sweetness. "You have brought me peace, Caroline." He wondered if she knew just how much that peace meant to him. "I thank God for the day you came into my life."

She raised her brow and pursed her lips. "I didn't come into your life, Wade. You found me."

"How did I get so lucky?"

She pressed her head against his shoulder. "I'm not sure about you, but as for me, I took a page out of Jonathan's book and wished upon the moon and the stars."

HEART OF TEXAS

CONSTANCE O'BANYON

Casey Hamilton has nowhere to go, no place but the Spanish Spur ranch to make a new home for herself and her little brother and sister. And when none of the local men will work for her, when trouble seems to dog her steps, she has no choice but to hire the loner with the low-slung guns strapped about his lean hips. She knows he is part Comanche, a man who'd fought his share of battles; is he a gunslinger as well? Is that why the past seems to haunt him? Either way, his silver eyes hold secrets too deep for telling; his warm lips whisper warnings she dare not ignore; and his hard arms promise that in his stirring embrace she will find the true...*HEART OF TEXAS.*

MOON RACER
CONSTANCE O'BANYON

Somewhere in the lush grasslands of the Texas hill country, three brothers and a sister fight to hold their family together, struggle to keep their ranch solvent, while they await the return of the one person who can shed light on the secrets of the past.

Abby learned to ride and rope and wrangle as well as any of her brothers, but Major Jonah Tremain is looking for a lady. Abby tells herself she doesn't care that the major is engaged to a proper Eastern-bred miss, but when she looks into his searing blue eyes and feels his lips against hers, she decides to teach him the error of his ways—only a Texas wildcat can do justice to passion such as his, and she plans to match him kiss for kiss.

Dylan

NORAH HESS

Dylan Quade is a man's man. He has no use for any woman, least of all the bedraggled charity case his shiftless kin are trying to palm off on him. Rachel Sutter had been wedded and widowed on the same day and now his dirt-poor cousins refuse to take her in, claiming she'll make Dylan a fine wife. Not if he has anything to say about it!

But one good look at Rachel's long, long legs and white-blond hair has the avowed bachelor singing a different tune. All he wants is to prove he's different from the low-down snakes she knew before, to convince her that he is a changed man, one who will give anything to have the right to take her in his arms and love her for the rest of his life.

Dorchester Publishing Co., Inc.
P.O. Box 6640 __5058-7
Wayne, PA 19087-8640 $6.99 US/$8.99 CAN

Please add $2.50 for shipping and handling for the first book and $.75 for each additional book. NY and PA residents, add appropriate sales tax. No cash, stamps, or CODs. Canadian orders require an extra $2.00 for shipping and handling and must be paid in U.S. dollars. Prices and availability subject to change. **Payment must accompany all orders.**

Name: ______________________________

Address: ______________________________

City: ______________ State: __________ Zip: ____________

E-mail: ______________________________

I have enclosed $__________ in payment for the checked book(s).

CHECK OUT OUR WEBSITE! ***www.dorchesterpub.com***

____ *Please send me a free catalog.*

Windfall

CINDY HOLBY

1864: Jake awakens from months of unconsciousness with his body healed, but his mind full of unanswerable questions. Is there a woman waiting somewhere for him? A family? A place he belongs? Shannon walks away from her abusive father and the only home she's ever known. Can a soldier with no past be the future she's prayed for? Grace tries to be brave when the need to capture a traitor rips her lover from her arms. Will it take even more courage to face him again now that his seed has blossomed within her? Jenny's grandfather's beloved ranch becomes a haven for all those she holds dear, but now the greed of one underhanded land baron threatens everything they've worked for. How can she keep the vision of her murdered parents alive for the generations to come?